Broken Leaves of Autumn

ELI HAI

Translated from Hebrew by Amit Pardes
Copyediting of the English edition: Susan Uttendorfsky at Adirondack Editing

Contact: elihai@012.net.il

ISBN-13: 978-1534781924
ISBN-10: 1534781927

Chapter 1

The heavy heat rising from the fiery dunes exhausted the many palm trees scattered along the deserted street, and their branches drooped, submitting to the forces of nature. Even the minuscule cloud above halted its movements. It seemed as though its strength abated in the face of the blazing sun. The air rested in place, refusing to create the slightest breeze that would relieve his stay under the sun.

Jeff Farmer wandered up the deserted street toward the bus station. After walking the short distance, he felt a sharp pain piercing his right foot. He wasn't barefoot, yet the canvas shoes he wore didn't prevent the burning heat from permeating his flesh and slowly singeing his feet. The blazing sun had no mercy on him either. It sent its fiery rays down on him, and Jeff felt its devastating heat in every part of his body. His cheeks reddened, and the sweat pouring from them mixed with the thin film of dust covering his face. He hurriedly pulled a bottle of water out of his shoulder bag and weighed his possibilities: should he wash his face or drink the water? The water wasn't as cool as it was when he'd left home. Nevertheless, he drank from the bottle eagerly, until he emptied its contents.

He looked around in a desperate attempt to find shelter from the exhausting heat. His eyes carefully scrutinized the tiny town that looked abandoned. He rejected the option of returning home, even though he knew the bus he was waiting for wasn't due for another hour. What would he do in the meantime? Where would he find shelter from the terrible heat that fell on the desert town, leaving its residents shut-in in their homes? Dejectedly, he did something wrong and even dangerous. He took advantage of the fact that the house next to the station looked empty, leaped over the fence, sprawled under a tree, and took off his shoe. He lifted his right foot and studied it carefully. The foot was red with a huge blister in the middle. He stood up and hobbled to the nearby tap, hoping the water would ease the pain. But he immediately pulled his foot back when the hot gush of water just aggravated the state of his sore foot. *Just what I need right now*, he thought with disappointment. *Maybe I'll postpone my trip to a different date, a better one?*

After all, that was what Pam requested. Requested? More like begged, cried, and whatnot. She did almost everything to try to stop him from leaving home, leaving her and his mother vulnerable to the whims of a cruel, foolish, mentally unstable father.

Pam was his only sister. Even though she was twenty-six, and three years older than he, she looked like a girl. She was short and plump, her body lily-white, her face flushed and freckled. Her light-blue eyes stood out strongly in contrast to her thick eyebrows and curly red hair. Her sloppy attire and unkempt face kept the few young men in town away from her, and not even one suitor knocked on their door. Their father abused her and made her life a living hell, while their mother stood aside, unable to save her. He was her only ally, and now he wanted to leave, as well.

For years, he yearned to leave the remote town in the heart of Arizona, but fear of leaving his mother and sister with his crazy father dissuaded him. However, even that fear didn't prevent him from dreaming of the day he'd leave home and build himself a new, different life, somewhere else, far from where he was born and raised.

Jeff gently massaged his feet, and doing so, recalled the last two times he ran away from home. The first time was when he was only twelve years old. It happened during a noisy fight in which his father hit his mother in the face. When he saw his mother rolling on the floor, blood pouring down her lips, he felt mindless with anger. In a rage, he launched himself at his father—who looked amused by the entire matter—and hit him with his small fists. It was then that his father's face flushed with rage, and his eyes spit fire. He shook off his son, slapped him, kicked him in the stomach, and showered him with a collection of his regular curses: "You're the spawn of the devil, boy! You and your sister were born in sin—a sin committed by your ungodly mother. If not for that sin, you wouldn't be here, you little bastards. I wish you were never born!"

Jeff was insulted to the depths of his soul, and despite the sharp pain in his body, he got up, left the house, and set out in a crazy and aimless sprint. He didn't care what would happen to him; he just wanted to get away from that cursed house. After running for fifteen minutes, he stopped dead in his tracks. To his disappointment, he'd noticed no one had followed him. No one cared about him, not even his mother. Maybe she regretted his birth as well? Maybe she also believed that if not for him, her life would be better. Perhaps he and his sister were the source of all of the family's maladies? During his short life, his mother had demonstrated so few gestures of affection. Sometimes she stared at him indifferently, as though he wasn't even her son, but a stranger. Did she also blame him for the sins his father accused her of? And if so, what was her sin in giving birth to him and his sister? Perhaps that sin was bringing them into this world? During those hours, endless questions spun in his head, until the sun set and a heavy gloom settled on the town. Only then, he returned home, holed up in his room, and endured his pain silently until he fell asleep.

The second time he left was more serious. It happened two days after he'd turned seventeen. He remembered that Sunday morning well; his mother and sister had gone to church while his father still slept. According to what he'd planned for a long time, he'd collected his few belongings in his rucksack and left the house. As planned, he hitched a ride with Joe, the neighbor's son, to the next town, Casa Grande, and from there hoped to hitchhike to Phoenix. He hoped that this way, he'd save the meager amount of money he'd toiled to earn during many months. In the big city, he'd definitely find a job, and this would be the beginning of a new life. And indeed, in the beginning, things went according to plan. Joe's pickup brought him to Casa Grande. From there he hitched a ride with a truck that took him all the way to Saxton, about twenty-five miles or more from his home. In Saxton, he tried to hitchhike, but to no avail. After two weeks, he ran out of money and had to return the way he came. Ever since, he hadn't tried to leave home but was convinced that the next time he'd succeed.

"Damn this foot. Why now?" he whispered to himself angrily and continued massaging his foot, until the large blister burst, and transparent, viscous liquid poured from it. The pain was so intense that he felt his foot burn. Maybe he should postpone the trip? This wasn't how he expected to start his journey, which would be difficult anyway. After thinking it over quickly, he decided he had to continue what he'd started. This time, it was final! He'd leave this damned desert and never come back! Okay, maybe just the once, to retrieve his sister.... He also thought about his mother but knew she wouldn't agree to leave the house she'd lived in for so many years. Furthermore, who knew what would become of her in several years? Would she live until then, or would she be too old to travel? Even though she was only forty-nine, she looked much older than her age. Her pale, delicate face was already creased with wrinkles; Jeff didn't know if they were caused by life's hardships or the desert sun. Her blue eyes squinted sadly, and her blonde hair was peppered with gray that she didn't bother to dye. In her youth, she had been a beautiful woman, and in fact, up until several years ago, she was still pretty. Jeff recalled that well. He remembered how the townsmen envied his father, sometimes even openly.

"Hey, John, your wife is pretty, a real hottie," they'd tell him, "and you're a fool. Such a fool that you prefer to sit in a bar and drink, instead of enjoying yourself in her arms."

"I wish my wife looked like yours," the others laughed.

"You can have her for yourselves," his father would slur slowly in the way of drunks, wallowing in his drunkenness, his mouth spitting fumes of alcohol.

Well, that was a while ago. It had been years since men had envied his father. Jeff felt his heart clench in sorrow for his poor mother. He didn't even think about his father. As far as he was concerned, he could drop dead on the street! Why should he care about a father who'd just piled trouble on him, his mother, and his sister? Why should he have mercy for such a stupid, selfish man, to whom liquor was the purpose of his life? Even if his father died in agony, he wouldn't feel sorry for him. The opposite was true. Maybe he'd even dance on his grave, as the old saying went. Who was to blame for him abandoning his home? His father! Who turned his youth into a nightmare? His father! So why shouldn't he rejoice in his father's death?

When he was small, he was convinced his father was at least the legendary John Wayne. He was a tough, strapping cowboy, with a straight, proud walk, and he trained his horses with an iron fist. But more than that, he was a great father, who dedicated a lot of his time and energy to his children and wife. However, several years later, everything changed. His father became a mean drunk who beat his children and wife mercilessly, and alcohol consumed him, body and soul.

His father was a lazy man. Most of the time he didn't work, so the burden of their livelihood fell on Jeff's weak mother, who worked in a sewing factory from morning until dusk. His father lounged all day in the bar, drinking himself silly, and in the evening, he'd drag himself home. Sometimes, he'd stumble on the way and fall asleep in the street. Then Jeff would go looking for him, at his mother's request, and when he'd find him, he'd carry him on his shoulders, dragging him all the way to his bed. The old man would vent the majority of his frustration on his mother and Pam. In the past, he even used to beat them until he drew blood. When Jeff was a child, he didn't even think of trying to intervene to save them. In the beginning, he would look at his rampaging father, and only after he calmed down a bit, would Jeff attack him with his little fists, trying to stop him from hitting them. His father would shake him off like a rag doll, brutally flinging him on the floor, and continue beating his mother and sister. When he grew into a powerful youth, he had the strength to restrain his father, and indeed, when he was at home, his father ceased with his physical violence, making do with verbal abuse. "You fucking little whore," he'd say to his daughter, and to his wife, he'd say, "You're a shitty Christian. The day will come when the Holy Mother will punish you for all your sins. Yes, woman, you're a shit Christian. Why do you even bother going to church? You're an adulteress, and the church is for decent folk, not for cheating sinners like you, you piece of shit." And his mother held her tongue and bore her pain silently.

"Why do you let him talk to you like that?" they asked their mother more than once.

"What am I supposed to do? Does a drunk man have a brain in his head? Does he understand what he's saying?" she always responded dismissively, putting her finger against her temple as though to indicate their father's mentally unbalanced state. Sometimes, it seemed to Jeff as though his mother was deliberately keeping the conversation brief. Was it because she herself feared his father's vitriol? Or perhaps she was hiding some sort of secret? Could there be truth in his father's words about them being born in sin and adultery? And why did he hate them so?

By the time he was fifteen, Jeff had already started working. He found a job in one of the town's diners, first as a dishwasher, and after a while, as the head cook's assistant. Sometimes, he had to work until the small hours of the night. One day, he returned home at midnight. To his surprise, his mother and sister weren't home despite the late hour. His father was sprawled on the couch; the smell of alcohol fumes from his mouth filled the house, reaching Jeff's nostrils. He sensed immediately that something was wrong. "Where are Mom and Pam?" He tackled his drunken father and shook him.

His father mumbled something incoherent that Jeff didn't understand. "What did you do this time, you motherfucker?" Jeff yelled.

"Mmhm, I..." his father mumbled, turned around, and continued his drunken slumber.

When Jeff entered the kitchen, he immediately realized what happened. The floor was bloodstained. In a panic, he ran to the clinic. When he burst in, he saw his sister lying on one of the beds, a nurse tending to her. His mother sat on a bench at the side, weeping soundlessly. Jeff turned fearfully to the bed and looked at his sister. Her face was bruised, her eyes filled with anxiety. She looked at him without saying a word.

"Did he do this to you?"

Pam didn't answer, just continued to stare at him in fear.

"The bastard hit her. He broke two of her teeth, and there are stomach injuries, too. I hope her ribs are intact. I just don't understand how a father can hurt his daughter like this," the nurse answered in her stead.

"Bastard! I'll end him! I swear I'll kill that fucker!" Jeff slammed the wall with his fist.

Since that incident, it seemed as though Pam's heart had broken. Her spirits, which weren't high to begin with, seemed to plummet and become more and more dark, and she shut herself in her room. Was it fear that she felt, or perhaps she was afraid to expose her battered face and broken teeth? She spoke sparingly, and when she did, her stammer was stronger. The doctor recommended they take her to a psychologist, but his mother refused with incomprehensible obstinacy. "She'll get over it on her own," she decided.

After that incident, his mother summoned her nerve and went to file a complaint at the Sheriff's office. The Sheriff agreed to lock up the abusive father. However, two weeks later, he released him after warning him not to repeat his violent actions.

Over the years, his father's strength waned. Old age and alcohol weakened him. He made do with verbal abuse and his attempts to hit his mother and sister were unsuccessful. When he tried to hit them, they pushed him away as easily as though he were a child.

The week before, Jeff turned twenty-three. That day, the die was cast. It was time to leave home. All that was left was to wait for the right time. His opportunity was quick to come. It was after a loud fight—one of many—with his drunk father. Not that there was anything unusual about this fight. It was a fight like any other, which took place almost every day. Yet, this time he felt he couldn't endure the sight of the pathetic drunk he called his father.

"You're the most loathsome, meanest person I've ever met in my life. It disgusts me to see you constantly drunk!" he hollered at his dad.

"Well then, get the hell out of here, leave home. You're useless anyway, and more trouble than you're worth!" his father yelled back.

Jeff was surprised by his reaction. His father cursed and shouted abuse frequently, yet he'd never demanded that Jeff leave.

"Don't worry. I'll be gone in the very near future," he said and looked directly at his surprised father.

"What are you doing?" Pam asked him when she saw him packing his belongings in his bag.

Jeff didn't answer. He raised sorrowful eyes to his sister and studied her. He could still see where her teeth had been broken, although two new teeth had been implanted instead of the broken ones.

"A-a-a...are you leaving?" Lately, her stammer had worsened, and she could barely finish a sentence.

"I'm sorry, Sis. I can't do this anymore. I have to get away from here. I have to find a future somewhere else," he finally answered, his voice quiet. However, he felt moisture gather at the corner of his eyes.

"W-w-w-here will y-you go? W-w-wha...t will you d-do?" Pam's face was frightened.

"New York," he replied quietly.

"N-new York? A-a-are you crazy? W-w-within hours y-you'll have nothing to eat! W-w-what will you live f-f-from and w-w-what will you do for work?" she persisted.

Pam was right. Jeff knew it wouldn't be easy, but he didn't care. What was better, staying here, rotting away in the desert? Was he supposed to spend the rest of his life in this cursed place? What choice did he have?

"Don't worry, Sis, I'll manage. I'm positive that I'll find a job in no time at all. And when I get settled a bit, I'll come back to visit you, and who knows, maybe I'll take you away from this place," he soothed her while she cried.

"B-b-but until you come back, w-w-what will I do?" she finally asked the question Jeff had been so afraid of. He didn't know how to answer that, and Pam cried some more.

"It'll be okay, Pam, it'll be okay. Don't worry," he rushed to reassure her as though she were a little girl, without giving her question much thought.

"D-does M-m-mom know?" Once again, she posed a difficult question.

"No," he responded dryly. "It's better that you tell her later. I prefer that she know when I'm no longer here."

Pam nodded. She'd calmed down some, which filled him with relief.

The night before his journey, he couldn't sleep. Endless thoughts and questions plagued him. Everything he knew about the big city he'd learned from the movies. Was it true that its skyscrapers kissed the sky? And what did a skyscraper, that was half visible and half hidden among the clouds, look like? And what if a skyscraper got hit by lightning during the cold winter months? What would happen then? Would all its inhabitants suffer injuries? After that, harder and more complex questions came to mind. Where would he live? Would he find a job immediately? And if not, how long would his money last? And if he wouldn't find what he was looking for, would he become homeless, one of those many people who slept under bridges, in abandoned houses, in charred fields, and on filthy sidewalks? A shiver ran through his entire body, shaking him. Toward dawn, exhaustion defeated him, and he fell asleep.

He heard the roar of the engine of the approaching bus. Jeff hurriedly pulled on his shoe. The blister on the bottom of his foot continued to bother him, but he chose to ignore it. He ran to the station and arrived there just as the bus pulled over. Excited, he got on the large vehicle. He sat in the back row, surrendering his burning body to the cool air that drizzled from the air conditioning vents. His tension was apparent in his sweaty face. The journey to the unknown was starting.

The bus quickly pulled away, leaving a long trail of dust billowing over the asphalt road covered with desert sand. Jeff turned his head in an attempt to send one last look at the place where he'd grown up. But apart from the dust covering the town, he couldn't see a thing.

Chapter 2

The double-decker bus stopped again at the station. Jeff stared out at the bustling street. The large houses, covered with dark, little bricks, looked like the exact replica of those that he saw at the previous station. Once again, he questioned himself if he should get off at this station, but something inside of him prevented him from doing so—something that he had no logical explanation for. It was as though his body was paralyzed, unable to move. While he sat, petrified in his chair, the bus pulled out of the station and continued.

He boarded a bus in Midtown Manhattan on the way to Brooklyn. The moment he arrived in New York, he wanted to get to Brooklyn. Why did he choose that burrow? There wasn't a special reason, apart from the fact that he was told that all the other places were too expensive or too dangerous, which was why he preferred to go there. He didn't have a definite destination in the borough, and therefore, at the beginning of the bus ride, he decided to let the bus lead him, allowing fate to control his situation.

The packed bus gradually emptied. In the end, it came to its final stop, and the last passengers got off and went their way. When Jeff saw he was the last passenger, he also hurried to leave the bus. He walked through the unfamiliar neighborhood, his excitement growing. It was mid-August. Outside, it was so hot, humid, and suffocating, that he had a hard time breathing. He surveyed his surroundings until his gaze rested on a mini-market near the station. It'd been hours since he'd last eaten, and apart from two gulps of murky faucet water from the toilets in the bus station in Manhattan, nothing had come to his mouth.

A huge billboard announced in large, bright red letters of "Moishel's Mini Market." Jeff walked in. He noticed a small help-wanted sign on the front door, but for the time being, chose to ignore it. First, he'd eat, then he'd focus on it. The large store was empty of customers so that all attention was focused on him. Jeff ignored the inquisitive looks and collected a loaf of black bread, a small jar of mayonnaise, and a large pack of sliced salami. Then, he carefully chose a tomato, cucumber, some pickles, and a soda. Behind the counter stood a man who looked to be in his mid-sixties and, at his side, a young man. They looked strange, with their short white shirts, from underneath which peeked thick strings that dangled down on wide black pants. On their clean-shaven heads, they wore black skullcaps, large enough to cover their entire heads. Long sideburns curled on both sides of their face, from ears to chin.

New York was a strange city. When he disembarked from the train that brought him from the airport to the center of Manhattan, he couldn't stop staring at the passersby, most of them odd-looking. Although he had seen characters such as these in countless movies, they now seemed more amusing. Not only the people set his imagination on fire, but also the skyscrapers that emerged from the asphalt like mushrooms and covered the sky. In Phoenix, there were also skyscrapers, which he saw for the first time the day before, however, there weren't as many, and they weren't as tall as these buildings.

"Five dollars and three cents," said the young man, who looked about his age.

Jeff fished in his pocket and pulled out a fistful of change. He put it on the counter and started counting the required sum, under the curious young man's watchful gaze. Then he collected his produce in a paper bag, thanked the salesmen, and left the store. As he walked toward the door, he still felt the man's stare.

He walked quickly to the public park on the other side of the street. After a slight hesitation, he chose a bench under one of the trees and started eating. As he ate, he thought about people and how fragile they were, how dependent on food. Without food, several hours could pass, and they'd feel the misery of hunger. He remembered the stomach bug that had plagued him several months ago. He had vomited and emptied his bowels constantly and hadn't eaten for three days. He'd felt like a rag and had almost fainted. When people were hungry, nothing interested them, their thoughts focused only on the food that would fill their stomachs. If you put off the nursing of a newborn, if only for a moment, the baby would scream as though he hadn't eaten for days. Sometimes, hunger forced people to leave their countries and families and to wander great distances. And what was most horrific was that sometimes a man would kill for a loaf of bread. One loaf of bread was sufficient to cut off a whole life. And not only people. Animals would also eat each other when they were hungry. Only two days ago, he'd watched a documentary on the animal channel and saw how a pride of lions had ruthlessly torn apart an innocent, helpless gnu in order to appease their hunger. The moment they'd filled their stomachs, they'd sprawled on the ground, like pets that wouldn't hurt a fly.

He hoped to find a job soon so he wouldn't starve.

He continued scarfing down the sandwich he'd prepared and thought about the next rich meal he'd eat if he'd be lucky enough to eat. Back home, he'd decided not to spend more than ten dollars a day on food until he found a job. When he finished eating, he gulped down the entire bottle of soda. An excellent meal for the price he'd paid, he concluded contentedly and returned to the store to read the "help-wanted" notice. "Cleaning company seeking worker," he read carefully. When he wrote down the details, he was happy to come across the opportunity to find a job on his first day in the city.

"Looking for a job?" he suddenly heard the young salesman's voice.

Jeff turned to him and nodded.

"You're not from here, right?" The man shook his head, his sideburns swaying right and left.

"No, I'm from the south," Jeff replied honestly, well aware that his drawl gave him away.

"The minute you came into the shop, I knew you weren't from here. You Southerners have an easily identified accent," the man said with a smile and revealed teeth as gleaming and white as the shirt he wore.

Jeff didn't reply. He was starting to feel impatience in the face of the man's nosiness.

"Nice to meet you. The name's Ahron." The man extended his hand, still smiling, and his pleasant smile seemed to deflate Jeff's irritation.

"Nice to meet you. I'm Jeff." He shook his hand uncomfortably, wondering what the smiling man could possibly want from him.

"How long have you been in the city?" Ahron asked.

"I've only just arrived today."

"Today? You've got a place to sleep?"

"No. I've just arrived, and I've hadn't had time to look for a place. I'm sure there's a little hotel in the area, just until I find a room," Jeff replied, his excitement growing.

A place to stay, that was the most important thing for him now. Before he arrived in the city, he was told to try his luck in Brooklyn, where he could find a room at a reasonable price. But his fear that he wouldn't find a place to live continued to plague him. He had five thousand dollars, a sum that was supposed to tide him over for several frugal months of rent and living expenses until he found a job. But the sight of the homeless people in the big city, which he'd seen on television, continued to haunt him. He wondered if this Ahron guy had any news for him. Was he just asking or did he have a tangible offer? Jeff came closer. The strange man no longer annoyed him. He was even starting to like him. "I may be able to help you find a job and a place to live. My parents have a basement apartment in the building where they live, three blocks from here. If you want, I can take you to see the apartment. In about half an hour, we're closing for the lunch break. What do you say?" He looked at Jeff, waiting alertly for his response.

"That's fine with me," Jeff answered without hesitation, surprised by the sequence of events, which had been kind to him up until now.

"Great. After we go see the apartment, we can go to my brother-in-law, Menachem, to see if the note he put up in the shop is still relevant. I think it is. He always needs workers. Everyone uses his cleaning services. His company cleans everything: houses, offices, cars, even garbage rooms," Ahron joked.

After half an hour, Ahron closed the store, like he'd promised, and they made their way together to the basement apartment, which belonged to his parents.

On the way, Jeff learned about the amiable young man's family. "I have ten brothers and sisters," Ahron told him proudly. "Seven brothers and three sisters. Reuven, the oldest, is twenty years older than me, and Rivka is the baby, six years younger than me."

"You don't say!" Jeff said admiringly. "So many brothers and sisters? The largest family in Eloy had four children."

"Yes, well, you must've noticed by my clothes that my family is a Hasidic Jewish family," Ahron explained. "According to the Torah, we're required to fulfill the commandment to procreate. You've heard of the Jewish Torah, right?'

"Yes, I've heard of the Jews and their faith, although, by the age of fifteen, I'd already left school and started working. But in the restaurant where I worked, there was a woman who talked all day long about Jews," Jeff said and started to laugh, his laughter contagious enough to get Ahron started too.

"You laugh like my sister, Rivka. I swear it's uncanny, how your laughter reminds me of her.... She also has this odd, rolling laughter that immediately attracts attention."

"How old is Rivka?"

"Seventeen."

"Still a child," Jeff decided.

"A child? Not exactly. In the community, she's already been mentioned with much respect. In our community, it's customary to get married at eighteen. So, in less than a year, she'll marry, and in two years, with God's help, she'll be a mother."

"No way! She's practically a child!"

"Why does that surprise you? You must know that there are places in the world where girls get married at fourteen, sometimes even at twelve."

"And you think that it's all right?" Jeff persisted.

"No. In my opinion, it really is too much, but factually, it happens."

"Does child marriage happen nowadays as well?"

"Yes, but in the past, it was much more common."

"And how, exactly, will your sister marry? Will a groom come down from the sky? If, by the time she's eighteen, she doesn't have a man, what will she do?"

"*Shidduch*," Ahron answered, in an Ashkenazi accent.

"*Shidduch*? What's a *shidduch*?"

"In our community, every person has a match before they turn eighteen. The parents look for the groom or bride. That's how my parents found me my wife. I knew who my wife would be since I was sixteen. Our Rivkel also has an intended groom. Her Avraham-David is a mensch, bless God."

"And if your sister doesn't want the groom your parents chose for her?" Jeff persisted.

"The choice isn't hers to make," Ahron said decisively.

"I don't believe it! What you're actually saying is that if she doesn't want him, they'll force her to marry him."

"Not exactly. We accept things unquestioningly; that's how we were raised, so there's no actual need to force us. In unusual cases, the match, the *shidduch*, is unsuccessful, and then, what's the problem? You find another *shidduch* until, in the end, it succeeds," Ahron concluded.

"And what if she doesn't love him? Or, let's take you, for example. What if you don't love your wife? What then?" Jeff continued asking difficult questions.

"Don't worry, my friend. I love my wife very much. She is, after all, the mother of my daughters. And how can you not love your wife, the mother of your children?" Ahron said, looking at Jeff in amusement, as though wondering about the question.

"Daughters? You have kids? At your age?"

"Yes, that's right. I have two lovely girls. You have no idea how much fun it is to be a father when you're young, at the height of your virility," Ahron replied, pleased with himself.

Jeff was silent for a moment, trying to imagine himself as a young father, but he snapped out of it immediately and concluded, "I don't think twenty-three, not to mention eighteen, are good ages to be parents. To assume the burden of child-rearing at an age that you're still a child yourself doesn't seem smart to me. Besides, the fact that you're not the one deciding who and when you marry seems problematic in itself." He noticed Ahron was listening, yet still smiling calmly, as though he knew things of utmost importance that Jeff, himself, had no knowledge of.

"I'm interested in one thing," Jeff continued. "How can so many people live in one house? In my house, for example, even though we weren't rich, my sister and I each had our own bedroom."

"First of all," Ahron said, "my parents' house is big enough for a large family. Second, there were times when some of the household members lived in the basement. And now the house has emptied because everyone got married. The house is almost empty, and even the basement has been vacated. And that's the apartment I'm going to show you."

While they walked and talked, they arrived at a tall building with a large entrance. On the side, was a small path leading to a staircase. Ahron turned onto the path and slowly walked down the stone stairs, most of which were cracked and broken. Jeff followed him cautiously, carrying his bag on his back; it suddenly seemed heavy. When they arrived at the front door, he noticed it was broken and falling apart. A heavy gloom engulfed the house. There wasn't even a small window to let in a bit of light. Ahron switched on the light, and a strong white light washed the foyer. Jeff noticed a small animal scampering quickly across the room and disappearing under the bed standing at the center of the room.

"Are there mice in the apartment?" he asked apprehensively.

"Maybe. It's been a while since someone lived here. The last person who lived here was me, and that was three years ago. When I lived here, I caught one mouse, and then I was forced to rent an apartment somewhere else because Miriam, my wife, refused to live here. She's scared to death of mice," Ahron said and burst into laughter. After he'd calmed down some, he asked, "But you're not afraid of the poor little creature, right?"

"No, I'm not afraid," Jeff replied, although the thought of sharing his living quarters with mice or rats didn't especially appeal to him. Yet, what choice did he have? Was he better off sleeping under the open sky next to other people living on the street?

"Here's the bathroom." Ahron opened the bathroom door, which emitted a shrill creaking sound, as though angry that its rest had been interrupted. Jeff peeked inside and was horrified by the sight that met his eyes. The walls were peeling, the ceiling was covered in mold and cobwebs. The floor was uneven as a result of broken tiles, and the large bathtub had lost its original color, rust stains decorating it. Ahron opened the faucet. Murky water gushed out. "It's been a long time since anyone used the water, and rust accumulated in the pipes. Open it for a few minutes and the water will come out clear," he apologized.

After that, they moved on to the kitchen, a small, narrow room. Jeff studied it and decided that it wouldn't be an easy feat, but he would manage to shove in a small refrigerator, a cooker, and maybe a small table and chair. In the middle of the room, there was a sink, also broken. Jeff sighed, not bothering to hide his disappointment.

"No one has lived here for a while. This is what happens when a house stands empty for a long time. There's no one to take care of it," Ahron apologized again.

Jeff hesitated. What should he do now? Politely refuse and go look for someplace else, more inhabitable? What would he do if he didn't find a place to sleep? Where would he sleep tonight?

"And how much will it cost me to rent this dump?" he asked, not trying to offend, but attempting to negotiate a better price.

"I'll talk to Papa. I'll try to convince him that in exchange for fixing up the place, you can live here for a year, rent-free," Ahron answered with a smile, like someone who knew the value of a good bargain.

"Fair enough," Jeff rejoiced. He started calculating right away and came to a conclusion that with a reasonable investment, he'd be able to turn the apartment into a place that was inhabitable, as well as aesthetically pleasing.

Calculating gain and loss, he could manage to save up some money, providing he got the lease for several years, of course, and on the condition he get a job.

"You forgot to call your brother-in-law about the job," Jeff remembered.

"You're right. The first thing I'll do when I return to the shop will be to call him. I promise. And in the meantime, look for a place to sleep. Next to my shop, there's a small hostel. Rent a room there until you finish renovating. While you're there, you're welcome to eat meals at my house. Unfortunately, we're not allowed to have people sleeping over…. Surely you understand," Ahron continued as they made their way back to the shop.

"Thank you, Ahron! Really. This is the most surprising day of my life. In my wildest dreams, I never would've believed this would happen. That on my very first day in New York, things would work out for me."

He was extremely touched by the help and warmth of the young Jew. There were no Jews in Eloy, yet he'd heard a lot about them. Some people also said things about them that he found unpleasant to listen to. And yet, on his very first day in the big city, populated with millions of Jews, he discovered that things weren't so, at least, not in regard to Ahron.

On that very day, Jeff rented a room in the hostel next to Ahron's house. At night, he slept soundly and summoned strength for the following days.

Chapter 3

From the sixty-second floor of the large building, the large park sprawled majestically. The towering trees, the abundant greenery, the wide lawns, and the animals running around the park gave the place the feel of a dense forest, as though there wasn't a bustling city nearby.

Eve turned to the window and looked down to the street with satisfaction. From her vantage point, the people below seemed to rush to and fro like grasshoppers. A feeling of elation engulfed her, and she rubbed her hands together in glee. Her eyes gleamed with happiness when she watched the two computer screens on her desk. The colors flickered as though dancing in joy.

She returned to her desk and tapped on her keyboard. The day's trade in stocks ran on the screen. "I did it again," she murmured to herself with a smug smile. She took a deep breath and continued to study the results of the day's trade. Dow Jones increased by one percent, while Nasdaq increased by one-and-a-half percent. A rough calculation showed that this day would yield half a million dollars, not to mention that in the last month, the profits from the investment portfolios she managed reached four and a half million dollars. She earned two and a half percent of that sum, so after deducting her expenses, her profits would be one hundred thousand dollars! What more could a person ask for?

But something else thrilled her even more. She pressed the intercom and called in her secretary.

"Yes, Eve, what do you want?" her secretary asked.

"Come in quickly, Jessica, I have something interesting to show you," Eve called, not bothering to hide the excitement in her voice.

"Here, look," she said, pointing at one of the numbers flashing on the computer screen.

"What exactly?" Jessica had a hard time figuring out what she was seeing.

"Can't you see? I broke the one hundred barrier! Since I've arrived here, one hundred million dollars have accumulated in my investment portfolios! Would you believe it? One hundred million! That's a good reason to celebrate, don't you think so?"

"You're brilliant, Eve! Brilliant! I'm not surprised. I always knew you were our smartest trader. Now you have a good reason to demand a fat bonus from the bosses. And while you're at it, get one for me, too." She winked at Eve, a wide smile on her face.

"You want a bonus, sweetheart?" Eve winked back. "Work for it. Drop everything you're doing, and prepare a detailed report including all the transactions we did for all the clients, and the accumulated profits from each and every transaction. When you're finished, arrange a meeting with the boss for me."

There weren't a lot of women in Wall Street's elite. However, Eve was one of them. Her rise to the top was dizzying. Only four years had passed since she'd graduated from New York University, and since, she had become one of the best brokers in the city. In the beginning, she managed a small investment portfolio for a company that chose to invest its money in shares. She remembered her many efforts to convince the company's managers to trust her.

"Why do you think you'll succeed when so many, much more experienced people than you, failed? You're young, inexperienced, and unskilled in matters of the stock market," said the CEO, who had interviewed her before she got the job.

"Exactly because of that. Because I'm young and inexperienced, I'll be cautious with the clients' money. In the beginning, give me small sums, and if I succeed, increase them," she logically coaxed the CEO.

Her unwavering self-confidence and mainly her stunning beauty and impressive appearance left its impression on the company CEO, and he agreed to hire her for a trial period. Obviously, he didn't regret his decision. By the first month, Eve had accumulated gratifying profits, and her investments gradually grew. Her success at work led more companies, as well as individuals, to approach her, requesting that she find them profitable channels of investment. In the beginning, her income was relatively small and was based on a weekly salary of several hundred dollars. But, hand in hand with her success, her status and income grew. Only two years later, she was transferred to the mother company, "Stock" and became the company's leading broker, the one who set the trend. Thus, for four years, Eve bought and sold equities of all sorts: shares, debentures, options; she mainly specialized in future transactions. Her success became absurd; it was enough that she decided to purchase a certain share, for the value of that share to rise. Rumors that Eve bought a certain debenture would spread and immediately many other brokers would jump on that share, which in fact would cause demand surplus and an increase in the price of that debenture. Her high position gained her a private secretary, who, with time, became her friend and confident. Her handsome income allowed her to buy a prestigious three-room apartment in the heart of Manhattan and a fancy Mercedes jeep.

Not that she lacked for anything before. Her father was one of the largest real-estate brokers in town, and his high income allowed him and his family life in the lap of luxury. Eve never lacked a thing, if it was expensive clothes and games in her childhood, or designer dresses and shoes when she grew older. Her father outdid himself when he bought her a flashy, expensive sports car when she turned eighteen. But when she graduated from college, she decided to make it on her own.

"If you succeeded, and you started from the bottom, so can I," she said and returned the keys to the sports car to him. Her father wasn't surprised. He even seemed satisfied with the way his oldest daughter chose to embark on a life of independence.

"Don't worry, she'll find her way and succeed, and if not, she'll come back to us very quickly," he assured his concerned wife after Eve packed her bags and left home. But Eve had no intention of coming back.

She was twenty-five, a shapely woman, tall and beautiful, with curly black hair and big green eyes. No doubt, she was the prettiest woman in the huge office building where she worked. Her dizzying success and beauty caused men to circle her and crave her company, but she didn't want any of them. She concentrated all her efforts on the thrilling trade of equities and, apart from a few hookups, never had a serious relationship with any of the men she met. When she had just started working, she showed some interest in Paul, the broker who taught her some trade secrets, but after several dates with him, she discovered he was married. Besides, the truth was that men held little interest for her.

All this was true until one evening, while she took her shower, and she started thinking about the guy who cleaned the outside of the windows of her office. His face, reflected through the thick glass, haunted her all night long until she finally fell asleep. She didn't remember what exactly attracted her attention. His casual attire, his tall, masculine body, or perhaps his big, wise eyes? And perhaps she admired his courage, suspended in the air so high above the ground, only a steel noose holding him so he wouldn't fall? A lot of courage and strength was required for that job. She was so lucky that not even the tip of her shoe was at risk at her job, while this window cleaner, who barely made a living, was risking his life hanging in the air. Life wasn't fair, she thought with a smile, but luckily, I'm on the side of success.

In the morning, she stopped thinking about that guy. Shares kept her busy, and she dedicated herself to them with all her energy. But when her workday reached its conclusion, she was surprised to see that she was thinking about him again. About his chiseled, muscular body, writhing along the length and width of the window trying to reach every corner with his wet rag. About his tan face, shadowed with a light stubble. When she drew closer to get a better look at him, he waved and smiled at her, but unfortunately, just then he moved to another window. Eve sighed. The man's appearance left her restless.

Paul ambushed her in the hallway. "Well, how was your day?" he asked, as though it was something he did routinely.

"Successful," she replied curtly.

"How about we go out today?"

Eve shook her head.

"We haven't gone out for quite a while. I have an idea how to take over companies. Interested in hearing it?"

"Paul, stop it. I don't want to go out with you and you know why And besides, I'm already committed to someone," she lied for reasons unknown to her.

"Who's the happy man?"

"See you tomorrow," Eve cut off the conversation, leaving her suitor mortified and confused.

In her apartment, scrubbing herself under the shower, she continued thinking about that guy. Was window cleaning the sum of his job? Maybe he also cleaned offices, and one day, he'd barge into her room? Tomorrow, she'd check where he worked and when he may return.

Later, untypically, she went to the mirror and studied her entire body. At first, she examined her smooth face and long neck for a long time. Then, she studied her small, high breasts decorated by big, pink nipples, which Paul had declared absolute perfection. In the end, she focused on her shapely legs and firm backside, the desire of every man. Satisfied, she curled up in her bed, and quickly fell asleep.

In the morning, unlike every day, she woke up early and arrived at the office two hours before the day's trading opened. She asked Jessica to urgently summon the maintenance director.

"Didn't you say you're absolving me today from secretarial duties so I could prepare the report?" Jessica joked. But when she saw Eve's tense face, she called the maintenance director.

Several minutes later, a huge man entered Eve's room. He was about seven feet tall, dark-skinned, in his fifties. Eve remembered using his services in the past when a water pipe exploded in the office and threatened to destroy all the investment portfolios. The maintenance director's quick, energetic thinking, closing the main faucet, prevented a colossal disaster.

"How are you, Mr. James?" she inquired politely.

"Fine, Ms. Eve. And how are you feeling?"

"I'm feeling great," she answered with a smile.

"How can I help you?"

"I'm curious to know how you hire the services of the window cleaners." She pointed at the large window.

"Window cleaners aren't employees of the building. They belong to a contract company," he replied, surprised at the odd question.

"Which company? Do you know?" Eve continued her investigation.

"I don't really remember. I think it's something like 'Menachem Maintenance Services.' If you want, I can check and get back to you," he answered.

"Yes, I want. And the phone number, too, please."

"Yes, Miss," he replied obediently. After a slight hesitation, he asked, "Why are you asking, Miss? Do you need a window cleaner?"

"Yes, certainly. Next time, I'd like my window cleaned from the inside, too," she said, without noticing that the window was gleaming clean.

"We clean the windows from the inside ourselves. The contracting company cleans only from the outside. In order to clean windows from the outside, you need special equipment, and that's the reason we hire the contracting company," he explained at length, surprised Eve didn't know that. In the end, he asked, "Would you like me to send one of the building's cleaners over here?"

"No, no need. As you see, the window's clean. You can go... and get back to me with the number," she instructed him, concluding the conversation.

She turned on the computer, and just for a second, for the first time since she started working after graduation, she felt as though her occupation was insipid and didn't interest her. After several minutes, the maintenance director returned with the desired number, and even though, trading had started, Eve took the scrap of paper with the number and dialed immediately.

"Menachem Cleaning Services, good morning," a female voice greeted her.

Eve hesitated.

"How can I help you?" the switchboard operator continued in a courteous, professional voice. Yet, Eve couldn't get a word out of her mouth.

"Hello, who's on the line?" the switchboard operator insisted.

Eve hesitated for a second. I'm starting to act like a dumb schoolgirl, she thought desperately, and right after that, placed the receiver in its cradle. She held her head in her hands, and for the first time, realized that something within her had changed. Again, the tall man fired up her imagination. She turned her gaze to the window. His smiling face seemed reflected in it, as though carved on the glass for all eternity.

At the end of the day, Jessica entered with a portfolio overflowing with papers. "I finished preparing that report like you asked me to. The results are better than you thought," she announced happily.

"Put it on my desk. I'll go through it later," Eve replied indifferently, still staring at the window. And Jessica was surprised by her dreamy expression.

She was prepared to swear that since yesterday, that report, which had fascinated her boss more than anything, had suddenly become worthless.

Chapter 4

Menachem, Ahron's brother-in-law, greeted Jeff with a smile. Like Ahron, he was a friendly, smiling man. Even though he was only several years older than Ahron, he already overlooked most of the cleaning and moving business in the city. He had plenty of vacancies, but most of them involved the hard work of cleaning and moving. Of all the jobs offered to him, Jeff preferred to clean windows. Cleaning windows was a hard, risky job, yet Jeff chose it because he thought it sounded easier than the other jobs, and furthermore, the pay offered in exchange was the highest: five bucks for a four-meter square window. Menachem told him that a good worker could clean up to sixteen windows in four hours of work. A simple calculation showed him that his monthly salary would be two thousand five hundred and sixty bucks. Two thousand five hundred and sixty bucks! Unbelievable! A fortune! Much more than what he made in Eloy.

"This Monday, God willing, you start working," Ahron told him when he came to the basement apartment for a quick visit. After studying the apartment, he said, "I can't believe my eyes. You've made such a lovely place for yourself. Well done, Jeff."

For two weeks, Jeff labored on the renovations in the small apartment. He hired a laborer, and together, they cleaned and painted the walls, replaced the tiles, and installed a new toilet as well as new sinks and faucets. They replaced the rusty bathtub with a new, state-of-the-art shower stall and shower head. The old light fixtures were replaced with chandeliers and cheap, colorful lampshades that Jeff bought at the flea market. On the walls, he hung paintings. He added some furniture, not top-of-the-market, but good enough to beautify the apartment and make the place a cozy home one wanted to spend time in. Of course, before he moved in, he didn't forget to fumigate the apartment. He really didn't feel like sleeping with creepy-crawly friends. On Monday, he already began work at his new job.

At the end of the first day, he came home exhausted, bone-weary, and desperate. He was convinced he'd made an awful mistake choosing this job. Even though he was strong and muscular, his shoulders screamed with pain. His hands felt paralyzed from the hard work. But more than anything, he was disappointed that he'd managed to clean only half of the windows he'd intended to clean. *If this is how things will be in the future, I'll reach only half of the potential salary*, he calculated gloomily. He sprawled on his bed and thought of his day. But no more than several minutes had passed before exhaustion overwhelmed him, and he sank into the sleep of sweet labor.

The next days were even harder. His aching body became weaker, and exhaustion subdued him. He thought of resigning, and only his financial situation prevented him from doing so. After the expenses he spent on living and renovations, he had two thousand dollars left. He couldn't afford to leave his job. He found solace in making new friends, and his closest one was Rico.

Rico was a Puerto Rican in his thirties, married with three kids. He was tall and strong, which allowed him to perform the task of window cleaning with amazing ease and skill. When he noticed Jeff was having a hard time with the job, he constantly helped and encouraged him. "Don't worry, brother," he promised after Jeff expressed his desire to leave the job. "I felt like shit, too, when I just started here. With time, you stop looking down, and then, your capacity increases. Your body adjusts to the job and stops aching. And if you leave, what will you do? It's very hard nowadays to find a job. And if you do find another job, it'll be exactly like this one—hard labor. Why would you want to do that?"

He managed to convince Jeff to keep at it. In the beginning, when he first climbed up to the roof of the building, he wasn't paying attention to the great height he was at. Later on, he was tied to the harness with straps, a large crane carrying him up. At first, he was suspended in the air, and then he was slowly lowered to the window of the top floor. Looking down at the street stretching beneath him, he felt so dizzy he thought he would pass out. He clutched the chain to which he'd been tied, terrified he'd slip and fall. For several long minutes, he swayed in the air, unable to move a limb. He couldn't even sip some water. It took another fifteen minutes, as well as the encouragement of his coworkers, for him to take out his rags and start cleaning the window.

Slowly, he adjusted to his new work and surroundings. Like Rico said, the aches abated, and suddenly, the work wasn't as hard. He equipped himself with a Discman, listened to music, and sometimes he even sang while cleaning the windows. And so, summer passed. In the winter, he started doing various maintenance jobs. Every few days, he'd go to Rico's and eat the delicious food his wife prepared. He was also a guest at Ahron's house, and the two became fast friends.

But the nights were hardest. When he lay down to sleep, he was swamped by waves of loneliness. He was attacked by bouts of homesickness, especially for his sister. On his first day in New York, he called home to talk with his mother. Her voice was cold and alienated.

"How are you, Mom?" he asked.

"Fine," she answered dryly.

"I'm sorry I didn't say good-bye..."

"You didn't have to! The important thing is you're happy now," she replied laconically, but her anger was evident in her tone. Was it because he didn't say good-bye, or for some other reason? When he asked to speak with his sister, his mother told him Pam wasn't at home, but he had a feeling she was lying. Two weeks later, he sent her letter, in which he told her what was happening with him, and promised to come visit soon. His letter went unanswered. After a month, he sent another letter, which went unanswered, as well. He'd expected his mother to ignore his letters, but why didn't Pam answer? Maybe she was mad at him, too? Mad that he had abandoned her and left her alone with their parents, in her deteriorated mental state. No doubt, she was mad at him and rightfully so. That's why she wouldn't answer.

Every day, he went to the mailbox, hoping to find a letter addressed to him, but to no avail. At the end of summer, he finally received the much-hoped-for letter from his sister. It was written in sloppy, unclear handwriting, which indicated she was agitated. Pam apologized for not answering for such a long time. She wrote how much she missed him. In the end, she asked about his welfare in a formal manner and wished him the best in all his ventures. When he finished reading the letter, he felt as though something was wrong. The next day, he called again. This time, his sister was on the other side of the line.

"He....llo," she answered with difficulty.

"Hey, Pam, it's me, Jeff. How are you, sweetheart?"

When she heard his voice, she started crying. Several long minutes passed until Jeff managed to calm her down and gently prompt her. She told him that their father was very sick, and their mother wasn't at her best either. She told him that she was depressed, that her stutter had increased, making it hard for her to talk with people.

"What's the bastard suffering from?" he asked first about his father's condition, and not necessarily because he was worried about him.

"H-h-h-h...is l-liv-ver isn't o-ok-kay. T-the d-d-d...octor says that it's no longer functioning, and he has only a few more weeks to live," she stuttered, sorrow absent in her voice.

So, the old sinner was dying? How about that? His birth father was on the verge of death. On the other hand, who said he was his dad? Maybe the mean old drunk wasn't even his father. Perhaps there was truth in the accusations he'd hurled at his mother, that they'd been born in sin. And if it was true, how come he never heard all sorts of malicious rumors and gossip from the townspeople? And yet, he and his father had a strong resemblance. They were both light-skinned and husky, with blond hair and big blue eyes. The more he thought about it, the more he realized that the possibility that John the bully wasn't his dad was almost impossible. Yet, even so, their bond was no more than a biological one, and they had nothing between them worth feeling sorrow for. That man was single-handedly responsible for his sister's mental state and was the reason he left home. Jeff couldn't feel any compassion for him. As far as Jeff was concerned, the man he called his father could croak.

"And Mom?" he continued asking.

"I-I t-t-think s-s-she's sad b-because of him."

"And you, Sis, what's going on with you? Why is your stammer worse?"

"I-I d-d-don't know. E-ever since my t-t-teeth were broken, it j-j-just g-g-got w-w-worse."

Her stammer had become heavy, to a point that completing a full sentence took a long time. In the beginning, he listened to her patiently, but as the conversation grew longer, he became impatient and started cutting her off, completing her sentences and waiting for her confirmation. It seemed she sensed that because, at the end of the conversation, she said, "It's hard for me to talk. It's better that you write to me." And Jeff did as she requested.

In the beginning, his letters were answered, but as time passed, her letters became far and few between, and then they stopped altogether, leaving him agonized with worry. He decided that in the spring, he'd take a few days off and go visit her and his mother.

The loneliness that was his lot at night grew worse in the winter. That was when he acutely felt the absence of a woman. And it wasn't that he didn't have opportunities. The opposite was true. On his first day on the job, the chubby, smiling secretary who greeted him and wrote down his personal details, asked him out on a date, but he rejected her politely. Then, Rico offered to introduce him to one of his family members, Laura, "a world-class beauty," he said. "Puerto Rican girls will eat you alive," he added with a wink, and Jeff gave in.

Rico was right. Laura did "eat him alive" on their first date, but she didn't capture his heart. After several dates, he realized she wasn't what his heart desired. And there was also the cute, nice girl he met every morning at the bus station on the way to work. They greeted each other with a good morning while they waited together for the bus. Once, she even sat next to him and started a conversation. She asked what he did and where he lived, but beyond that, nothing happened. Maybe something will happen, Jeff thought each morning, when he got off the bus and said good-bye to her. But he didn't make his move, and one morning, he arrived at the bus station and to his regret, she wasn't there. The feeling of missed opportunity followed him for days.

Sometimes he thought about Ellen. Ellen was a thirty-five-year-old divorcee, who worked with him at the diner at Eloy. She also relieved him of his virginity when he was seventeen. Now, he yearningly recalled her voluptuous body, her large breasts, and her pouty lips, which sucked eagerly on his tongue. Even Ellen, a woman whom he didn't even love, became the object of his desire during those lonely nights. He imagined curling in her arms, while she wrapped him in the heat of her soft body, scattering kisses all over him.

The yearning for a woman's body didn't abate, so he called Laura the man-eater again. She rejected him. Desperate, he ordered a woman off one of those websites. The sexual encounter calmed him a bit, but the sum she demanded, one hundred and fifty dollars, forced him to waive services destined for horny men. Among all these women, there was one mysterious girl. Not a girl, but a real woman, probably several years older than himself, perhaps even married. He saw her only once, at the end of summer, when he cleaned the windows in the enormous building where she worked.

"Millions of dollars are made in this building," Rico declared importantly.

"What's so special about it, besides its size?" Jeff asked.

"Oh, I wish you and me could walk into the joint. These are the offices of the largest brokerage firm in the world. Which means, they only invest for people who have at least a million bucks. Get it? A million bucks," Rico replied. After a brief pause, he added jokingly, "And I, Rico, am short of only one dollar to enter the gates of this building."

"Here, take a dollar to make up what you're missing," Jeff laughed. Then he sighed and said, "A fictional sum that I'll never in my life have. Come on, bro, back to reality. Let's go up to the roof. Otherwise, we won't have money to eat."

They collected their work tools and hurried to the elevator that led them straight to the roof of the building.

"And that's nothing," Rico stated, while he helped secure Jeff in the contraption. "Wait until we clean the windows of the Twin Towers. Then you'll see a real skyscraper! Those two are concrete monsters that will endure for another million years," Rico said and whistled appreciatively as he helped Jeff shimmy down.

Jeff moved from window to window, until he reached the window on the sixty-second floor, where he saw her. While he meticulously polished the glass with a rag, he noticed her in her luxurious office. In the beginning, she was on the phone and didn't notice him. She clacked on her keyboard while constantly talking on the phone. But then she gazed at the window, finally noticing him. In the beginning, she glanced at him without much interest. After a while, she looked at him again, and since, didn't take her eyes off of him and followed his work in amazement. For a moment, he thought she was gesturing with her hand that he come in, but that was impossible since the window was sealed shut. From his vantage point, he noticed her shapely body and her beauty. A moment before he finished the window, she suddenly abandoned her desk and approached the window, examining him closely with her large green eyes, and signaling something with her hand that he didn't understand. His breath hitched, to a point where he could hardly wave at her. And then, the harness in which he sat, lifted and quickly carried him to the next window.

The amazing woman disappeared.

After that brief, strange encounter, Jeff thought a lot about that woman, and mostly pondered how he'd meet her again. He amused himself with the thought that if he had a million dollars, he would go to her and ask her to invest them for him, thus gaining the opportunity to meet her again. And actually, why not? Granted, he had only seven thousand dollars that he'd painstakingly saved up, but weren't they enough to request investment consultation? When he met her again, he'd ask her where to invest the money, and maybe, who knows, she'd give him some good advice. He'd already heard about people who turned a thousand dollars into a million in less than ten years. And if he was lucky, he'd have, if not five million dollars, then at least fifty thousand. Just thinking about that sum excited him greatly.

All through the first months of winter, his thoughts jumbled in his head: sorrow for his sister, the money he may earn, and the desire for a woman. Mostly, his longing for the mysterious woman from the window on the sixty-second floor. And then, just when it seemed as though nothing would happen, it did.

One day, at the height of winter, Jeff and two other workers were summoned for urgent repairs in a fancy building in the heart of Manhattan. When they arrived at the building first thing in the morning, a uniformed doorman received them.

He led them to the area by the elevator.

"Who's in charge?" he asked.

"I am," said Jeff, who had the most seniority and experience.

"The door's broken, and you have to change its hinges." The doorman pointed at the door leading to the stairwell next to the elevator. Then he added, "And in the stairwell between the fourth and fifth floor, the ceiling plaster is crumbling. It needs a new coat of plaster and paint."

Jeff chose to fix the door next to the elevator and instructed the other two workers to fix the ceiling in the stairwell. He kneeled and took out his work tools, just as he heard the ding of the elevator, which stopped at the ground floor. The elevator door slid open. He heard the rap of high heels as the woman wearing them emerged from the elevator. Jeff raised his eyes to her and recognized her immediately—the beautiful woman from the sixty-second floor! She wore a short, red skirt that showed off long, shapely legs sheathed in black stockings. Through her white shirt, he could see a blue lace bra.

For a second, he thought their eyes had met. But maybe not? Perhaps, she hadn't even noticed him? To his disappointment, she emerged from the elevator and hastened her steps as she walked toward the exit. Had she not noticed him? Or maybe she did and chose to ignore him? Jeff concluded resignedly that she had, but apparently, his presence hadn't left any impression on her. And why should such a beautiful, rich woman show interest in him? Why would she be interested in a poor, uneducated guy like himself? She was probably married, and if not, she probably had many suitors, all of them rich, wealthy men from mid-Manhattan. In their previous encounter, she seemed to show interest, especially when she approached the window, and it seemed as though she had wanted to say something to him. But that had happened so briefly, just a fraction of a second before he moved on to clean the nearby window. The entire matter was just a figment of his imagination and nothing more, he concluded sorrowfully. People see what they wish to see, and to prove it, she had just passed by him, so close he could've touched her, and she hadn't even noticed him.

Reeling from the intensity of the encounter, he could barely turn his head to follow her rapidly disappearing image. Yet, then he saw something unexpected. He watched her cross the threshold and leave the building, already resigning himself to the fact he would never see her again, when she stopped. It looked as though she were hesitating, reconsidering something, deliberating whether to continue or turn back. In the end, she turned around and retraced her steps, until she stood two meters from him. Jeff lifted his head and stared at her in wonder, unable to hide his amazement at her beauty, which was even more astounding from up-close. He straightened slowly and looked straight at her, filling his lungs with her intoxicating scent. She stared at him as well. They looked at each other for one long minute, without a word.

"Hello," he finally managed, with no little difficulty, to say, breaking the awkward silence. "You're the lady from the investment firm, right? I cleaned your window last summer."

"Right," she whispered, having a hard time hiding the flush in her cheeks.

"Do you remember me?" he asked.

Not only did she remember his handsome face, but she also longed for the day she'd meet him again. "Oh, I remember," she replied shyly, surprised at herself. She'd never been shy before in the company of the opposite sex, not even as a teenager.

"Nice to meet you. Jeff." He extended a hand that was shaking from yearning and stress.

"Nice to meet you. Eve," she replied and shook his hand with one that was just as shaky. Then she smiled, and he smiled back.

"Why are you laughing?" he asked even though she wasn't.

"Never mind," she said, and suddenly her expression became serious. "When you have time, I have a table at home that requires some fixing up. Can you do that for me?" She remembered that her dinner table had one loose leg, and was glad to find an excuse to meet the cute guy again. She hoped good things would result from that future meeting, certainly better than the excited, ridiculous adolescent encounter they were having now.

"Yeah, sure," he replied happily.

"Great," she said, her eyes shining.

"And then you can help me." He remembered his original plan. "I have a small sum of money, and I don't know what to do with it. I was told you're an investment advisor. Would you be willing to recommend a fitting investment for me?"

Eve smiled in satisfaction. She took out a business card and gave it to Jeff. "Call whenever you want to meet…"

Jeff was sure he heard a note of seduction in her voice. A strangely delightful feeling encompassed him, a feeling he'd never felt before. He shoved the card into his wallet and returned to his tool box. At the end of the workday, just before he left the building, he approached the mailboxes in the foyer. On the mailbox of apartment seventy-two, he found her name: Eve Klein.

Chapter 5

A heavy silence descended on the Jewish neighborhood in Brooklyn. The synagogue goers had gone home and left the street silent and abandoned. The relentlessly falling rain took a short break. Only the many puddles were a silent testimony to the heavy rains that fell only minutes before. Dim beams of light shed by the street lamps glittered in the big puddles and induced a mystical atmosphere. The somewhat murky water seemed to conceal a mystery that no one had yet discovered.

Jeff walked quickly between the puddles on his way to Ahron's house, which was about twenty blocks from his basement apartment. He had wrapped up in warm clothes and took advantage of the brief dry spell. Despite the considerable distance and the overcast weather, he chose to forego the subway or bus. Usually, he didn't walk a lot, but it was the Shabbat, and he knew that traveling on a Shabbat was forbidden by the Jews.

It was another one of his many visits to his friend's house. Recently, his visits to Ahron had become even more frequent, and their friendship grew stronger. They met or talked on the phone almost every day. Even now, as he started walking faster because of the intense cold, he pondered for the hundredth time about the odd relationship between himself and the amiable young Jew, who was seemingly so different from him. Both of them were of almost similar height, and both had big blue eyes, yet apart from that, they were almost entirely different. Ahron's complexion was pale, and compared to Jeff's tanned face, he looked even paler. Ahron was skinny and fragile, while Jeff was lean and muscular. But their main difference was in their attire and hairstyle. Ahron was always meticulously dressed in a white button-down shirt and black slacks, while Jeff dressed casually in jeans and T-shirts. Ahron's head was shaved, while a golden mane covered Jeff's head. To those looking at them from the side, the differences seemed vast. They didn't even have common recreations. Their friendship was based mainly on the heart-to-heart conversations they held. More than once, Jeff wondered whether the fact that he lived by himself caused Ahron and his wife to invite him over as their guest, or perhaps his presence in their house really was important to them. He couldn't find a clear-cut answer. He didn't even concern himself with the question whether a Jew was permitted to have a gentile as his guest on the Shabbat evening.

The break in the rain had reached its end, and it started pouring again. Soaked to his bones, and panting from the long, exhausting walk, he knocked on his friend's front door. Miriam, Ahron's wife, dressed so modestly that Jeff thought it was completely over-the-top, welcomed him hospitably. Hanna'le, Ahron's four-year-old daughter, rushed toward him happily, jumped into his wet lap, and screeched joyfully, "Uncle Jeff, Uncle Jeff, I'm so happy you came!"

"Sweetheart, I'm glad I came, too," he said and lifted the child from his lap so as not to get her Shabbat clothes wet.

"*Oy*, you're so wet! Here, wipe yourself off." Miriam rushed to bring him a large, fluffy towel.

Jeff took the towel and wiped his hair. After doing that, Hanna'le ran to the armoire in the living room, took a large black yarmulke out of one of the drawers, and returned to him. Jeff bent down and allowed the young girl to put the black skullcap on his head.

"You don't have to put on a yarmulke. Don't let that little rascal control you," Ahron said, and didn't bother to hide his pleasure from the unique bond between the tall, muscular man and his mischievous little daughter.

"No problem. It doesn't bother me, and you can see for yourself how happy it makes her," Jeff said. He picked up the toddler and lifted her high as she screamed with joy.

"I brought something to make the meal a success," he said and held out a bottle of red wine. "Strictly kosher. And the wine made its way here on foot" He smiled at Ahron and Miriam.

Ahron took the bottle and looked at the label. "Indeed, very strictly kosher. I also believe that you walked over here, but unfortunately, I'm not sure if according to the Halacha, we can drink wine received from the hands of a gentile. I'll ask the rabbi, and if he approves, I promise I'll use the wine for the *kiddush* next Shabbat."

"Don't take offense, my friend," he said when he saw the hurt look on Jeff's face. "In Judaism, there's logic in everything. Things aren't decided randomly. Sometimes, even we common folk don't understand why things are done in a certain way. We do as the adjudicators decree and don't ask questions. Accept things simply, as well. Your intentions were good, and that's what matters."

A troubled silence fell on the living room and only Hanna'le's shrieks, while still in Jeff's arms, pierced the silence.

"Now, leave Jeff be and go get your chair because everyone is sitting down to eat," instructed Miriam in an attempt to ease the atmosphere.

"Are you all right, my friend?" Ahron asked.

"I'm fine. I'm sorry. I don't always think how the other side will accept things. I always expect people to act according to my logic, and what can you do that my logic doesn't always work as it should?" Jeff recovered.

"I understand. Let's forget about it and sit down to eat. I'm very hungry. Look, the table is full of delicious treats," Ahron smiled.

Before they sat down to eat, Ahron said the *kiddush*. Then they washed their hands, and only then, did they sit down to eat. At the end of the meal, everyone sang songs, and although Jeff didn't understand a word, he found the singing pleasant. Sometimes, he'd find himself humming some of the songs sung at the Shabbat meals, those that he remembered from previous times. After they had finished singing, Ahron said the *Birkat HaMazon*, the "Grace after Meals." Immediately after that, everyone abandoned the table and moved to the spacious sofa in the living room. Miriam served tea, and they all drank with pleasure.

"What are those songs you sing at the table?" Jeff asked curiously.

"Those are the Shabbat songs. In these songs, we express the delight we get from that particular day. It's important for us to convey that same delight around the dinner table. This way, we thank God for the food we eat and the day of rest he so kindly gave us. This is what we call *oneg* Shabbat, which means Shabbat entertainment," Ahron replied contentedly, enjoying the conversation that evolved on the subject of the holy day.

"And why don't you sing in English?"

"The songs are a combination of Hebrew and Yiddish, that's the reason. It'll sound strange to you, but there are Hebrew words in the song that I, myself, when I sing them, don't always understand. Funny, isn't it?"

"I've heard of Hebrew, but Yiddish? Does that even exist?"

"Yiddish is the language the Jews spoke in Europe in order to distinguish themselves from the Gentiles," Ahron explained.

Jeff still thought Jewish customs were weird.

Why didn't they eat all types of meat? And why wasn't television one of the Shabbat's entertainments? Ahron was talking about Shabbat entertainment, and was there anything more entertaining than a good TV show in the evening?

"Are there no televisions in all Jewish homes?" Jeff asked.

"No," Ahron laughed. "Unfortunately, there are Jews who aren't religious and don't maintain the sanctity of the Shabbat. They have a television, which they watch on the Shabbat. But we belong to the

Ultra-Orthodoxy, a sect of Judaism, and we think it's a corrupting appliance."

"The computer is also a corrupting influence. I heard children can watch profanity on it, God forbid, and the television shows shallow programs that don't contribute a thing to the education of children," Miriam contributed her opinion to the discussion.

"That's true," Jeff admitted. "A large part of the programs shown are utter garbage, and children are better off not watching them. Even I get bored sometimes from programs that tons of people are crazy about. But there are other programs you can learn from, for example from the Discovery channel and National Geographic."

"Right, but there's always the risk that things will get out of control and children will prefer the forbidden things. For the avoidance of doubt, it's better without the television and computer," Ahron tried to wrap up the discussion, which displeased him.

"I, for example, never watched television, and I don't feel that there's something missing in my life," Miriam supported her husband's argument.

"I don't believe it! How's that possible? Not even incidentally, while wandering in a shopping center, for instance?" Jeff persisted.

Miriam shook her head. "I don't go to shopping centers! Those places are also corrupting! Of course, I've seen a television, but I've never watched a program, not even once."

"So how do you keep up to date with what's happening in the world, and how do you commemorate and watch your joyful occasions if you have no television and computer?" Jeff wondered.

"We can listen to the news on the radio in the car. And important events, we videotape and keep on a cassette. But we mostly take pictures, like in the old days. There's no better way to preserve the past," said Ahron, who'd had enough of the conversation. He got up and went to the armoire, where he opened a drawer and took out three big albums. "This is our wedding album, this is our girls' album. In the third album, are the pictures of my extended family. Here you can also find pictures of the family pre-World War II."

Ahron placed two albums on the table and gave Jeff the third. Jeff looked through the album and examined the older ones. Pictures from the past, especially from WWII, fascinated him. Something in the fading images intrigued him. More than once, he wondered what his life would've looked like had he been born in the nineteenth century. He probably would've been a farmer, lived in a wood cabin, raised vegetables, and gathered hay to feed his cows. From time to time, he would've taken his wagon and ridden into town to buy provisions. And when he'd returned home, his wife, short and stout, wearing a long dress covered with a white apron, would've welcomed him with a smile. When he thought about life in the past, he always felt as though he'd have been better off living then.

He paused on one of the pictures. Ahron rushed to explain with undisguised pleasure, "That's my big sister and her two children. And this is my brother Shimon, who did Aliyah to Israel. Now he lives in Mea Shearim in Jerusalem." He said the word "Aliyah" in Hebrew.

"What's an Aliyah?" Jeff asked curiously, while he continued to study the images, which seemed to look back at him in amazement.

"Every Jew, who chooses to immigrate to Israel, the land of the Jews, makes Aliyah," Ahron explained.

"Interesting picture," Jeff said, pointing at a big picture that portrayed the faces of three young, pretty girls, wearing tattered clothes. Their light eyes were sad and anxious. They were very similar, and Jeff assumed they were sisters. In the background, old houses crowded side by side. The picture was so old, that the black and white had faded into a blurry gray.

"This picture was taken in Ghetto Warsaw during WWII. You can see how frightened they are, the poor girls," Miriam contributed.

"Who are these girls?" Jeff asked.

"These are the Kaminsky sisters. This one is Gietel, my grandmother, may she be of blessed memory. My father's mother.

She passed away three years ago. This is her young sister, Aunt Rachel. Aunt Rachel, may she live a long life, abandoned our way of life. She immigrated to Israel right after the war, married there, and until this day, she lives on a kibbutz. She must be seventy, maybe more. The last time I saw her was five years ago. She came to our wedding," Ahron explained at length.

"What's a kibbutz?" Jeff lifted his head and looked at his friend questioningly.

"It's a communal way of life that exists in Israel, similar to a way of life that existed in what was once the USSR," Ahron said curtly. He didn't like going into long explanations about the secular, abominable lifestyle customary in the Holy Land.

"And who's the third girl?" Jeff pointed at the thin girl, who out of all three, looked most tormented. Her face looked tense and portrayed profound sadness.

"Ach," Ahron sighed. "That's Hanna, Grandma Gietel's twin. The Nazis, damn them, transferred the Jews to the concentration camps, and took her, too. We don't know what happened to her. She was probably taken to the gas chambers, where she died. My little Hanna'le, may she live a long and prosperous life, carries her name."

Jeff had some general knowledge about the mass murdering that the Nazis committed against the Jews, Gypsies, and others. In school, he learned a bit about WWII and the Nazis' cruel massacre of the Jews. He'd also heard that most of the executions were done in the gas chambers, but in school, they didn't go into detail. He never gave much thought to the tragedy that occurred during the war. Why would he? It had happened many years before he was born and thousands of miles from where he grew up. Even if the victims had been Christians, he wouldn't have given it much thought. But now, staring at the tormented faces of those innocent, helpless girls, he felt something deep inside. He felt acute distress settling on him.

"Tell me more about those death camps," he requested.

"The Nazis, damn them, decided on an act called The Final Solution. Mass systematic destruction of the Jews. Not another random killing, but an organized genocide. Almost all of Europe's Jews were put on trains and taken to labor and death camps, built especially for that purpose. The minute they were taken off the train, they were stripped of their clothes and taken to the gas showers, where they suffocated to death. Then, the bodies were taken to the incinerators. So, ruthlessly, women and men, children and the elderly..."

"Gas showers? I'm not sure I understand," Jeff said, horrified.

"Yes, showers that the Nazis, damn them, inserted gas into, instead of water. You understand? Instead of water coming out, gas did. The epitome of evil," Miriam said.

"And they didn't resist?" Jeff wondered.

"When they boarded the trains, they were told they were taken to labor camps. Some, those who were healthy and strong, really were taken to the labor camps. Those taken to labor camps had a number tattooed on their arm. My uncle has a number like that to this day. The others, who were 'useless,' were instantly taken to the showers," Miriam explained.

"To this day, there are pictures that perpetuate the suffering that the Jews went through in the Holocaust. But what shocked me more than anything are the pictures of the shoes. Mountains of shoes! And the horrific thought that goes through your head is that behind every pair of shoes is a person who's no longer here," Ahron added with wet eyes.

"Monstrous," Jeff whispered in shock and continued staring at the picture, as though hit by lightning, paying mind to the clumsy, shabby shoes on Hanna's feet. He tried looking at the other pictures in the album, but the picture of those three girls kept flashing before his eyes. However, it was Hanna's frightened eyes that wouldn't give him peace.

When he returned home, he couldn't sleep. He kept thinking of the gas chambers in which millions of people found their deaths. He fell asleep just before dawn, but his sleep was a restless one.

In his dream, he stood in the middle of a sunny green field, full of flowers of all color. While strolling pleasurably, he noticed a distant grove, full of trees with bright green branches. As he admired the magical scene, he suddenly felt cold. So cold that even his winter attire couldn't warm him up. He carried his eyes to the sky and saw black clouds covering the sky. When he looked down, the flowers disappeared, and prickly bushes took their place. The trees shed their leaves, which dried up and turned black. The colorful scene faded, and the green field became dark and gloomy. And then he noticed them, a pair of threadbare shoes, hidden in one of the bushes. When he came closer, the shoes started to multiply, until they piled into a mound. He tried to retreat, but the mound grew larger until it became a huge mountain of shoes. Terrified, Jeff looked around, but the only thing he saw was an endless chain of mountains. All of them shoes. Baby shoes, children's shoes, men's shoes, and women's shoes. Then he noticed the shoes moving. First, they moved quietly and slowly, and then in an ear-splitting racket. Jeff started running for his life, and the shoes chased him. As he ran on, the shoes grew fewer and fewer, until only one shoe remained, a stubborn shoe that continued jumping along, the sound of its terrifying steps growing louder and louder. In a minute, it would hit his back and overcome him. From afar, he noticed a ramshackle shed that looked empty. He ran toward it, and when he arrived, he locked himself in one of the rooms. The pursuing shoe continued to knock on the door for a long time. In the end, it gave up and left. A distressing silence fell on the room. Jeff examined his surroundings. The room was small and narrow and empty. In the beginning, he was there alone, but gradually, many people started streaming in: women, men, old people, babies. Barefoot, naked, they entered the room, and it grew more and more crowded. Everyone pushed everyone. A silent mass that swayed from side to side, like a pendulum. Even if they breathed their last, they would remain standing. It was so crowded that no one would fall. Jews. The number burned on their arms exposed their identity. Jeff studied his arms. Thank God! He didn't have a number like the rest of these people. Then what was a Christian like himself doing among this herd of persecuted Jews? There must be a mistake that would be immediately corrected. He'd report this, and everything would be fine. Suddenly, he noticed Hanna, the girl from the picture. She stood in a corner of the room, her hands crossed behind her back. Unlike all the other people in the room, she wore the same clothes she wore in the picture. He tried to call her, but couldn't make a sound. Then, he raised his hand and waved at her, but she didn't notice him. Like all the others, her eyes were focused on the ceiling. Right over his head, a thin iron pipe protruded, and started permeating the damn gas into the room. Like the devil, you couldn't see it or smell it, but you could easily hear the rustle of poisonous air slowly creeping out of the pipe and spreading, with infuriating, cruel slowness, into the small, crowded room. Suddenly, the suffocating stench of urine and feces overwhelmed him. Fear had paralyzed the people in the room so strongly that they couldn't control their bowels.

"It's a mistake! A mistake! I've been brought here by mistake. I'm not a Jew!" he screamed. However, no one paid attention to his screams, and the gas just continued spreading from the ceiling, slowly, stubbornly. Jeff started to feel his throat close. His breaths became short and quick. Next to him, a lifeless woman stood, her weakened hands still clutching her dead baby, pressing it to her chest. And there was a little girl, too. She stood petrified, only the tears streaming from her blue eyes to her pale lips indicating she was human. Behind her, an old man froze in place while clutching his throat, in a desperate attempt to bring even a bit of oxygen to his lungs, his wide eyes refusing to believe. Jeff also opened his mouth, but there was no air. From the corner of his eye, he managed to see Hanna's head droop, her eyes rolling back in her head. And just one moment before he suffocated like everyone else, he made one last attempt to breathe. Jeff mustered what was left of his strength, took a deep breath, but instead, what came out of his mouth was a terrible scream that shook him and jerked him awake. His body was wet, as well as his pillow and sheet.

He hastily jumped out of his bed, as if it were a suffocation demon threatening to cut his life short, and ran to the kitchen. With trembling hands, he poured himself a glass of cold water. His head hurt and his legs were shaky. What was the meaning of that terrifying dream? Never before had he dreamed such a terrifying and tangible dream. He returned to bed and slept until noon.

The phone ringing woke him. At first, he considered not answering, but it just continued ringing. In the end, he gave in, got up, and answered. On the other side of the line was his mother.

"Dad died last night," she wept quietly.

Jeff wasn't surprised. Since that conversation with Pam, he expected a call notifying him of his father's death. Jeff accepted the news with mixed feelings. On the one hand, his death put an end to the ordeal that his father put his family through. On the other hand, he felt sorry for his mother, who was clearly sad, despite his father's abuse.

"When's the funeral?" he asked, even though he knew he wouldn't attend.

"Tomorrow. Can you make it?" she asked hopefully.

"I'm sorry, Mom. You'll have to manage without me. I can't leave work, and to tell you the truth, I don't want to come," he said truthfully.

His mother was silent. So was he.

"In a few more months, I'll get a few days off. When that happens, I'll come visit," he tried to cheer her up.

But his mother didn't answer. All he could hear was her quiet sobbing.

"Mom!" he called suddenly.

"Yes," she answered, and stopped crying.

"Don't worry, Mom. It'll be okay. If you need something, tell me. I have enough money. Tomorrow, I'll wire you enough money through Western Union to help you pay off funeral expenses."

"Thank you," she said.

"Good-bye, Mom."

"Good-bye, son," she replied and hung up.

She'd always called him Jeff, never "son." And now, when they were so far away, she called him "son." Maybe now that his father was gone, something would change in her?

After that conversation, he continued thinking about his dream. His identification with the Jews in World War II surprised him.

When darkness fell, he heard a knock on the door. At first, he wasn't sure, but then he heard another knock. He hurried to the door. When he opened it, a surprise awaited him.

Chapter 6

Saturday afternoon, it rained without a pause. The sound of the downpour permeated the house, breaking the silence. Rivka or Rivkel, like everyone called her, was almost alone in the big house. Her mother slept soundly in her room, and her father had left for a Torah lesson at the synagogue before the afternoon prayer. Calm overcame her. She lay on her bed contentedly, grasped her pillow with both hands, pressed it to her slender body, and rolled on the bed. The pillow against her breasts and stomach was pleasing. Her nipples pebbled, and a feeling of delight spread through her body. Only one more year, one year, until she too would come of age, leave home, and be alone with her intended. And thank God, she had a *shidduch* and a good one at that.

"Abraham-David comes from a good, well-to-do home, and most important, he's a prodigy in the Torah," the matchmaker promised. And why wouldn't he be? Why wouldn't she deserve a worthy husband? All her brothers and sisters were married, and all of them had exceptionally successful spouses. She was a fine girl as well, and she also deserved a good *shidduch*, she concluded to herself in satisfaction. After that, she raised her head and thanked God. She'd already seen her intended groom. Once she had seen him when the matchmaker had introduced the two families. The other times, she'd watched him at the synagogue, mostly during morning prayer on Saturday. Luckily, she liked him.

Her intended was a tall, thin man, with the smooth face of an angel, like a newborn baby. He had a protruding chin with a small dimple in the middle and large, upturned nose. He had small, deep-set brown eyes that were soft and tender. He always dressed well, as a Hasid of his position should. A black striped suit of the latest fashion covered a white shirt and a tie, and on his shaved head rested a fancy black hat. Long brown sideburns curled down the sides of his face and almost reached his shoulders. Indeed, every time she looked at him, she was content. Blessed be the Lord, who sent her an excellent groom.

Abraham-David was, without a doubt, the desire of every girl in the Hassidic community. Although they had never held a conversation, neither at her house or at the synagogue, more than once she'd heard his voice when he was called upon to read the Torah in the synagogue.

He had a clear, pleasant voice. She wondered what he thought of her. Did he also consider her a good match? Did he like children? She loved children and wanted many, even ten if possible. And he? She'd already heard about matches that had failed because one of the spouses was sterile or didn't even want children, God forbid, and that, despite the commandment to procreate. Then she decided to calm down; she had no doubt that that wasn't the case regarding them, and that Avraham-David loved children just as much as she did.

While she thought about her intended, she clambered off her bed and went to get an apple. She ate contentedly, and her large light-blue eyes followed the traces left by her teeth. So sweet and juicy, she thought and took one bite after another. The fruit of paradise, she concluded. Suddenly, she jerked her arm up in alarm and threw it as though it was a burning piece of coal. The apple rolled on the floor, until it stopped in the corner of the room, collecting dust that damaged its perfect beauty.

Rivka's face paled, and her lips quivered slightly. Eating an apple was explicitly forbidden! She'd eaten again without a blessing. This time, she skipped the "*bore pri haetz*" blessing, which blessed the fruit from the trees. Her fears grew stronger when she recalled that just this past Shabbat evening, as she prayed in the synagogue, she heard Rabbi Ziegel's sermon. Rabbi Ziegel, who was considered a great adjudicator, said that eating fruit without a blessing was the same as stealing. Eating without thanking God, who had given us that food, was the same as stealing, the rabbi adjudicated resolutely. And she, Rivka, was not a thief, God forbid!

This wasn't the first time she'd stumbled. A week ago, she'd gobbled up a slice of cream cake, and only when she'd finished eating it, did she remember that she didn't say the "*Mezonot*" prayer. And there was that time when she went to bed and fell asleep without saying the evening "*Arvit*" prayer. In the middle of the night, she'd jerked awake in fright, her entire body trembling from fear. In an attempt to atone for her sin, she'd sat on her bed, and read the "Shema Israel" and five more chapters from Psalms. Only then, did she go back to sleep. But these sins were nothing compared to the sin she committed last Thursday. A sin of true lawlessness. And she had no one to blame but herself, for this time she'd sinned clear-mindedly.

She and Dvora, her best friend, had snuck into one of Manhattan's shopping centers. The decision to do that was unbearable and wasn't made easily. Dvora had tried many times to commit the terrible, daring deed, yet she was unsuccessful.

"What sin is there in two girls taking an innocent walk in the city?" Dvora persisted.

"You're crazy! What business do we have in the city?"

"I'm not crazy! You're crazy!" Dvora retaliated. "What's crazy about two girls getting on the bus and going to the city center?"

"Okay, don't get mad! I promise I'll think it over," Rivka said, trying to cool her friend's ire without any intention of keeping her promise.

"Well, have you considered my offer?" Dvora asked several days later.

"What offer exactly?" Rivka asked oh so innocently.

"You're kidding, right? Our trip into the city, of course! You promised you'd think it over."

"Honestly? I didn't really mean it when I said that. Enough with this craziness, Dvora. There's nothing for us in the city!" she replied.

"Sometimes, I think you're totally stupid. Can you explain to me, once and for all, what's so awful about us seeing and knowing what's going on around us? We don't live in an empty world. Events that shock everyone are happening right next to us, and we just close our eyes. The rabbis control us and forbid us from doing almost everything. Why should we listen to a bunch of old men whose only wish is to lock us up at home and leave us ignorant?"

Dvora's harsh and unexpected attack astounded Rivka.

"*Oy vey!* What are you saying? You mustn't talk like that. You'll be punished by forces above," she gasped in alarm.

"The fact of the matter is that, although I think like this all the time, nothing's happened to me. I'm healthy and whole. And I'll let you in on a secret: several weeks ago I took the subway into the city, all by myself, and I actually had a lot of fun."

"To the city? All by yourself?" Rivka paled.

Dvora nodded, and her eyes twinkled.

"The fires of hell will consume you at the end of your days, and nothing will be left of you," Rivka flung at her.

"Will you relax with that nonsense! It's just an innocent stroll in the city."

"A city full of abomination is not an innocent stroll. You'll end up like Mrs. Zliekowitz, who was banished from the Hasidic community until she went crazy, and now she's in the madhouse," Rivka stated decisively.

"Yeah, such a disaster. I hope they'll banish me, and I'll be free of this prison. And reading books in secret, as opposed to the rabbis' opinion, is not a sin!"

"That's not the same thing at all," Rivka said uncomfortably.

"Why?" Dvora said defiantly.

"Because… because… because reading adds knowledge, while a walk in a city filled with lasciviousness is a disgraceful act that conflicts with our ways." Rivka could barely find the words, but she articulated them tastefully, just like the books she read.

The two girls had been reading fiction, poetry, and philosophy of all kinds for quite a while. However, while Dvora loved plain fiction, Rivka focused on science books. She especially loved books that taught about the universe. Not that she doubted the creation of the world by God Almighty, God forbid.

She felt as though, this way, she was learning about the creation in a more thorough and profound way. The two girls had always felt like confidants, and together, they'd secretly devoured the written word. They'd been very close friends since childhood. Together, they adhered to ways of the Torah, unquestioningly and unthinkingly. Reading did expand their horizons, but it didn't cause them to doubt, even slightly, the truthfulness of the way their parents had paved for them.

At least, that's how things were until that point, because lately, it seemed as though Dvora had lost it. Her mind and mouth were filled with heresy, to the point that sometimes Rivka considered abandoning her good friend. She was afraid that some of that heresy would stick to her. Was the fact that a *shidduch* hadn't been found for Dvora the reason for those fissures in her faith? Perhaps, her good friend was envious of her and wanted to drag her to forbidden places, and thus, to cause her to fail? Or perhaps, she'd experienced something that totally made her lose her mind? Rivka was convinced that she was better off taking a step back from their friendship, which seemed more dangerous than ever. But something in her wouldn't allow her to do so. She loved Dvora deeply, of that she had no doubt. Would abandoning her be the honorable, fair thing to do? Wasn't it better that she speak to her heart and set her back on the straight path? But perhaps Dvora was right? Not completely right, yet, maybe there was a grain of truth in her words? What was the harm if they went into the city for a short outing? From the day she was born, she'd never left Brooklyn even once. She didn't know a thing, apart from school, synagogue, and the houses of friends and relatives. Her only aperture to the world was through the books hidden in the back of her closet. This certainly wasn't a life well lived, but when she got married, everything would change. She and Avraham-David would travel the world, thus satisfying her curiosity.

Her friend Dvora had no doubts. Her first sexual experience had changed her opinion from one extreme to the other. She gave her virginity to a boy she barely knew, and ever since, had met him regularly and experienced a new world, full of insatiable thrills and passions. She kept the relationship a secret from Rivka, afraid that it would frighten her friend, and she would cut off her ties with Dvora. But that didn't stop her from trying to cajole her to go out together to the big world. Without understanding why Rivka eventually succumbed to her friend's caprices. Perhaps *yetzer hara*, the inclination to evil, also raged within her?

One day, they secretly snuck out and traveled straight to the shopping center in the heart of Manhattan. They went from store to store and studied the daring dresses presented, alas, in front of everyone. Rivka couldn't stop looking around in fright, terrified someone she knew would walk by and see her.

"It's promiscuity to wear a dress like that, which doesn't cover a thing," she whispered in her friend's ear while Dvora studied in amazement the transparent red dress on the dummy in the window.

"I'd actually like to try that dress on. At least once," Dvora said and winked at her friend, and both of them burst out laughing. The idea that the buxom Dvora would wear a dress with such a generous neckline amused both of them.

"Let's go inside. I want to try it on," she said.

"God forbid! That does it! I won't even consider it! If you go in, I'm leaving!"

"So wait for me outside, scaredy cat. And look at me from outside. Believe me, you'll have something to look at." Dvora laughed.

Before Rivka had time to react, Dvora entered the store, leaving behind a shocked and confused Rivka. She approached the salesgirl and pointed at the dress in the window. The salesgirl gave Dvora a thorough once-over, went to one of the shelves, and returned with the desired dress. Several minutes later, Dvora emerged from the changing room with a victorious smile. Rivka almost fainted when she saw her friend. Under the transparent dress, her racy blue underwear and transparent bra were easily noticeable. Her large breasts threatened to burst from the narrow dress.

"Take that off and get out of that shop right now, crazy!" Rivka shouted from outside. "All we need is someone to notice you, and that's the end of us."

"You're crazy," Rivka told her friend when she emerged from the store. "I am now positive you belong in the madhouse."

"Indeed, I am. I'm crazy, but at least I'm crazy and happy," Dvora replied, and her eyes danced happily.

"I didn't know that those innocent dresses you wear hide such daring undergarments. How do you have the guts to wear bras and panties like those? And where did you get them from?"

"From here," Dvora answered succinctly.

"From here?" Rivka's jaw dropped open in shock.

"I bought them in this shop several days ago. Remember, I told you I was in the city?"

"Yes, I remember. Now let's go home! I've had enough for one day," Rivka demanded.

"It's your turn now," Dvora said suddenly, ignoring her friend's anger.

"My turn? With the transparent dress? Are you out of your mind? I've had enough of your craziness; I want to go home!"

"You know what? I have an idea. Not the dress. Try on a pair of pants. Don't be afraid! I'm curious to see what you look like in a pair of pants."

"No," Rivka said resolutely and started walking toward the exit of the shopping center.

"All right, calm down." Dvora hurried after her. "It took us so long to get here, and already you want to leave? Let's stay here for another half hour. Just a half hour, I promise."

"A half hour and that's it? Not one minute more, and no nonsense, and you'd better keep your promise."

They continued going from shop to shop until they entered a large electronics store. The store was heaving with consumers. The noise was deafening, and colorful lights flashed on the television screens. Rivka stopped and stared at one of the television screens. A masculine man appeared on the screen, wearing shorts, and diligently demonstrating exercises. For several long minutes, she curiously followed the flexible, sinewy athlete's movements.

"Hey, Rivkel," Dvora swooped on the opportunity. "I didn't know you noticed men. If Avraham-David knew... there goes the *shidduch*..."

"Don't be mean. He just reminds me of that guy who lives in our basement, the one who rented the place from my brother. And what do you mean 'notice'? He's a *Christian*!" Rivka almost spat in anger.

"Okay, sweetie, calm down, I'm just joking. Even if you do desire other men apart from your intended, it's fine with me."

"You're crazy. I've had enough of you today!" Rivka concluded, and they started making their way to the subway.

At the station, they noticed a couple kissing. Rivka covered her eyes with both hands, and Dvora burst into laughter at the sight of her shy friend.

When they sat at the back of the car, Dvora whispered, "Say, have you ever tried it?"

"Tried what?" Rivka asked.

"Touching there," Dvora looked at her friend's lower stomach. "I don't understand what you mean," Rivka really didn't understand what she meant.

"Touching here," Dvora gestured at her vagina.

"Are you crazy? What's wrong with you today? You've lost your mind completely!" Rivka hissed, horrified, and turned her head away so her friend wouldn't notice her flushed cheeks.

"You should try. It's the most wonderful thing in the world..." Dvora whispered in Rivka's ear.

"I'll pass on that pleasure!" Rivka bit out decisively.

"It's called *masturbation*, sweetie," Dvora teased her friend. "It's this supreme feeling that I can't even describe in words. You should try it once."

"Stop, please stop. I don't want to hear anything else," Rivka cried out and closed her ears. It seemed as though her anger had achieved its purpose. Dvora fell silent.

That night, lying in bed, Rivka couldn't stop thinking about what she'd seen that day. She kept seeing her friend wearing that transparent dress, her curves visible, like the women who sold their bodies in houses of inequity. Then she recalled the moans of delight of the girl at the subway station. Was it love or just wanton acts meant to satisfy cheap passion? When she thought of it, she was overcome by an odd feeling. Her body trembled with excitement. Hesitantly, she touched herself lightly, first her breasts and then down there, in that forbidden place. She wanted to understand that thrill her friend talked about. In her imagination, she saw her neighbor from the basement lean toward her, kiss her, and passionately knead her breasts. Her hands continued to stroke herself, and a forbidden pleasure, the kind that she'd never felt before, started spreading through her body. She moaned. Her head threatened to explode. And then, just before she reached satisfaction, she panicked and jerked her hands away. Slowly, the excitement passed, replaced by shame and regret. The excursion into the city and her hands on her body seemed now like a crazy journey of lasciviousness and abomination. She tried to delete the day's events from her mind, but unsuccessfully. Only then, did she notice that the object of her passion wasn't Avraham-David, her intended groom, but the neighbor from the basement apartment. Rivka remembered their first meeting. It was in the evening, during one of her many visits to her brother's house. Usually, when the front door opened, little Hanna'le would run to her. But this time, Hanna'le was sitting on the lap of an unfamiliar man. He read the little girl a story from a book they were holding together. The child was so fascinated by the story, that she didn't even bother to glance at her aunt. Under different circumstances, Rivka would've been offended, but now, looking at the handsome, intriguing young man, she forgot all about Hanna'le.

"Meet my sister, Rivka. Remember I told you about her?" Ahron stopped Jeff's storytelling in order to introduce her.

"Sure, the one who laughs like me and is going to get married. Pleased to meet you. I'm Jeff." The tan blond man got up, bowed, and smiled at her, but didn't extend his hand.

"He's already learned that our women don't shake hands with men," Miriam explained smugly to Rivka, who stood shy and flushed.

During that entire evening, she couldn't stop sneaking looks at the young man who'd charmed her so. There was a reason Ahron chose him as his friend, she thought.

Rivka got out of bed, lifted the eaten apple from the floor, and threw it into the garbage. Then, she took the mishnayot and started reading. Reading mishnayot helped one atone for one's sins, the rabbis promised. While reading, she focused on the words, although not very successfully. In the beginning, the betrayed Avraham-David snuck into her thoughts, and later, gradually, without her noticing, Jeff consumed all of her thoughts. She stopped reading, put the book on the table, sprawled on her bed, and then, curled her body and thought about everything that had happened to her lately.

She noticed that up to the day she'd met him, her life had been amazingly tidy. She prayed all the prayers, read all the Psalms chapters, and above everything, never ever forgot any of the mandatory prayers. Not even once! And now, who would believe it, but in one month she'd stumbled four times! Four times, God forbid! And God punished, too. He saw and followed her actions, read her mind, and would certainly judge her harshly.

He would punish her terribly. He would probably put her to death by torture, as befitting a sinner like herself. And all this, why? Because of a Christian, who had bewitched her and scrambled her brain.

But perhaps the change she was going through wasn't about him? Why was he to blame? And if it wasn't him, what was the source of that wantonness that had overcome her? Was it all Dvora's fault, leading her astray and enticing her?

She thought about it tirelessly, until she finally reached the conclusion that the man she'd first met a month ago at Ahron's house, and later saw time after time in the neighborhood, was the reason for the confusion that plagued her and threatened to consume her.

She started Saturday properly: went to synagogue, prayed devotedly, and when she came home, washed her hands, said her prayer, and ate the food her mother had prepared. When she finished, she devoutly said the *Birkat HaMazon*, and then went to her room. In her room, she tried to think only about Avraham-David, and she'd actually succeeded until she took a bite from that apple. Yes, the apple that had caused Adam and Eve's misdemeanor in paradise had also tripped her, and since, all her thoughts had wandered toward Jeff.

She imagined his appearance. His smooth, tan face, sea-blue eyes, and blond mane. But more than anything, she thought about his strong, masculine body. He wasn't skinny like Avraham-David. His body was sturdy and tan, like that man she saw on television at that mall that was filled with immorality. Once again, she fantasized about her body pressed to his, and how he'd embrace her with his muscled arms, and then kiss her tenderly, whispering words of love. Suddenly, the most forbidden thought of all sprung to mind: how she yearned to spend some time alone with him. Yes, alone. Consequences be damned! Indeed? Was she brave enough to go to him? Could she desecrate the name of God, and do that terrible thing? And if so, then how? Sneaking into his house wasn't a complicated mission, but what would happen to her if she got caught? And if she managed to get all the way to him, would she have the nerve to kiss him like she'd imagined? Would she get to taste the flavor of love?

Love?

Of course, it wasn't love! Was it possible that she, a God-fearing Jew, fall in love with a Christian? And if not, how to explain her powerful desire to spend time with him? Was it just sexual desire? No, it was not! Desire was the lot of wanton girls, and she wasn't a wanton girl! Well then, what could be the reason for the thoughts that had plagued her and threatened to drive her mad? There was only one conclusion. When she thought about it, her entire body trembled: she was in love!

Darkness had fallen, and the rain had stopped. Rivka left her room and went to the living room to hear her father pray the Havdalah. After the Havdalah, she snuck out to the street, where her legs carried her to a place she feared more than anything. The place that could change her life from one extreme to the next.

Chapter 7

Darkness fell slowly on the Brooklyn boulevard, carrying a mysterious opaqueness. The soft golden lights of the street lamps barely lit the path leading to the basement apartment. In the weighty silence, the rustle of drainpipes, as the rainwater poured from the rooftops and splattered on foggy streets, was easily heard. It was cold, very cold. The many layers she wore didn't prevent the cold from penetrating her clothes. Temperatures were close to zero and threatened to freeze her hands. Despite the cold, a film of sweat covered her body and her head burned. Her excitement increased with every step she made. She walked slowly, barely dragging her feet, which suddenly became unbearably heavy. Suddenly, she started shaking, shudders increasingly wracking her body the closer she got to the steps leading to Jeff's apartment. Her heart raced crazily, like the heart of a sprinter swallowing distances as fast as possible. She stopped in her tracks, breathed deeply, trying to find some calm in the storm raging in her soul. She was well aware of the fact that she wasn't supposed to do this. What did a Jewish girl have to do in the house of a Christian man who lived alone? For a moment, she considered retracing her steps, but as though the devil himself urged her on, her feet continued walking, carrying her to the unknown. When she arrived, she knocked so softly on the door that she herself could hardly hear it. When there was no answer, she knocked again, this time, harder. When she heard his approaching footsteps, she panicked, whirled around, and climbed up the steps leading to the deserted street.

"Rivkel, is that you?" She heard him calling her by her nickname like her friends and family called her.

She stopped. Then she tried to turn to him, but she seemed frozen in place.

"Rivkel, why are you standing like that?" he persisted.

She turned to him slowly, hoping the flush on her cheeks would disappear and she with it. She yearned for the ground to swallow her, so great was her shame.

"Come on down. Why are you standing outside? It's really cold," he invited her in.

It was very cold. Only then did she feel the freezing temperatures. She walked down slowly and hesitantly entered his apartment.

"There, now you're warmer, right?" he said.

She nodded, still unable to find the appropriate words.

Jeff couldn't hide his surprise at the unexpected visit. It wasn't that he was displeased to see her, on the contrary. The harsh winter days forced him to spend most of his time in his apartment in oppressive solitude. And now, without preparation, he received a visit, and not just any visit, but a visit from his favorite girl. He questioned the purpose of her visit, for he knew that, according to her faith, she was forbidden to visit a man's house on her own.

After a brief silence, he said, "Make yourself comfortable, Rivkel. Sit down, and I'll make you tea to warm you up a bit." He pointed at the little loveseat and went to the kitchenette.

Rivka remained standing in place, silent. Only her wide, frightened eyes followed the sinuous movements the man who fascinated her so. She could hear a cat yowling outside. *He must be cold, too*, she thought. Did these howls hint at what the future held for her?

"I'm glad you're here. Finally, someone visits me at this crappy house, keeping me some company," he called from the kitchen. "Do you still have your coat on? The fire's burning, and it's hot here. You should take it off or you'll catch a cold when you go back out," he told her when he returned.

Wordlessly, Rivka slid out of her coat, unable to find the right words.

"I hope this is just a polite visit, and nothing happened to force you to come here," he continued. She shook her head.

"Good, I'm glad it's like that."

"I shouldn't be here," she mumbled suddenly.

"Sorry? I didn't hear you. What did you say?"

"I shouldn't be here."

"Why? What's wrong with this?" he asked, even though he knew the answer.

"Don't you understand? If anyone finds out I was here, I'll be in big trouble, and so will you and so will Ahron. He'll be blamed for opening his house to you and causing us to meet, and you, you can expect my father to run you out of here in disgrace," she said agitatedly. Suddenly, she realized the gravity of her actions.

Jeff wasn't surprised. Ahron had explained this to him before. "A woman isn't allowed to be alone in a closed place with a man who isn't her husband," he explained to Jeff, out of his fear that Jeff would arrive unannounced at his house and find himself alone with Miriam. And now, he was alone with his sister. What did that say about him?

He remembered the day he first saw her at Ahron's. He liked her from the start. She was a charming, vivacious girl, thin and tall, with curly golden hair and big blue eyes, her nose upturned and her cheeks pink. The many layers covering her couldn't hide her attractive curves. There was something magical about her that made him want to spend some time with her. Was it love? He'd never been in love before. So if he was, how would he know? One thing was for sure, spending time in her company at Ahron's house was really nice, and maybe even beyond that. He remembered being charmed by her looks, but he especially admired her wit, her maturity, and her wisdom. Her knowledge about world events surprised him and mostly surprised Ahron. He recalled the knowledge she demonstrated on the subject of the universe. "Scientists think there are life forms on other planets," she told them importantly. "And that our solar system is just one of many. And what's even more surprising, they think that parallel to our universe there are other universes. Can you believe it? And all this was created by God, His name be praised."

"I didn't know you knew so much about the universe," Ahron said, looking in bafflement at his sister. "To the best of my knowledge, this isn't something we're taught in school."

"It's just some things I overheard a woman say to her friend when I was waiting for a doctor's appointment," Rivka lied, her face flushing.

When she saw that Ahron was having a difficult time believing her, she added, "And besides, the Rabbi Melubavitz studied astronomy, too, did you know?"

"No, I didn't know. And besides, the Rabbi Melubavitz isn't our rabbi. You should remember that," Ahron responded sternly.

She'd interested Jeff back then, and now, here she was, a young fragrant flower, so pretty, just begging to be picked. What would stop him from reaching out, gathering her to his body, kissing her soft lips, and carrying her to bed? He was convinced that she would easily succumb, otherwise, why else would she come here? But he wouldn't do it. He wasn't a bastard. And she was an innocent, inexperienced girl. He couldn't have a real relationship with her. What would happen to her if someone found out she'd spent time in the company of a man, and a Christian at that?! No, he wouldn't do something like that. Hurting her was like hurting Ahron, his friend, a man who'd been so kind to him.

"You're right, Rivkel, you really shouldn't be here. It's best that you go now," he said with great difficulty and made a move to escort her to the door. "We'll meet at your brother's, where we'll be able to talk without fear," he urged her.

"I'm sorry I disturbed you," she said at last and walked toward the door.

Suddenly, she stopped and gave him a long, sorrowful look. Then, she walked back to him, raised herself timidly on her toes, and pressed against his body. She brought her lips close to his and whispered in a trembling voice, "Kiss me, please! Just once! I'll live in sin until the end of my days, if only you'll kiss me one time. Please, just one time."

Jeff was surprised, but before he had time to do anything, he felt her lips caressing his, hesitant, as though fumbling in the dark. Then he felt her tongue foraging into his mouth, which was slack from surprise. He heard her moan and felt her writhe in his arms, which held her tightly. Just for a second, he thought of picking her up and carrying her straight to his bed. Desire burned through him and madness consumed him. In a moment, he'd pick that forbidden wildflower that stumbled onto his path so surprisingly. As he burned with passion, misgivings tormenting him, she suddenly shoved at him, tearing herself from him, grabbed her coat, and fled tearfully, leaving him standing there, stunned.

"Rivkel, don't go, please stay," he managed to call after her before she slammed the door and ran up the stairs.

When she returned to her room, agitated and frightened, she was filled with remorse for the terrible crime she'd just committed. She'd sold her soul in favor of her body. She let carnal lust consume her. There was no greater sin. God wouldn't forgive her; He'd send the fires of hell to finish her, she was sure of that. "What have I done?" she sobbed quietly. "I'm worse than Dvora. Even she doesn't do things like this."

After a long time, she calmed down and thought of him again. She felt the sweetness of his lips and remembered his warm, strong body pressing against hers. Then she imagined how he'd cradle her in his arms, like a prince in a fairytale, and take her straight to seventh heaven, to a place where they'd live happily ever after.

Suddenly, she was sure of her feelings. She really, really was in love. And love knew no satiation. Her love was boundless. Her love was uninhibited. She felt an uncontrollable urge to press against his body again, to rest her head in his bosom and inhale his sweet scent. To send a caressing hand to his hair and face, and kiss him passionately. To entwine her tongue with his, and sink with him to the depths of sin and pleasure. She closed her eyes, and pleasure filled her. A full-bodied shiver ran through her. Once, thinking about kisses filled her with revulsion. She thought that kisses were the lot of immoral sinners. And now, in such a short while, everything had changed. Now, she knew what a kiss was. A kiss expressed powerful emotions and a desire to connect with one's beloved. Yes, she wanted to connect with him, and even, God forgive her, give him her virginity. Succumb to him completely and allow him to do to her whatever he wanted. From now on, she belonged to him, and only to him.

You wanton girl, she scolded herself angrily. This wasn't love. It was the diseased desire of any street girl. Yes indeed, she was wanton like one of those cheap girls who sold their bodies for fleeting satisfaction. She wasn't worthy of Avraham-David. She was damaged. Damaged! Lust had sunk its talons into her, and everyone knew that lust was the devil itself. That's it, she was a goner. The *yetzer hara* had controlled her, consuming both body and soul.

Confused by the events of the day, she fell asleep shortly before dawn. After a short, restless nap, she woke up. However, the moment she opened her eyes, she realized that her life had changed forever. She couldn't marry Avraham-David. Marriage was an eternal alliance based on a life of truth and trust. And even before entering this alliance, she'd betrayed Avraham-David's trust. She was no longer as pure as before. She was damaged, a deformity that couldn't be cured. She'd kissed a stranger. And that wasn't all. Even worse was that she constantly thought about that stranger, who'd stormed into her life, and now, her only desire was to spend time in the company of a man who wore around his neck a gold necklace with a cross. The thought scared her to death. Suddenly, her face was overcome with uncontrollable tics that she didn't understand. Frightened, she ran to the mirror and looked at her face, which looked distorted. She pressed her lips together and sucked in her cheeks in terror in an attempt to stop their spasming, but to no avail. Afterward, she went to the kitchen for a glass of cold water, hoping that it would help some. Yet, when she drank from the glass, she gasped and almost choked.

"What happened, Rivkel?" her mother rushed into the kitchen in alarm.

"Nothing! Really nothing, Mom. I may have swallowed too quickly, and the water went down the wrong pipe," she lied and hurried back to her room, leaving behind her startled and confused mother.

For an entire week, she barely ate or drank a thing. She hardly said a word. She spent most of her time in her room so no one would witness her corruption. Occasionally, her mother came to her room to bring her her meals.

"What are you going through, child? Does something hurt? Is something bothering you? Why aren't you eating the tasty food I bring you? I'm cooking especially for you, all the things you love…" her mother asked, and Rivka would wave her off with noncommittal answers.

Then, an unexplained illness plagued her. Her fever went up, the spasms in her face continued and even increased. Her concerned parents called the doctor, who gave her a thorough checkup. "This girl lives in fear," he declared. "I'll prescribe her pills that will calm her down. Don't worry, she'll start feeling better soon, and within several days, God willing, she'll be as good as new," he assured the concerned parents.

"With God's help, with God's help," they mumbled.

At the time, Rivka had turned off her cell phone, mostly because she didn't want Dvora to call her, and then, unintentionally, she,

Rivka, would reveal her feelings. She knew Dvora was the only person she could tell what she was going through, that she'd always find a listening ear with her friend, and that with her help, she'd be able to get through those difficult days. On the other hand, she wasn't sure she should talk with that instigator. Dvora could exacerbate her situation with her awful heresy. In the end, she decided she was better off not saying a thing and keeping her secret to herself.

But one hour later, Dvora came to visit. She burst into her room and yelled at her, "Why aren't you answering your phone? What kind of friend are you? I've called you dozens of times, both to the landline and to your cell phone, I've left you a thousand messages, and it's like the ground has swallowed you! You disappeared!"

Secretly, Rivka was glad that her friend came. Finally, someone would bring her back to life. But she couldn't answer her friend.

"Why aren't you saying anything? Don't you have anything to say? Cat got your tongue?"

"Stop, Dvora. Please, just leave me alone," Rivka said and burst into tears.

"You look awful, sweetie! What are those tics? God above, something awful must've happened to you... I think I can guess what it's about." Dvora's aggressive tone was replaced with a softer, placating one.

Rivka stopped sobbing and lifted her head. She looked at her friend. Did she know?

"That guy from the basement apartment... You have a huge crush on him, right?"

Well then, Dvora did know. The rascal had sharp senses. All her cunning friend needed was a brief slip of the tongue to find out everything. Rivka didn't answer, but her silence was as good as a confession.

"Back when we were in the city, I saw your eyes shine when you talked about him. Obviously, something's happened since then...

nu, tell me," Dvora continued, her expression amused from the new situation.

Rivka hesitated.

"*Nu*, come on. Spill," Dvora urged her.

"I kissed him," Rivka mumbled, and Dvora wasn't sure she'd heard correctly.

"I'm sorry, I didn't hear what you said. Care to repeat?"

"I kissed him," Rivka weakly repeated her words, and followed her friend's reaction worriedly.

"What do you mean you kissed him? Just a kiss?"

"Yes, a kiss. A kiss full of passion. A kiss full of sin. You do realize, Dvora, that I kissed a Christian man, right?" Rivka started crying again.

"Stop!" Dvora ordered. "Cut it out! Nonsense! Why are you crying? What are you, a little girl? So, you kissed a guy. Big deal!"

"You're crazy, Dvora!" Rivka responded angrily. "You're talking as though you come from another world. You know what will happen to me if anyone finds out. The rabbis will banish me, and my life will become a living hell. I'll be wedded to a third-class man. Probably a cripple, or a blind man, or an old man with ten children! You *know* that's how things are done here! So don't try to pretend you're progressive, okay?" she attacked furiously.

"What are you talking about? Who'll make your life a living hell, *who*? Rabbi Ziegel, whom everyone says he commits homosexual intercourse with his students? Or maybe Rabbi Shmilov, the Torah prodigy, who for years it's been rumored that he enjoys the company of prostitutes?" Dvora blew out a breath and then continued heatedly, "Oh, I know who you mean when you say 'rabbis.' You must mean the great adjudicator, Rabbi Ziegel, who sexually abuses every woman who comes to him for help. Yeah, well if those are the rabbis you mean, then they can all go to hell! I don't give a you-know-what about them."

Rivka stared at her friend with her mouth open. She, like everyone else, had heard the rumors about the community's rabbis, but she was sure that it was nothing more than evil gossip, which was rife among the people of the Hassidic community. *And even if that is the situation,* she thought, *why should I pry in the forbidden businesses of others?* And then came Dvora, and all at once, shooting off a clear-cut unequivocal rant, slung at her the ugly truth.

"You know, Dvora, how evil gossip is. How do you even know it's the truth? On this matter, the only thing to say is 'Those who guard their mouths and their tongues guard themselves from calamity.' You're better off not saying anything else about this. It's blasphemy." Rivka sat on the bed, grabbed her pillow, propped it against the wall, and leaned her head on it. She felt smug that she'd heatedly defended people she considered completely righteous. Just for a second, the spasms in her face stopped.

"'Those who guard their mouths and their tongues guard themselves from calamity,'" Dvora mocked. "You really think it's plain gossip? You're so naïve, Rivkel. Even worse, you're a total fool. Let me tell you a story and listen carefully. Just the other day, when I passed by the Beit Midrash, Rabbi Zeigel stood at the doorway. He called me and asked that I come to his room, claiming that he wanted my advice on something. Yeah, right. When I walked in, he started praising me, saying how smart and beautiful I am. He said that of all the young women in the community, I'm the only one who seems to him like an admirable girl. 'You can be trusted,' he said and came closer, putting his hand on my shoulder."

"And then?" Rivka asked in alarm.

"And then the dirty old man continued stroking me, and suddenly his hand slid under my shirt. I felt him knead my breasts. And mean old me, I let him get a bit horny, and then I jumped up and ran outside. I left the old pervert shocked and aroused," she concluded, laughing.

"I don't believe you," Rivka stated, even though she knew Dvora was telling the truth. Dvora had never lied to her.

"Oh, you believe me! Deep inside, you know I'm not lying. These are the people we live with, and you think I care? I don't because I know that one day I'm going to leave and live my life to my heart's desire." Dvora sprawled on the bed, rested her head on her friend's legs, and her vivacious face calmed.

"Even if it is true, it still doesn't change my situation. It's not like I can come to them and ask them 'Why are you punishing me while you're committing such awful things?' That's how things happen here, and you know it," Rivka said after she briefly thought it over.

"Regarding that, you're one hundred percent right. It won't help you, but at least you can live with yourself with a clear conscience." Dvora felt as though they were on the verge of a severe dialogue. She sat down, stretched, and prepared for what was going to happen. To her disappointment, Rivka remained silent.

"Nu, Rivkel, why aren't you saying anything?" Dvora urged her, disappointed.

"I don't know what to say. Even worse, I don't know what to do."

"I'll tell you what to do! Listen to your heart! Do what your heart tells you to do. Don't be afraid, because what are the ways of the world? What's life worth, if a person doesn't do what's good for her? On condition, of course, that she isn't hurting anyone?" Dvora infused a philosophical aspect into the discussion.

"And what about my parents and brothers and sisters? If I go with a goy, won't it hurt them?"

"It's their choice! If they get hurt, it'll be their own fault and, God forbid, you blame yourself," Dvora answered resolutely.

Rivka was silent for a while, and suddenly, her face lit up as though she'd found a treasure. "I think I'm finally getting it. But other than that, reading between the lines, it seems to me as though you're trying to protect not only me but mostly yourself. It seems as though you're searching for justification for your actions, not necessarily mine." She looked at Dvora victoriously.

Dvora was silent for a moment, as though caught red-handed, hesitating on how to proceed.

"Well, say something. What happened? Cat got your tongue?" Rivka mocked her.

"First of all, I want you to know that no matter what happens, I won't remain ultra-orthodox. I have no intention of marrying an ultra-orthodox Jew, going around with these restricting clothes and a bald head. I have no intention of giving up on my hair. If you want to give up on your golden curls, be my guest. Indeed, I'm protecting myself. And regarding this matter, you're right, I've gone much further than you. ..."

"What do you mean?"

"I mean that I've gone much further than you...I haven't been a virgin for the last six months."

"*What?* God forbid!" Rivka blurted, and covered her slack mouth with her hand.

"Six months ago, I met a lovely, beautiful guy. After a month of passionate courtship, I consented. On our fourth date, I gave him my virginity."

"And since then?" Rivka asked curiously.

"Since then, we meet once a week, sometimes even more. We make love in a secret place, and that's it." Dvora got up and strutted around the room like a woman of experience.

"And what about the future? Now, you're having fun, but what about your future?"

"Everything's going to be okay. I've already told you that soon I won't be here. And I meant that."

"Is he Jewish?" Rivka asked in suspense.

Dvora laughed.

"Why are you laughing?"

"Luckily for me he's a Jew. But it doesn't really matter. For them, the Hassidic leaders, he's as goy as they come. His name is Adam. He came from Israel three years ago to study here."

"And...does he love you?"

"I think so. He promised me that after he graduated, in six months, he'd take me with him to Israel, and we'd get married," she concluded with a smile.

For the first time in her life, Rivka was envious of her friend. Dvora was at peace with her choices and happy, while she was torn and unhappy. Did she have the strength to turn her back on the ways of the Torah? And if she did that, what would become of her? Would the Blessed Lord protect her? No! God supported the righteous, not the sinners. Yet, was she walking down the path of evil? Jews that weren't Hasidic, were they actually sinners? And if she chose to stray from the way of the Torah, could she ever be happy and in peace? While she tormented herself with these many questions, she hurried to the mirror and studied her hair. Her golden shoulder-length curls were so pretty, she had a difficult time imagining herself without them. No, she wouldn't shave her head! Whatever happened, no one would take her curls from her. Even if she married Avraham-David, no one would cut her hair by any means! Her head would remain full of hair as it was. When she thought about it, her eyes welled with tears, and her cheeks began to spasm again.

Chapter 8

Sunlight caressed Central Park, blending with its pleasurable sights. The sparse clouds moved aside, a kind of gesture for the majestic creation. At the sides of the path leading to strawberry fields forever, colorful birds jumped, tweeting joyfully and gratefully for the sun that extracted them from the extended captivity forced by winter. Squirrels peeked from among rocky crevices, suspiciously examining their surroundings, and then jumped hastily to the sprawling green, cheerfully wagging bushy tails, showing them off to everyone. The water of the lake started flowing slowly. Ducks and swans quacked with joy, splashing happily in the cold water, and under the water, a plethora of fish circled. Occasionally, they leaped out of the water to enjoy the fresh air and then dove in again, leaving behind them little whirlpools that looked like aquarelle paintings on a transparent canvas. Tourist-laden boats left the pier and sailed to the heart of the lake. In the treetops, leaves that not long ago looked frozen and droopy stretched in place as though awakening from a deep sleep, savoring the unexpected warmth summoned by nature.

An unusual day of spring had come to town in the midst of winter, and the surprised residents hurried to take advantage of it, thronging to the park. Groups of casually dressed youngsters gathered in every corner. Some of them played odd musical instruments and wouldn't stop singing, while the others danced with an abandon that brought to mind the contortions of acrobats in the circus. Eve was also there, among the crowds. Wearing a warm, custom-made coat, which adhered to the latest fashion, she strolled slowly, enjoying the sights and intoxicating smells, wondering why she'd kept away until now from this magical place, one of the city's pulsing veins of life. Although she worked close by, she'd visited the park very few times. For her, staring at the park from her vantage point on the sixty-second floor was more than enough.

When she reached the restaurant at the heart of the park, he was already waiting for her. He rose hastily to his feet when he noticed her, walked toward her, and offered her a seat, his smile emphasizing sensual lips and white teeth.

She remembered that smile, which had first captivated her when he'd smiled at her through her office window. She smiled back and sat down, not before taking off her coat.

"Hey," he said quietly, his eyes following her delicate movements.

"Hey," she replied, looking straight at him.

When their eyes met, her heart started beating quickly and a flush covered her face. He was so close to her. She noticed every last detail of his features. His big blue eyes, startling against his tanned face with its light stubble. His beauty embarrassed her, yet nevertheless, she couldn't tear her eyes away from him.

"How are you?" he asked politely.

"Good, thanks. And you?"

"Just fine. I'm glad we had a chance to meet," he said as he sat down.

"Have you been waiting long?" She changed the subject and surveyed the bustling, busy restaurant.

"Not really. Ten minutes maybe. Why?"

"I'm sorry you had to wait. I was afraid I'd run late. There were tons of people on the way, and I kept stopping everywhere to people-watch, so I kind of lost track of time. The park is full of buskers and funny dancers. It's impossible to just walk by without stopping a bit to look at them," she apologized.

"I know. I also stopped at several places, mainly where people gathered. The most interesting things always happen there. The human statues are the coolest. They just stand there for hours without moving, and all that effort for a couple of dollars. There was a guy and girl there who sat pressed together, their lips merged in an eternal mud kiss," he said, emphasizing the word kiss.

"I saw them, too. I think that by the end of the day, they'll have awful neck pains." She laughed and added enthusiastically, "This city can drive you nuts sometimes, right? Look what's going on here. We're in the middle of winter, outside it's so cold that any normal person would choose to stay at home, and still, the park is packed. A little sun and everyone's outside. ..."

"You really love this city, huh?"

"I love New York. It's an amazing city, and there's nothing like it in the entire world. What about you? Don't you like it?"

"I'm still learning. For me, everything's new. I've only been here for several months. Enough time to draw an impression, but not enough to fall in love."

"Oh, I'm so silly. I should've known. I heard something in your voice, you know. A southern accent."

"How could you have known? Not every person with a southern accent is new in town. There must be southerners in New York who arrived here years ago, and they still kept their accent."

"Right. I, for example, was born in New Jersey, but I've lived most of my life in this city. That's why I sometimes forget and think everyone was born here. Anyway, now we have an interesting topic to discuss. Let's order, okay? I'm starving," she said, her eyes searching for the waiter.

"Sure. I'm starving, too. I haven't eaten a thing since this morning," he answered, as though this wasn't their first date.

Actually, ever since they met by the elevator at her building, they'd met only once, briefly. Jeff called and asked her to find him an appropriate venue of investment, and she invited him to the office. When he arrived, she welcomed him gladly, and it seemed as though she'd prepared for a long meeting. She even ordered cookies and coffee for them. But disappointingly, before they had time to drink coffee, she was summoned to an urgent meeting with the boss.

"Rain check?" he asked hopefully.

"Sure," she smiled.

Before he left, he wrote a check and gave it to the secretary, who looked at the check and burst out laughing. "Seven thousand dollars! She won't bother herself for seven thousand dollars. I guess she has some other reason…and honestly, now that I look at you, I understand what it is." She winked at him.

Since that snatched meeting that proved, in a very painful way, the gap between them, they hadn't been in touch. He held her business card in his hands many times and wanted to call, but at the last minute, he changed his mind. He was afraid their differences were too acute, and that she didn't really want a serious relationship with him. And there were times when his curiosity to find out how much money had accumulated in his investment portfolio almost won out. Nevertheless, he curbed his curiosity and didn't call. If she wanted to get in touch, she'd find her way to him.

And that's what happened. The other day, in the late evening hours, just after he got into bed, she called. After exchanging polite chit chat, she asked, "We're expecting some nice weather tomorrow. Would you like to meet in the park, maybe take a walk?"

"Yeah, sure. Great idea!" he answered, not bothering to hide his enthusiasm.

"Great, so it's a date! We'll meet at three, eat something, and then take a walk in the park. Does that sound okay?" she asked, and immediately continued, "I'll have my secretary make reservations for us. I have a feeling all the restaurants will be packed tomorrow."

"A good meal always sounds good," he said even though he knew he'd still be at work at three o'clock.

When he curled beneath the covers, he decided to work only half a day the next day so that he'd be at the top of his game at their date. Who knew where things would lead to?

"So, how's the stock market?" he asked as he perused the menu.

"I don't think it's the stock market you're interested in, right?" she laughed. "You probably want to know what happened to your money."

"Of course! Have you seen someone who isn't interested in his own money?"

"Your money has almost doubled its value," she answered succinctly and dramatically.

"Wow!" he said admiringly. "It's barely been a month! Do you want to tell me that I now have about fourteen thousand dollars? God, I don't believe it."

"Believe it, my friend. These days, the stock market is hot." She enjoyed his excited response.

"Way to go. Seriously. Maybe you should sell the shares and realize the profit?" he suggested, even though he didn't know what his money was invested in.

"The moment you put your money in my hands, I'm the one who decides what to do with it. But don't worry, I know what I'm doing," she assured him.

"It's nice of you to think about my money even though it's such a small sum," he thanked her, tensely anticipating her response. Would a derisive note creep into her voice?

"Look, let's be honest. Of all of my investment portfolios, yours is the smallest, but that's what makes it the most challenging. For me, that's the most important thing." She smiled in satisfaction.

Jeff looked at her in obvious adulation. He always admired people who controlled the secrets of investment. Shares, bonds, and options were terms he'd only heard of. Specializing in the field always seemed to him beyond his comprehension.

"Is it hard?" he asked.

"Is what hard?"

"The stock market. Managing investment portfolios. Is it hard work?"

"The work itself is fascinating. It keeps you in suspense and demands concentration and endless follow-up. Take your eyes off the ball for one second, and boom, there goes the money. There's no doubt that it's an exhausting job, especially mentally. Why do you ask?"

"Just curious. I always thought managing investment portfolios was too complicated for me. I've always counted on my body more than on my head," he said, flexing his right hand and pointing at the bulging muscle with his left one.

"Yes, well, I don't have your muscles, so I have to use what I learned. It's certainly easier than the jobs you do," she laughed, without bothering to hide her admiration of his masculine body.

"I owe you something, too," he suddenly remembered.

"What?"

"A chair or a table, I don't really remember. One of them needed repair."

"Oh, yes. The table in the dining room. One of its legs is wobbly. I'd appreciate you coming by as soon as possible. It looks like it'll collapse soon, and I'll have nothing to eat on," she laughed.

"If it's good for you, we can go now," he suggested and hoped she'd agree.

To his surprise, she did.

"Don't you need tools?" she wondered.

"Don't worry. Glue will be enough. On the way, we'll go into a hardware store and buy some. You don't need anything more than that."

When they finished eating, she wanted to pay for the meal, but Jeff refused and insisted on splitting the bill. "After what you made for me in the stock market, I can afford it," he joked, and Eve acquiesced with a soft smile.

Fixing the table, which barely looked like it needed any fixing, took only a few minutes. When he finished, he noticed her standing close by, her face glowing with happiness.

"Would you like to stay for coffee?" she asked timidly, and he nodded with a tense smile.

"Great. I really appreciate your help," she said softly and came toward him. She was so close that the smell of her perfume flooded his nostrils. He inhaled deeply to calm himself, but instead, felt himself getting dizzy. His expression grew serious when he took that last step toward her. He felt her body, almost weightless, float and press against his. And then, he held her head and pressed his lips against hers in a long, uninhibited kiss, as though asking to infiltrate her heart. He heard her moan and sigh softly as she relieved him of his shirt. His chest bare, he squeezed her to him and embraced her wildly, almost ripping off her dress.

"No, not here…let's go to the bedroom. I feel more comfortable there," she whispered.

She took off her clothes and lay down on the bed, waiting for him to come to her. Her green feline eyes followed every move he made. For a moment, he stood over her, studying her. His eyes were worshipful. First, he looked at her long, shapely legs, then concentrated on her flat stomach. And when he made his way to her breasts, he felt his breath hitch. They were small and round, and at their center, were two sweet nipples that looked like two, cheeky wildflowers. Then, he stared at her face. He was willing to swear that he'd never seen such a beautiful face, not even in the movies. Her lips were full, sensuous, and inviting, hinting at what was to come. When he finally looked at her eyes, he understood why. Her eyes were alight with indescribable joy. Just then, he knew she loved him. He hurried to lie down next to her and their bodies converged.

"I love you," she admitted quietly after they'd made love, still panting from the exertion of their lovemaking.

"I love you, too," he answered unhesitatingly, and kissed her, willing to swear that he could kiss her like this forever. "From the day I saw you, I knew something strange had happened to me. In the beginning, I wasn't sure it was love. Only after I found myself thinking about you constantly, did I realize I was in love with you," she said, and rested her head on his chest.

Jeff looked at her silently.

"And what about you? When did you realize?"

"Me?" He was surprised. "Didn't you notice how I looked at you? I almost fell from that window," he laughed. "And since that wonderful moment, I've been thinking about you day and night, hoping we'd meet one day." Then he loomed over her, peppered her eyes, her nose, and her lips with countless kisses, and added, "But it was your eyes that captivated me. They totally hypnotized me."

"Stop," she laughed, amused by the way he'd kissed her.

Jeff stayed over at Eve's place that night. They couldn't tear themselves away from each other.

The next morning, they both dragged themselves to work exhausted and thought about each other constantly. They both realized they'd found love.

The financial and social gaps between them, the fact that she was two years older than him, all of these didn't bother Jeff at all. He knew his love for her was pure. He wanted her more than he'd ever wanted anything in his life. At work, when Rico teased him for catching a rich chick, Jeff only replied, "I love her so much that I don't care about her money."

And Eve, as her love for him grew, felt as though her work had become a secondary, almost unimportant factor. It reached a point that she sometimes forgot to sell or buy shares, thus inflicting damage on her investment portfolios. That didn't go unnoticed by her superiors, and one day she was summoned to their offices.

"What's going on with you?" one of the managers asked.

"What do you mean?" she asked with faux innocence.

"You're not on the top of your game. Something's happened to you."

"I don't understand what you're talking about," she insisted.

"We're talking about the fact that, lately, you haven't been focused on work. Your instructions are late, and as a result, our investors are suffering substantial losses."

"You're exaggerating. These are routine things. It happens that sometimes reactions are late. It's happened before. This isn't the first time," she said defensively.

"Maybe to others, but not to you. And I know what I'm talking about. It's true that other brokers make mistakes, but those are mistakes of judgment. Yesterday, you sold one option. At the beginning of the trade, the option was traded at thirty-five dollars and sixty cents. The transaction was executed at the end of the day when the value of the option went down to thirty-three dollars. Why?" asked the vice manager.

"Unfortunately, I made a late decision. All day long, I deliberated on the matter, and when I decided to sell, its price started to go down. It's not such a big deal."

"Do you really not understand or are you pretending? We're not talking about the fact that a lot of money went down the drain! Had it been a mistake in judgment, okay. You're allowed to make mistakes, too. We're talking about something that you're going through, something that makes you late to work. As far as we know, you make most of your decisions the previous day and execute those decisions in the morning. Yesterday, you came to work late, when the value of the option started going down," the vice manager reproved her.

Eve was silent. He was right. She had nothing to say in her defense.

"We expect you to snap out of it and return to function like you always have. The private phone calls that you do during the day are a disturbance to you, and you're better off postponing them to the evening," the manager concluded the conversation.

Eve knew that every one of their claims was correct. Jeff now filled a place previously filled by her work—the secret of her professional success, no doubt. And now, most of the time, she thought of him and fantasized about him. And when she wasn't thinking of him, she was talking with him on the phone. She couldn't wait to see him at the end of the day. In the evening, she'd arrive at his apartment as fast as she could, pick him up in her car, and then they'd spend time together until the small hours of the morning. Their relationship grew stronger, and the future looked rosier than ever.

"I think it's about time that you move in," she suggested one night.

"For now, I'm happy where I am. The transition from a small, modest apartment to a lavish one like yours is too quick for me. I need time to adjust to the idea. You have to understand, I've always relied only on myself… Let's wait for another opportunity."

He remembered Rivka's visit, as he rejected her offer, and couldn't imagine how quickly his life would change.

Chapter 9

"Love is pleasurable, like nothing else. Like a deceiving potion carrying the lovers and beloved through high clouds, to endless skies, to the top of the world. It possesses cures and power, which can strengthen the body and soul toward a dawning day. And sometimes love is evil, sucking the broken lovers to the depths of the earth, to the bottom of a pit. It brings with it grief and despair and sleepless nights. It has many faces, love does. Sometimes, it laughs; sometimes, it cries. Sometimes, it is calm; sometimes, stormy. Mostly, it is soft and caressing, but also harsh and searing. Man mustn't fear it, for it is the purpose of his life." Rivka reread the paragraph from the book Dvora gave her last night.

"Read," she'd demanded. "A little philosophy won't hurt you. Maybe you'll finally understand the difference between what's important and what isn't."

And Rivka read and read, greedily swallowing every note and every word, and the more she read, the stronger became her inner turmoil. Her mind was feverish with thoughts, her head threatened to explode. When she finished reading, her mind was made up, and she was as resolute as ever on the way she had to choose. She was in love, of that she had no doubt. Was her love strong enough to bring her to the top of the world, or would it drag her into the depths of the earth?

For two nights, she couldn't sleep, not even for one minute. She tossed from side to side, desperately trying to find a position that would allow a few minutes of rest. When sleep eluded her, she sat on her bed and waited for the morning to rescue her from her suffering. When dawn came, she got out of bed and wandered around the house doing nothing. She continued this way until late afternoon when fatigue overcame her, and she fell asleep on the couch in the living room.

Then she dreamed. As in Jacob's dream, she saw angels climbing down a ladder from an illuminated heaven. They all came to her as she sat on a chair in the center of a large courtyard. When the last angel climbed down, they started flying around in circles, until, suddenly, she noticed that one of them was Jeff.

"Jeff," she exclaimed happily. "You're an angel. I always knew you were an angel. Come to me, my love. Come to me, my angel."

"Shhh…be quiet. I'm not an angel. I'm flesh and blood, like everyone else," he whispered in her ear, then shed his white wings, threw them aside, took a chair, and sat down beside her. When he shed his wings, she saw the tailored suit he was wearing. Only then, did she notice her outfit: a white wedding dress covering her body.

"Indeed, you're not an angel," she agreed with him. However, after studying him carefully, she added, "But you're the groom, and I'm the bride. And we're both sitting beneath the canopy. You're mine, and I'm yours."

"You're right, you're the bride, and I'm the groom," he nodded and slid a gold diamond ring on her fourth finger.

Suddenly, she noticed the angels had climbed up the ladder again, and each, in his turn, disappeared into a dark black hole that had opened in the skies. She and Jeff were left alone. Here was the opportunity she had been waiting for, to spend time with him alone. She raised her slender hands and softly stroked his face for several minutes. Then she stroked his hair, until, suddenly, she gripped his neck tightly and pulled him to her. The strong, muscular man surrendered easily to her strength. She pulled off his clothes, and to her delight, he didn't protest. "Take it! Take my virginity, Take it from me. Deliver me from it. Do with me whatever you like!" she screamed at him.

He leaned over her, docilely obeying. She felt his muscular body press tightly against her own, felt his large hands spread her legs. Suddenly, a sharp pain pierced her narrow hips, like a knife penetrating her body, threatening to cut her in half. She wanted to cry, but then the pain subsided, replaced by a sense of pleasure that she'd never felt before. When he finished, he rolled off of her and lay down beside her. Just then, she felt calm and peaceful, until the blood began to trickle. First, it trickled from between her legs, then from every part of her body. She tried to stop what had become a gushing torrent, but in vain. She saw how the wave of blood that left her body washed the parched earth, which devoured it and turned red. When she looked for Jeff, she was disappointed to discover that he'd disappeared into the black hole like the other angels.

"Jeff, help me!" she shouted in panic, raising her head to the sky.

To no avail. Jeff wasn't there to answer.

Just then, she woke up, jumped, reached out, and felt her face, belly, thighs, and legs. When she finished, she examined her hands and discovered that it wasn't blood, but sweat pouring from her entire body.

"What was *that*?" she muttered in fear.

She ran to the sink in the shower. First, she washed her face, then looked at herself in the mirror. Gazing at her reflection, she couldn't believe this face was her own. She looked gaunt and tired, so weary that even the convulsions had ceased. Just then, she made up her mind. When she did, she finally calmed down. Tonight, God willing, inspired by the holiday, she would realize her love. Her body trembled.

"Rivkel, time to light the candles. Come, Papa is blessing," she heard her mother call her.

She hurried to the kitchen. She wanted to feel the atmosphere of this special day and hoped that Hanukkah, the miracle holiday would not pass over it.

"*Baruch ata Adonai Melech Ha'Olam, she'asa nissim le'avotainu bayamim hahem be'zeman haze*," she heard her father bless the lighting of the candles. *Blessed are You, Adonai our God, Sovereign of all, who performed wondrous deeds for our ancestors in days of old at this season.* When finished, they all sang the traditional "*Maoz Tzor.*"

When her parents left the kitchen, she stayed put and continued staring at the burning candles. Three thin pillars of wax protruded proudly from the menorah that lit the big house in a melancholy light. Their tiny flames flickered in an endless dance, as though they were happy about the holiday.

It was a Sunday, the second candle of Hanukkah. The festive celebrations passed over her so far. Her body throbbed with agonizing pangs of love. Her pains were severe, intolerable. But tonight would be different. She'd decided. A decision not readily accepted. There was still a way out. If she chose to marry Avraham-David, no one would know her secret. She would get her life back, and it would be comfortable and uncluttered. Like all girls of the Hasidic community, she would marry, bear children, and raise them in the way of the Torah. Her parents and her family would be happy and would support it. When she kissed her husband, her conscience would be burdened, but she'd get over it. She wouldn't be able to live a happy life with a man she didn't love, but her happiness was nothing compared to that of her parents and brother.

Yet, there was another way: to follow her heart, as Dvora had said. Completely abandon her way of life for a guy whom she'd desperately fallen in love with. Recently, she'd completely abandoned the religious laws. She hadn't prayed, nor blessed.

Faith in the Creator amounted to one blessing, or more correctly, request: to win Jeff's love. During those days, he was in her bones like a raging inferno, slowly consuming her heart and soul. She had to stop thinking of him, if only for a moment. There were times when she longed to go outside, run to him, embrace him tightly and cry out to him that she loved him. But she didn't do so. She was so afraid of the consequences of the meeting that it prevented her from doing so.

But tonight was different. Tonight was her night, her very own night. The die was cast. Tonight, she would go to him! Even if her legs crashed and she went blind, she would crawl in the dark on her knees and wait at his door. Already familiar with the nature of love, she would give herself to him until the end. She'd give him all of herself, both body and soul. She could no longer live a life of lies. God was following her from above at every given moment, that was for sure. The Almighty gave her life to live, so he wouldn't punish her. And what is sin? Was love a sin? God was merciful and compassionate and, therefore, would favorably judge her! God gave her a heart to love, and she would go after her heart! Tonight, God willing, when darkness fell, and after her parents fell asleep, she'd go to his apartment again. She no longer cared what happened there. Secretly, she hoped what happened to Dvora would happen to her: that she would lose her worthless virginity. Tonight, she would realize her dream. And if not, and she left the apartment still a virgin, her life would never be the same again. In fact, there would be no turning back after that. She had practiced and memorized the sentence she'd read. "Even hard and searing, man mustn't fear it, for it is the purpose of his life."

Shortly after lighting the candles and eating the donuts, her parents retired to their room. Rivka took a shower, put on her best clothes, combed her hair, wore makeup and perfumed. Finally, she wrapped herself in her coat and left the house.

A cold gust of wind greeted her as though waiting for her arrival. Sullen and angry, it whipped her exposed face mercilessly.

On the pavement, rolled strange eddies of autumn leaves, leftover from the autumn, which suddenly seemed so far away. With every step she took, tears welled up in her eyes. They were so many that it was hard for her to see the leaves intact. One rogue tear made it way down her cheek. At first, it was warm. However, after that, it succumbed to the cold and froze before it had time to reach Rivka's lips.

When Rivka reached the stairs leading to his house, she gripped the railing for fear of falling. Then she stood and looked around. It was almost completely dark, and even as she strained her eyes, she saw nothing. As she walked down the stairs, she was accompanied by an odd feeling that someone was following her. She paused again and looked back. She didn't see a soul. Standing there, she took a handkerchief out of her pocket, wiped her tears, blew her nose, and after some hesitation, she continued down the stairs until she reached his door. This time, she rang the bell, pressing long and purposefully so that there would be no doubt as to her intentions.

He opened the door. Wearing a T-shirt and shorts, he stood in front of her in all his beauty. The surprise was evident on his face. "You again," he said carelessly, disappointment evident in his voice.

She nodded, insulted, still standing in the doorway.

"Come in," he regained his composure, as though regretting his first sentence.

She walked into the house, and when he shut the door, she stood there, looking at him hopefully.

"I'm sorry. You came at a bad time, " he apologized.

"Why?" she asked quietly.

"Because I have to go out soon."

"Should I come another time?" she suggested.

"It's okay, you can stay a while. I still have time," he relented, fearing she'd feel rejected.

Rivka hesitated.

"Sit down, sit down," he urged her and pointed to a chair. "Is everything okay with you?" he asked after noticing how pale her face was.

"So-so," she replied with difficulty.

"I think you came here because you wanted to tell me something, right?"

"Yes, I have a lot to say…" she said, squirming in her seat uncomfortably. "You know, lately, since I met you at my brother's house, I…you know, I'm confused. Suddenly, I began to think I was living the life of a lie, a life that I don't belong to." She stopped talking, examining his response.

"And?" he urged her.

"Life outside resonated with me more. It's not that I stopped believing in God, Heaven forbid, but suddenly everything seemed different. Do you understand? Like I don't belong to the world I'm living in. I want to live like secular girls. Wear jeans and T-shirts, go to the beach in the summer and sunbathe, watch a good movie, or even go see a play on Broadway. Watch television without fear, openly read books and study Earth Sciences at the university. I know not everything is clean and beautiful on the other side, but I'm sure it would be better for me there," she blurted out.

"And what's all this got to do with me?" he wondered.

"Now, when I think about it, I realize I've always had doubts about my way of life. I didn't think about it deeply, as I do now. Everything I've done until now was what was expected of me. I never questioned that. I just did what everyone else did, without questions and doubts. You know, I have a good friend named Dvora. About two years ago, she and I started to read books secretly, you know, books that aren't related to religion. Those books helped me discover how stupid I was. Suddenly, a whole new world opened before me, the world that the Almighty, that even now I believe in, created for me. Once, we even sneaked to the city, you know, out of curiosity. We wanted to know what was going on. Other lives have always been in my consciousness. But only when I met you did I begin to seriously consider a change. Suddenly, I not only thought about things but also dared to do them."

"Like what?" he asked.

"Like what? Get to the city, come to you. In the past, I would never dare to do such things, and yet, this is the second time I've come here."

"Why?"

"Because I want to leave the Hasidic community and live far away from here with you." Her voice confident.

"Why me?" He wanted to understand more.

Rivka looked up at him sadly. "You really don't understand? Can't you see that...I love you? Are you blind? Do you not see that I've gone mad with love? When I met you, I thought you were a nice guy, fun to be with, talk to, nothing more. Suddenly, I found myself wanting to spend more and more time with you. I thought of you during the day, thought of you during the night, thought of you everywhere. I was on the verge of madness. I felt I had to come to you. You know, when I was here the last time you and I kissed you, I felt the clouds. I felt there was nothing more lovely than to kiss the man you love. Since I've been thinking only of you, and I don't know what to do..."

She looked up at him pleadingly, hoping he'd come to her, hold her. But Jeff sat down, buried his head in his hands, and said nothing.

"Take me, please. Take me to you, please." She stood up and then sat down next to him.

Jeff looked at her. He felt pity for the girl he was so fond of.

Rivkel," he said after some thought. "I think this is two different things. Let's try to compartmentalize. First, the life you live, or the life you want to live, has nothing to do with me. If you feel bad where you are now, you should leave. If you don't like the way you live, go. You're mature enough to decide your future. Don't let others determine how you live. I, for example, left my hometown because I thought it wasn't the right place for me and I needed to seek my future elsewhere. Since I met you and Aaron, I've asked myself how can anyone live in such a closed world, a world without openness, like the one you live in. You know what? Sometimes I think your brother chose me as a friend because, for him, I might be a window to a world he wanted to live in but couldn't. Perhaps, this is also why you want me. You want to leave, and without realizing it, you see me as a bridge to another life. Leave me aside. Go after your faith, and everything will be fine. I promise you that everything will work out." He looked very pleased with the way he phrased his words.

"And the second thing?" she asked tensely.

"I've thought of it a lot. I thought about you a lot since you were here. I don't think a relationship between us is a good thing," he said succinctly.

"But...but, I love you. Does my love mean nothing to you?" she asked desperately.

Stop, Rivkel. I like you very much. Maybe even more than I should. You're a beautiful and intelligent girl that every guy would love to get to know, but I'm Christian and you're Jewish! Even if you don't stay religious, you're still a Jew. Don't abandon your religion and faith for the man you think you like." As he talked, he looked up at the clock. It was seven. He breathed with relief. There was still time until Eve arrived.

"I don't care about your faith. This country is full of Christians and Jews that are intertwined with each other. If I can't have you, my life isn't worth a thing." She approached him and put her head on his shoulder. "You know...you won't believe it, but I love you so much that before coming over here, I decided to give myself to you. Yes, I'm ready to lose my virginity, and more importantly, I am ready to give you my soul," she said with tears in her eyes.

"No, kiddo. You don't love me. You only think you do, but that's not the case. Do you know what love is? You just said that you were confused. Once you give yourself to me, you'll regret it, but by then it'll be too late. It really is confusing to be marrying a person offering you a lifestyle you do not want. Your way of life should be your choice. Every person has the freedom to choose his way according to his desire and belief," he said, wiping her tears with his fingers.

"I do know what love is," she whispered indignantly and then persisted stubbornly, "Do you know what love is? What do you know about love? Huh, tell me what you know."

Jeff was silent.

"Well, smart aleck, tell me what is love? If you don't know, I'll tell you what love is," she exclaimed as excitedly as she had last night. "Love isn't a kiss on the lips or hug around the waist! No way! Love is giving unconditionally and without expecting anything back. Such is my love for you. I'm prepared to give you everything I have, even my life. Yes, my life!" Rivka began to cry again.

Jeff kept his silence. For a moment, he wondered if Eve loved him this way. Would she also be prepared to give her life for him? Could he give his life for the sake of love? He doubted it!

"Stop crying, kiddo. Stop crying," Jeff put his arm on her shoulder, wishing to comfort her.

"I'm not pretty enough for you," she blurted suddenly, and bitter laughter mixed with her weeping.

"That's not true; you're very pretty. One of the prettiest girls I've ever met, and I'm not saying this just to make you happy. The day will come, and you will see it. The day will come, and you'll recognize your own worth and your beauty. And on that day, you'll also find your love," he promised.

"So why?"

"Why what?"

"Why don't you want me?"

Jeff hesitated. He didn't want to torment her. Didn't want to tell her about his love for another woman.

"I told you, we don't fit," he lied reluctantly.

"And is this the only reason?" she asked. She wanted to be sure there wasn't another reason he'd rejected her.

"That's the only reason," he lied resolutely.

"And what do you think I should do now?"

"Go somewhere else. Don't be afraid. Leave this place you don't like anyway. Forget Brooklyn. You can build a new life somewhere else, and I am sure you will succeed. Do what I did, and you'll be fine."

"You're a man. It' easier for men to just get up and leave. It's different for girls. They're more dependent on the house. Look at me, for example, where would I go? How would I make a living? I can't afford even the bus ticket. I can't leave. I'm doomed. I want to leave, but I don't think I'm capable of doing so. If I'm lucky, no one will know I was here, and then I'll marry Avraham-David, have children and raise them with sideburns and a shtreimel. If I'm unlucky, my intended will abandon me, and I'll wait until they find a third-degree match," she concluded sadly.

"You're wrong. You're not thinking as you should. I cannot believe you're giving up so easily. If you marry Avraham-David against what your heart is telling you, you'll suffer your entire life, and you'll have no one to blame but yourself. Don't do it, Rivkel. Where will you go? That is a really difficult question, and I wish I could help you in this matter. If you decide to leave, I'm sure you'll also know where to. As for the money? Save! Save every cent that reaches your hands. When you have enough money, you leave. And if you run out of money, there will always be someone who's willing to help you."

Rivka did not answer him. From the way he'd welcomed her, she'd realized he wouldn't be with her. She decided not to cry anymore in his presence. She was proud of what she was and wasn't ashamed of what she'd done. She would return home with her head held high and wait for things to come. Maybe she'd marry, maybe not. Many questions would be tested, primarily the question of whether you can overcome the pains of love.

"I'm sorry, but I have to end the conversation. I have to leave right away. We can talk another time." Jeff glanced at the clock again. Time was running out. Soon, Eve would arrive, and he hadn't even taken a shower.

"Thank you for your time," she said, turning to go.

I'm sorry things are like this," he said as he leaned over and kissed her cheek, feeling his heart ache.

Rivka walked slowly up the stairs. When she reached the top step, she stood in place, panting from the effort required, suddenly. Then she stepped on the path leading to her house. On the way, she noticed a fancy jeep pulling over under the streetlight, just in front of the basement. A woman climbed out of the car. Rivka couldn't see her face clearly, but her wealth was evident in her clothes. The expensive fur coat wrapping her, her fashionable boots and narrow red skirt were evidence enough. The woman turned to the stairs leading to Jeff's apartment. Rivka watched her until she disappeared down the stairs.

She felt tears clogging her throat. She took a deep breath and walked faster. The street was quiet and deserted, and only the murmur of the wind broke the silence as it continued carrying the leaves, straight into her sad face, slapping her with incomprehensible rage. And one leaf, the one clinging to her coat, where her heart beat, was broken. Indeed, love was a bitch.

Chapter 10

Traffic was light on the roads. It started snowing when darkness fell, scaring away partygoers, most of whom chose to stay at home. Eve's vehicle was among the few gliding down the slippery road. She drove slowly. Snowflakes piled on the road, painting it white, but had no impact on the vehicle's steadiness. The big, powerful, four-wheel drive continued paving its way confidently.

The interior of the spacious car was warm and pleasant. The quiet purr of the engine and classical music didn't break the silence. Jeff was tired and preoccupied. He leaned back and yawned loudly, hoping Eve would notice and accelerate. The drive from Manhattan to Brooklyn seemed longer and more tiresome than usual. He yearned to arrive home, curl up under his down covers, and sleep.

"I love this weather. Snow illuminates the night and makes it so much prettier," Eve broke the silence, which had started to weigh on her.

"Uh huh," Jeff agreed without really paying any attention to what she was saying.

"Look under the lamplights. Look what a lovely sight. Snowflakes falling from the sky as though they intend on decorating the city for Christmas," she said, trying to sound festive.

"You should hurry up, honey. The snow's coming down harder, and we may get stuck on the way." This time, he urged her to drive faster, ignoring her observations.

"Don't worry. My car can handle harsher conditions than these. Even if the storm gets worse, we'll make it to your place. Last year, I was caught in the middle of a snowstorm when I drove from Manhattan to New Jersey for dinner with my parents. The jeep handled it beautifully and didn't give me any trouble," she replied, disappointed with his answer.

For the first time in their relationship, a note of complaint crept into her voice.

"And yet, you still better hurry," he bit out.

"Worst-case scenario, if I'm unable to drive back, I sleep over at your place," she winked playfully. She hoped it would improve his sullen mood. To her disappointment, Jeff remained silent, his expression impassive and preoccupied. Obviously, something was bothering him, something unknown to her.

"Did you enjoy the show?" she asked after a while.

"It was very nice," he replied succinctly.

"It was great, right? Beautiful. I haven't seen such a lovely show in quite a while," she tried again to revive the conversation but was unsuccessful.

Eve didn't understand Jeff's silence. She didn't know that during the entire show and after, Jeff had been thinking about Rivka. He yearned for things to be different. He really did try to concentrate on the amazing performance, to feel the excitement the rest of the spectators had felt, but he couldn't. He sat through the show, thoughts of her consuming him. His concern for Rivka was genuine and deep. She was important to him. Was it possible he loved her? Was it possible to love two women at the same time?

Watching a Broadway show had always been a wish of his. For years, he dreamed of sitting in one of the spacious seats in a fancy theater, watching the play. He would even go to the opera, which wasn't really his bag. And he never hid this desire from Eve. "Six months in the city, and I haven't had the opportunity to go to a show. Mostly, because I didn't have anyone to go with," he hinted.

And an infatuated Eve had worked hard to procure tickets to a new musical that had just opened on Broadway, acclaimed by everyone. Using her connections, and for two-hundred and fifty bucks a ticket, she'd made his dream come true. And now, to her disappointment, he remained indifferent to what he'd seen and heard, and that, despite the fact they had sat only several feet away from the stage.

"You were telling me about your landlord's daughter, and then the show started, and you stopped. Do you want to tell me now?" Eve decided to change the subject.

"Are you a mind-reader?" he asked seriously.

"No. Why?"

"Because I was just thinking of her," he said.

"What exactly were you thinking about?" she inquired, offended that the neighbor's daughter was the source of his bad mood. On the other hand, at least now he was willing to talk. It looked as though the subject was very close to his heart.

"I think she's really miserable."

"Why? What happened to her? Is she sick or something?"

"No, she's not sick. Although maybe she would be better off if she were sick. You can recover from an illness after several days. But she's been suffering for quite a while. Who knows when her suffering will be over," he said thoughtfully.

"Go on," she prompted.

"Rivka is a good, decent girl. She's seventeen and a half, and the sister of a good friend of mine, Ahron. The guy I've told you about. Remember?" Jeff inquired and stretched, preparing himself for a long conversation.

"Yeah, I remember, although to tell you the truth, your relationship has always seemed weird to me."

"I don't always understand it either. But I'll have you know that Ahron is very nice and friendly. I have a great time visiting him, and you'd be surprised how often we find common subjects to discuss. Anyway, this evening, a couple of hours before you picked me up, she came to see me," Jeff paused, trying to think how to continue.

"Why did she come?" Eve asked, troubled.

"She came to ask for my help. Ahron and Rivka belong to a sect of Hasidic Jews. You know, the ones who wear pantyhose and big black hats and grow long sideburns. You know who I mean, right?"

"Sure, you can't live in New York without encountering them occasionally. There are even a few in the stock market. Boy, those Jews are zealous about their religion and way of life. Once, I walked into the elevator, and one of those guys was in there. The minute I walked in, he covered his eyes and got off the minute the elevator stopped. You'd think he'd seen a leper. They don't have an easy life."

"True, their lives aren't easy. As long as you believe this way is the right way, you're okay, but when you stop believing, your life becomes ten times harder. Rivka stopped believing, and that's a problem. She claims she's sick and tired of the life she lives, and she prefers to lives like other girls. She wants to leave home, and that's a bit complicated because she can't just get up and say she's leaving home and go live on her own. Her parents won't give her their blessing like yours did when you left home. Their problem is that the minute you abandon your faith, the family severs all ties with you."

"That bad?"

"Even worse. There are families who mourn those who've strayed from their way of life, as though they're dead. For them, they simply don't exist anymore. When Ahron told me that, I was totally horrified."

"But what does all this have to do with you?" She was anxious for him to get to the point of the matter.

"She wants me to help. She says she loves me and asked me to be her accomplice when she runs away from home." His answer surprised her.

"Love?" she repeated alarmed.

"That's what she said. She says she's fallen in love with me and wants to run away with me."

"And you agreed?" she asked tensely.

"No! I told her a relationship between us is hopeless and if she wants to leave, she should leave. She should do what I did and not be afraid. I told her she had to do it on her own. It seemed as though my answer had disappointed her. She definitely expected more. When she left, she looked so miserable, and I couldn't help her. During the entire show, I kept thinking how I could help her, and if I should tell Ahron about it. Obviously, I should keep her secret, but I'm still afraid he'll get mad at me for not telling him about it. What do you think?"

"I don't know. It seems like you shouldn't interfere because you can get into trouble. Don't forget that her parents are the ones renting out their apartment to you. You can find yourself out in the cold, just like that. I've already heard awful stories about their chastity squads. Someone told me that their thugs beat the crap out of a guy and a girl, innocent passersby, who weren't even Jews, for kissing on the street."

"And the police?"

"Most of the time, the victims don't press charges, mostly because they're part of the community. I'm asking you to be very careful. I think you should cut your ties with her, the sooner, the better."

"That's very easy to say, but what if she comes to me again? I'm not sure I'll be able to tell her to leave. I hope she'll snap out of it and manage on her own," Jeff concluded, hoping that Rivka's issues would take a turn for the better without him needing to interfere.

"Is she pretty?" Eve asked meekly.

"Amazingly beautiful," was his answer and she fell silent.

When Eve pulled over by his apartment, he leaned in, and kissed her longer than usual, as though trying to prove to her and to himself that he had only one love, and it was her. Then he waved good-bye and climbed out of the car. When she drove away, he lingered a bit on the street, following her car until it disappeared. Then he hurried down the stairs, reluctant to let the increasingly heavy snow pile on his clothes. He glanced at his watch. It was half past one in the morning. This time, they finished their outing earlier than usual. Maybe it was better this way, Jeff thought as he stripped his clothes and climbed into bed. Tomorrow, he had an especially busy day, and he wanted to arrive refreshed to work. After several minutes, Jeff disappeared under the covers and fell into a deep sleep.

Loud knocking on his door shattered the tranquility in the dark apartment. Jeff wasn't sure whether he was dreaming or if someone was actually knocking. When he heard the doorbell ring, he realized he wasn't dreaming.

Sleep-dazed, he shuffled toward the door. Before opening it, he turned on the light and glanced at his watch. It was three a.m. Who was the nutcase coming to his apartment at this hour? Rivka again? If she was coming here at three in the morning, she had to be in an awful state.

Yet, when he opened the door, a frightening surprise waited for him. Four thugs, their faces masked, burst into the house, and before Jeff had time to realize what was happening, a punch in the face felled him. He tried to drag himself to his feet and fight back, but he was outnumbered by the four thugs. They overpowered him easily, mercilessly pummeling his body and face. Even after he lay on his stomach, groaning with pain, one of them kept on beating him. The brute stopped only when the blood streamed down Jeff's battered face.

"Don't lift your head, you son of Belial, Balaam Ben-Beor. Stay where you are. The slightest move and you're dead, you bastard," one of them ordered him.

Jeff, who was unfamiliar with the names they flung at him, remained still. Fear paralyzed his painful body.

"Do you know who we are?"

Jeff shook his head, barely. When they burst into the house, he'd realized the trouble he was in. Even though they were masked, their shaved heads, black yarmulkes, and sideburns that curled to their shoulders made it clear enough where they came from and their intentions.

"You should know. We're not burglars or looters. We're doing a justice. You've hurt us badly. You've violated the honor of a daughter of Israel." The spokesman was probably the leader of the four.

Jeff was silent, still finding it difficult to digest the trouble that he'd landed in.

"Do you understand the significance of your actions?"

"I didn't do anything," Jeff struggled to prove his innocence.

"You really don't understand? You pig-eating bastard, I'll show you, you fucker," one of them yelled and kicked Jeff in the ribs.

The impact of the kick rattled his entire body. He couldn't breathe and felt as though he was going to faint.

"Avraham, stop! Stop beating him! Are you crazy? A kick in the ribs can kill him. From now on, you do only what I tell you to do, understand?" the spokesman addressed the man who kicked Jeff. This time, the voice was clearer. Apparently, the man chose to take off his mask. "It's late, so we won't make this long. According to our knowledge, you lured our Rivkel here, thus violating her honor. How could you do such a thing? How could you hurt people who've only been kind to you, who gave you a house to live in, huh?"

Jeff raised his eyes. The spokesman's face was exposed. He didn't look like a good-for-nothing, rash youth, but a man in his forties. From his words, Jeff realized that everyone knew of his relationship with Rivka.

"Well, let's hear what you have to say for yourself," he prompted Jeff to speak.

"She came here of her own free will. I didn't ask her to come. She came by herself, I swear," Jeff replied, blood still pouring from his lips.

"Do you know the damage you've caused, you Antiochus? You've erased an entire holy family from the face of the earth. The marriage of a kosher daughter of Israel with her intended will be null and void, and both she and her intended have lost, and all because of a *goy* like you," the man screamed at him, totally ignoring Jeff's denial.

"But I've already told you, she came here of her own free will," Jeff repeated stubbornly.

"It doesn't matter at all. You could've rejected her. Instead, you chose to welcome her in your house, and the devil knows what you've done to her."

"Nothing happened. I didn't touch that girl. I swear I didn't touch her," Jeff said, hoping to convince the man.

"Then why did she come here? Please explain to me why she came?"

"To talk. She came to talk," Jeff said briefly, reluctant to expose Rivka's secret.

"Talk? About what exactly? About what exactly did you and she talk? What can you possibly have in common with her?" he insisted derisively.

"We just chatted! Nothing special," Jeff lied for lack of any other option.

"We'll check that out," the man said, unconvinced. "Anyway, we hope you got the message. Stay away from our Rivkel, and if not, you'll meet a bitter end. You have forty-eight hours to pack your things and leave the borough. You understand? Not only this apartment but also leave Brooklyn. You also don't have to pay the remainder of the rent, Moishel already knows you're leaving. I hope things are clear and that I won't have to come back here, understand?"

Jeff didn't answer.

"I asked if you understand." The man leaned over him, grabbed his hair, and wrenched Jeff's head toward him.

"Yes, I understand," Jeff choked out on a painful groan.

"I almost forgot. Don't come to work either. I'll send Menachem a message regarding your resignation."

Jeff nodded.

"That's it, guys. I think our work is done here. Let's go," the man said, and the group hurried out of the house.

Jeff remained on the floor for several long minutes. Then, he picked himself up with the little strength left in him. First, he sat on the sofa, examining his limbs and face. His jaw, lips, and nose were throbbing with pain, and his ribs threatened to fall apart. He tried to stand, but it took him several attempts, and only then, after a great effort. In the end, he dragged himself to the phone and called for help. After several minutes, an ambulance arrived and took him to the hospital.

"Two cracked ribs and a broken nose. Ten days of bed rest, and you're as good as new. For your own safety, I'd like you to stay the night so we can supervise you. Tomorrow, if nothing unexpected happens, we'll send you home," the doctor concluded after studying his X-rays.

In the morning, he called Eve, and she rushed to the hospital.

She was horrified when she saw him. "Who did this to you? Were you in a fight?" she asked in alarm while she stroked his face.

Jeff tried to smile but was unsuccessful. His bruised jaw hurt, and he grimaced from the pain.

"What did the doctors say? Did you get X-rayed? You don't have any fractures?" she asked anxiously.

"Calm down. I'm fine." He tried to laugh again. This time, he was more successful.

When she calmed down, he told her at length what had happened during the night after she'd dropped him off.

"Those bastards! Animals! They could've killed you. I told you they were incorrigible nut cases, and that you should watch out for them. I warned you," she said, stroking his hair and forehead. Then, she tenderly kissed his bruised lips.

"It's not that bad. I'll survive. I learned something new first hand," he laughed again and then groaned from the pain that the laughter cost him.

"What are you going to do now?" she asked.

Jeff looked at her, and after thinking it over a bit, said, "In my pants pockets, there are the keys to the apartment. Have someone go there and pick up my stuff. Do not, under absolutely any circumstances, go there yourself. Don't take a thing but my clothes. I'm not interested in all the rest."

"Where should I move them to?" she asked and rubbed her hands together with obvious glee, as though she already knew the answer.

"If your offer still stands, bring them to your place," Jeff said and lifted his eyes to her hopefully.

"Of course, my love, of course." She leaned over him and kissed him again on his lips. She didn't even try to hide her satisfaction at the opportunity that had fallen into her hands.

"Don't you have to go to work?" he asked, hinting that she leave. His sleepless night was starting to catch up with him, and he yearned to sleep.

"Don't worry, I'll leave in a few minutes," she replied, slightly insulted.

"I didn't mean to make you leave. I thought trading was opening, and it's important you be there, right?" he apologized.

"Work can wait a bit. The situation with the stock market isn't great now, and nothing will happen if I'm a bit late."

"I hope all the bruises disappear by the holiday," Jeff changed the subject, gently touching the swelling that decorated his face.

"God! Good thing you reminded me. We're invited to my parents next week for the holiday meal," she said, tensely waiting for his response.

"I see you love driving in the snow to New Jersey. You're better off not going alone, right? Driving in the snow is dangerous..." He winked at her.

"I knew you'd agree," she said happily, kissed him, collected her stuff, and left.

Jeff spent his first days at Eve's apartment resting and lounging about lazily. Mostly, he watched television and read the newspapers. Once in a while, he turned on the computer, surfed the Internet, and played computer card games such as Solitaire Spider. A month later, after he'd recuperated, he left the apartment to search for a job. Despite his tremendous efforts to find work, nothing came up.

"I have got to find a job," he thought out loud, one evening. His frustration was evident on his face, due to his extended period of inactivity.

"I can talk to Daddy. I'm sure he can find you something," Eve offered earnestly.

"Are you crazy? No way! Working with your father would be the height of stupidity. One little fight between you and me, and your dad would kick me out of a job. One little fight between me and him, and you'd kick me out of the house," he said, then burst into laughter, which she joined.

"You're right. A logical and amusing thought," she said after she'd calmed down.

"So what do we do?"

"You know, Jeffie, I have an idea for you," she said after thinking matters over a bit.

"What is it?"

"You and I can open a business together."

"What?"

"You heard me. We'll start a business and be partners."

"Not on your life! You have a fantastic job. What do you need another business for?"

"I won't leave my job. Partnership doesn't necessarily mean that all the partners are active. I'll be a silent partner. The one who invests the money and doesn't work," she explained.

"Nope. No way!" he refused decisively.

"Why not? Sometimes, I don't understand you, Jeffie, I really don't. I think it's an excellent idea. You'll have a job, and I'll make some money on the side. What's wrong with that? I've been searching for new investment channels anyway."

"I'm glad you're optimistic, but a business is not the stock market. During the first years, almost every business loses money. That's what happens until the business establishes itself. In the restaurant I worked at in Eloy, the proprietor was constantly complaining that he was losing money. Every week, he whined that he was taking money out of his household account, literally out of his children's mouths, to maintain that goddamn business. So tell me, if there are losses, who'll cover them?"

"I actually think that if we plan wisely and put together a good business plan, we won't suffer losses. I'm positive. We just have to think of something that suits your talents," she said, getting more excited by the minute, as though she'd just started her financial path.

"Eve, cut it out! You can't be serious. Partnership demands a large financial investment, and as far as I know, you have the required money, but I don't. And please don't tell me you'll invest my share instead of me because if your investment goes down the drain, I'm gonna feel real bad," he said resolutely.

"Nonsense. Not every partnership needs identical financial investments. There are partnerships where one person brings the money, the second brings the knowledge, and the third brings initiative and work. You and I will build a business in which I'll bring the required funding, and you'll do all the work. We'll split the profits fair and square, fifty-fifty. I think you have undiscovered skills. Trust my instincts on these matters," she coaxed him.

"And if the partners have disagreements?" he asked while pressing against her body and kissing her.

"I know a place where they can solve all of their disputes." She winked and pointed at the bed in the bedroom.

"That makes sense. Solving disputes between partners in this method is definitely an alluring solution," Jeff conceded and carried her to bed.

Chapter 11

Rivka's visit to Jeff's apartment was discussed widely among Brooklyn's Hasidic members. By the next morning, the rumor that a good Jewish orthodox girl had been in a goy's house spread like wildfire. It wasn't long before everyone, from young to old, was talking about her. Other matters were pushed aside, and Rivkel became the topic of the day. And when tongues wagged, there was no stopping them. Like a tsunami of lava furiously washing the slopes of the mountain, consuming everything in its way, the gossip reached every house in the Hasidic community, labeling Rivkel a "*shiksa*." At first, rumors said that she was seen entering his apartment. Some were willing to swear that Rivka was seen through the window, kissing the goy. Others let their imagination run wild and said that they saw her leaving the scoundrel's apartment, wearing a dress stained with the blood of her lost virginity. The moment the situation reached that stage, Rivka's fate was doomed.

Was it coincidence that revealed her secret or perhaps Divine Providence? Maybe it was retaliation for her many sins, the revenge of God, or perhaps just plain bad luck?

Later on, she found out. One of the men, a yeshiva student, was on his way home from the yeshiva. When he passed by the basement apartment, he noticed a suspicious shadow moving about the place. At first, he thought it was a thief who'd intended to break into one of the houses. He changed direction and followed the suspicious shadow. When it disappeared into the basement apartment, he sneaked quietly to the front door, brought his ear close, and listened. But to his surprise, it wasn't a thief. On the other side of the door, a man and woman were having a conversation. He couldn't hear everything, but from the content of the conversation, he understood that a daughter of Israel, who planned on abandoning her holy way, was in the house. He lay in wait for more than an hour, until she came out, and when she did, her face was revealed under the street lamps. He recognized her with certainty. From that moment onward, it was like a snowball. The young man alerted his friends from the yeshiva, who went to the rabbi, who summoned Yehuda, one of Rivka's older brothers. Yehuda, a hot-headed, zealous Jew, didn't hesitate regarding his course of action. With the rabbi's encouragement, he collected three young men, all members of the chastity squad, and together, they went to pour out their wrath on Jeff. The Hanukkah miracle that she'd so desperately hoped for passed Rivka over this time.

The next evening, two of her brothers, Reuven and Yehuda, came over and conferred with her parents. The looks they sent at her and the sound of her mother's sobs told her everything she needed to know. She understood that her secret had been exposed and that her fate was sealed.

"Why are you whispering? If you have something to say to me, say it," she mustered her courage and approached them.

"You corrupt girl! You'd better be quiet now," Yehuda raged at her.

"Why are you calling me that?" she asked, deeply insulted.

"Why? I'll tell you why, bitch!" Yehuda's face turned red with rage. He attacked the fragile girl, and before any of those present managed to stop him, he slapped her across the face with all his might. The unexpected blow flung her to the floor. After that he raised his arm, fully intending to punch her.

"Stop! Don't hit her, please!" Their mother grasped his shirt and pulled him away.

"Get up." Her mother grasped her arms and helped her stand.

"Enough of this, Yehuda. Hitting won't solve the problem," Reuven, the oldest brother, ordered.

"She should be severely punished. We should beat her like we beat him. She's no different from him. There should be equal justice to those two wantons. They were both accomplices to sin, and if the *goy* was punished, she should be punished, too," said Yehuda, after reluctantly complying with his mother's and brother's requests to stop hitting his sister.

"You hit him? Are you crazy? You are crazy! What did you do to him, huh? What did he do to deserve a beating? He didn't do a thing! It was me! The guilt is all mine! It's me who's sick and tired of this life, and I went to find solace with him. I'm to blame!" Rivka burst out, and then looked straight at those present, and added while sobbing, "And maybe not? Maybe I'm not to blame. I'm not to blame that I was born into a life that isn't for me. Maybe God wants me to be different and not like I am now. Maybe God sent this man here to open my eyes and make me understand that the life I'm living is a life of lies. That's it, I don't want to live here anymore. I want to leave! Get as far away as I can!"

"Don't say that, child. You shouldn't talk that way. It's blasphemy." Her mother started weeping again.

"You're wrong, Mother. This isn't blasphemy! Listening to your heart's calling can't be blasphemy! No! It's God's will!" Rivka wept in her mother's arms.

"That's it? So easily you're throwing away everything we've been raised on? And calling it a life of lies! What's wrong with you, Rivkel? What? You're throwing an entire life into the garbage! How dare you? How can you turn your back on God like this?" Reuven persisted furiously.

"Easily? Easily you say? Do you know how many sleepless nights I've had! My life has become a living hell! I've struggled with all of my replenished strength. I've struggled day and night! There wasn't an hour, a minute, that I didn't struggle, but what can I do when it's not in my hands? What can I do when I lost the fight? And you, Reuven, I'll have you know that I'm not renouncing God Almighty and I never will," Rivka cried amid sobs.

"Such a naïve little lamb," Yehuda mocked.

"You *bastarddddd!*" The scream that ripped out of Rivka's throat was so fierce that everyone fell silent.

A tense silence fell on the house, shattered only by her mother's quiet weeping.

"Please, Mother, don't cry. If there's sorrow in my heart for what I've done, it's because of you, because of you and Papa." Rivka tore herself away from her mother and approached her father, who stood apart, looking suddenly so old and helpless.

"At least you have a measure of remorse," Yehuda continued stubbornly.

"You're Haman the Wicked! A heartless man! That's what you are. A violent hoodlum. You have nothing but violence. Back when you were in the yeshiva, you used to run around with all those hooligans and beat up innocent passersby. I heard the stories about you. You have no right to interfere in my life. Go mind your own business!" she yelled at him, her face red with anger.

"Haman? How dare you, bitch? That's what you call me? You scum! Luckily we're all married, otherwise, we'd have to enter a flawed match!" Yehuda jumped on her again, and when Rueven blocked his attack, he added furiously, "You don't live in an empty world, you fool. You have a proud, respectable family whom you've brought shame upon. Don't you care about that? I'm your big brother, and it's my right to interfere in order to protect my family. And I'll have you know, if you won't talk to me with respect, I'll beat you senseless, you slut."

"Enough, enough with the violence. Stop fighting. We're still a family. We have to think clearly what to do. How to get out of this mess," said their father, who until now, stood hunched in the corner, silent and stunned.

"Oy, the mess," her mother, who'd stopped crying, repeated after him.

A loaded silence fell on the room. Everyone looked troubled and thoughtful. However, while everyone was thinking of how to save Rivka's honor, she was thinking about Jeff. What really bothered her was the fact that he'd been hurt because of her. What was he going through now? How did he feel? What did he think of her? He was probably mad at her, blaming her for all the trouble that had fallen on him. There was no doubt that the blame was all hers. She shouldn't have gone to him. Of this, the sages said, "Think on the end before you begin," and she hadn't thought at all.

"What happened to Jeff? Was he hurt? Where is he now?" Rivka broke the silence and addressed Reuven, ignoring everyone else.

"I don't know. I wasn't there. From what Yehuda told me, you don't have to worry about that gentile. He got beat up a bit and kicked out of the apartment. Overall, he was punished for his actions. In any event, he doesn't belong in this neighborhood," Reuven tried to reassure her.

"Is this the way of the Torah? 'Her ways are pleasant ways, and all her paths are peace.' Isn't that what you taught me? Instead of checking and asking me what exactly happened there, you gathered your bullies and rushed to beat him up, as though he were no better than a filthy criminal. Is this how decent people behave? Is this the way of the Torah, on behalf of which you act? Answer me!" Agitated, she turned to Yehuda, and her words surprised everyone.

"Fine, here, I'm asking you, what exactly happened there? Maybe you can tell me what you were doing, alone, in a single man's home. Did you learn Torah lessons together? And if so, who did you learn about? About Moses or perhaps Jesus Christ?" Yehuda mocked her, hinting that her dramatic outburst hadn't impressed him. When he didn't get an answer, he continued seriously, "In this community, there are rabbis, and we act according to their ways. Those who stray must be punished. I acted according to the rabbi's commandment."

"That's your rabbi, not mine!" Rivka said, bringing on her head the wrath of everyone in the room.

"Those who guard their mouths and their tongues keep themselves from calamity. Watch what you're saying," Reuven warned her.

"I told you she was a slut," Yehuda said.

"If my own brother says I'm a slut, what will everyone else say? Who knows what rumors are spreading about me outside? Everybody probably thinks he came to me. And that wasn't what happened, Mother. I swear, we only talked. There was nothing between us, I swear to you." This time, she said what she had to say quietly.

"Innocent lamb. In a minute, you'll be asking us for a reward for your actions," Yehuda ridiculed her again.

"You nasty, merciless man!" Rivka screamed, launched herself at him, punched his chest with her small fists, and then ran to her room and shut herself inside.

The decision to stay in her room during the following days wasn't Rivka's or her concerned parents'. The extended family gathered and gravely discussed the new situation. A serious dispute arose among the siblings. Yehuda, who was the most zealous of them, suggested locking her in the basement apartment until they found her a new *shidduch*.

"But who told you she needs a new *shidduch*?" their mother asked in despair.

"What's wrong with you, Mother? What sane father will marry off his son to that *shiksa* after what happened? We have no choice! We have to lock her up! She has to learn a lesson she'll never forget. If we don't, she'll return to her evil ways," Yehuda explained to his siblings, who were shocked by his fanaticism and malice.

"I agree," said Margalit, Rivka's older sister. She was the only one who supported the idea.

"Don't exaggerate, Yehuda. It's enough that she stays locked in her room. That's not an easy punishment, considering the state she's in," Reuven addressed Yehuda, in an attempt to moderate his suggestion.

"You won't lock her anywhere! You won't do with her what Joseph's brothers did to him. As it is, people on the street will abuse her and turn her life to hell. No one will have mercy on her. We have to use methods of persuasion with her. We may have to find her a *shidduch* with someone from a place far away from here, a place no one will know about her past," their father interfered in the discussion. His voice was stern, indicating to his children that he was the one who would decide what would happen.

"And where exactly do you suggest we send her?" Reuven asked bemusedly.

"I don't know. Maybe Israel?" Their father's voice trembled.

"Israel? The land of Israel will be holy only after the coming of the messiah. As long as the messiah hasn't arrived, we will not acknowledge that land of heretics. This is the reason we're all here and not there," Yehuda ruled.

"That's not accurate. Shimon lives in Israel, and he lives among a sect of our Hasidim. They live there exactly like we live here, only segregated from their surroundings," their mother corrected him.

"They're not one of us. The minute they decided to live in that heretic state, they're not one of us," Yehuda insisted.

"I think you're exaggerating. All of you. We don't have to lock her up or send her away from here. She's our little sister, and it's our duty to help her as much as we can. Right, she did something very wrong and shamed us all, but we're still family, and we have to help her, not hurt her," Ahron interfered for the first time in the discussion in an attempt to ward off the weight of the punishment.

Since Ahron found out about the meeting between Rivka and Jeff, he'd been walking around grieving and ashamed. His world lay about in ruins. On the one hand, he felt betrayed, but on the other hand, he was weighed down by guilt. He was inconsolable with sorrow. He wanted to set things right because he felt responsible.

"Shut up! You have no right to say anything. All the trouble started when you let a goy into your house. If you had some brains in your head, this never would've happened. How could you? I don't understand how you could've let him into your house," Yehuda attacked him.

"Rabbi Ziegel allowed it. Hospitality is allowed," Ahron responded curtly, but hurt was all over his face.

"You're wrong," their father addressed Yehuda. "Ahron isn't to blame! This is from the heavens. God Almighty wanted this, and there wasn't a thing we could do to change it. From now on, we'll all pray that God will fix Rivka's errant soul and set her back on the path to righteousness."

"How? How did this wickedness fall upon us? A mindless, corrupt girl in such a respectable family. I can't understand it," Yehuda lamented, finding it hard to accept his sister's sudden transformation.

"She isn't exceptional. Ultimately, she's like all of us. She's still a little girl, whose thoughts are still unripe. Take a cluster of tomatoes who've all grown on the same vine. Four tomatoes will be red and sweet, and the fifth will be green and inedible. After some time, the green one will ripen and be like the rest of the tomatoes and maybe even better. We need patience. Rivka will redeem herself," their father tried to assure them with words of wisdom.

"And if, God forbid, she's pregnant?" Margalit insisted, unhappy with her father's lenient approach and determined to exacerbate the discussion.

"*Oy vey!* Don't you dare say that again!" her mother said angrily.

"Stop trying to stir things up, Margalit. She says that nothing of the sort happened, and I'm satisfied with her answer," Reuven supported his mother.

"And you believe her? You believe that during all the hours she spent there, nothing happened? On my life, you and mother are innocent. We should take her to a doctor to check her. He'll be the one who'll decide if she's a virgin or not," Margalit said decisively.

"Why are you exaggerating? *Hours*? She wasn't there for hours. Sometimes, I find it hard to believe that this is the way you talk about your little sister. Instead of helping her, you're making things difficult for her. Maybe you're jealous of her?" Ahron intervened, so angry by Margalit's words that he felt he had to retaliate harshly.

Margalit was twelve years older. Eight births and binge-eating that knew no repletion had caused her a concerning weight gain. She already weighed more than one hundred kilos. Her short legs barely carried her, so that she spent most of her time sitting at home idly. Her despairing husband rejected her and hadn't come to her in months. Ahron had no doubt that his older sister's frustration was what caused her to harden her heart against their rebellious little sister.

"Me jealous? Have you no shame, to talk like that? What would I be jealous of a rash little girl who desecrated the name of God? I have no reason to be jealous of her; I'm happy as I am."

"Whatever. I prefer not to answer," said Ahron, who didn't want to exacerbate the argument.

After a hard, scathing discussion, it was decided to entrust the care of the black sheep to the dependable hands of the oldest brother, Reuven.

"First of all, know that you've gravely damaged the honor of the family. Our good name was known to all, and that's gone. From now on, you stay in this room, and you're not coming out. You'll eat your meals here, except the Shabbat meal. You can leave only to use the bathroom and shower. Nobody intends on following you, but if you try to leave the house, I swear that with my own two hands, I'll lock you in the basement like Yehuda suggested," Reuven warned her, and Rivka accepted the verdict docilely.

She didn't say a thing.

Two days later, her parents summoned the matchmaker. She gathered Rivka and her parents in the living room and announced sadly, "I'm sure you know that Avraham-David and his family have washed their hands of the *shidduch*. A successful effort is lost, and now my assignment will be seven times harder."

"That's it? That's how it ends? No forgiveness? Rivka swore to us that the two of them only talked and nothing more. Nothing happened between them. The rumors on the street are all barefaced lies," her mother lamented.

"Dear Yehudit, you don't know what's true and what's not. You weren't there, after all. Rivka herself admitted that she was alone with him. In that, she broke the laws of seclusion, which in itself is gravely forbidden, and there's no forgiveness for it. I went to Rabbi Ziegel to ask for his advice, and he didn't even want to hear about it. 'She can go to hell,' he said to me," the matchmaker sealed their grave.

"God help us that a rabbi should speak that way!" Yehudit said angrily.

"Did you speak with Avraham-David's parents?" Moishel asked.

"I did."

"And what did they say?"

"Over their dead bodies. His father used those exact words. They drove me away in disgrace, and I couldn't do a thing."

"What will happen to Rivka now?" Moishel continued.

"God is Almighty. God willing, we'll find her another *shidduch*. But I'll make it clear to you that he won't be of the best."

"What do you mean?" Yehudit asked even though she knew where the matchmaker was going.

"I mean that the boy will have a certain defect. A man that no one is waiting to grab. Maybe lame, maybe old. I don't know. What I'll find, I'll find."

"And is there someone like this?" Moishel asked, his expression dark.

"To tell you the truth, I already have someone like that. A one-off, and if you don't hurry up, that someone will disappear, too."

"And who is this man?" the parents asked together.

"You must know that this match is difficult for me. The difficulty is both on the bride and the groom's side. It requires a lot of effort and many meetings. Therefore, for that reason, this *shidduch*, naturally, costs a bit more," she answered and waggled her fingers to indicate the salary she deserved.

"Don't worry, Gietel, you'll get what you deserve down to the last cent," Moishel said. He took a deep breath and asked somewhat apprehensively, "How much are we talking, more or less?"

"Not more or less. Exactly. Five thousand," she replied.

"Five thousand is a lot… but, nu, what can you do? Go on, tell us who he is," he prompted her.

"The Birnbaums, a very respected family, have a boy a bit touched in the head. Not something serious you should worry about. He functions like a normal person. He even has a job," Gietel said.

"So, what's the problem?" Yehudit probed.

"Sometimes, you know, he has these unexpected rages, and when that happens, it's a bit unpleasant to be around him," she explained apologetically.

"In other words, you're saying he's crazy," Moishel interpreted her words.

"God forbid! Not crazy *crazy*. Those kinds of people are put in the madhouse. He's just a bit touched. So, like I said, a month ago, the parents came to me and asked me to find someone appropriate for the boy. What do you think?" Gietel nervously followed their reactions.

"How old is the boy?" Yehudit asked.

"Thirty-three."

"*Thirty-three? You're* crazy! As old as that, and you call him a boy? Under no circumstance! Find her someone else. Our daughter, despite what she's done, deserves something a bit better than that," Moishel said angrily.

"The choice is in your hands. This is the situation, unfortunately. There aren't a lot of options. You want it, take it. You don't, God will have mercy. From above, someone else will be sent."

"What do you say, Rivkel? Why aren't you saying anything? This is your future we're discussing, daughter. Say something," Moishel addressed Rivka, who hadn't said a word since the meeting had started.

"What? Sorry, what did you say, Papa?" Rivka jerked as though awakening from a long, exhausting dream.

"I asked what you think about the match Gietel suggested."

"I'm not interested in a match, and I don't want anything. Do whatever you want, just leave me alone." She got up and went to her room.

"Leave her alone now. Things are very hard for her. It's understandable. The higher they climb, the harder they fall, that's what she feels. She'll come to terms with the new situation in a couple of days. Anyway, I want to ask you to think carefully of what I offered." Gietel got up and made to leave.

"I don't think it's a good match. Look for something else," Moishel expressed his opinion and glanced at his wife.

"Are you serious? Tell me, are you serious? Do you think she's better off with a lame or blind man? Because if you do, I have several of those, if you want to listen." Gietel, who had them right where she wanted them, sat back down.

"No! We've had enough for today. Give us some time to think it over, and we'll give you our answer next week," Yehudit dismissed her.

"By the way, I forgot to ask. It's very important for the *shidduch*. Is she still a virgin?" the matchmaker asked in a whisper.

"Yes, she's a virgin! Now leave," Moishel bit out and walked her to the door with a furious expression on his face.

"Heartless, greedy woman. For a thirty-three-year-old *meshugeneh*, she wants five thousand dollars," he complained.

"Thirty-three-year-old *meshugeneh* or ninety-three-year-old *meshugeneh*, what other choices do we have? That's the will of God and that's what will be," Yehudit said in despair, and Moishel looked at her quietly.

Chapter 12

From his seat on the fifth floor, Jeff surveyed the floor in satisfaction. Masses of people swarmed all over the department store and bought everything in reach: clothes, household utensils, cosmetics, toys, electrical appliances, and computers. Long lines waited at the checkout stations. Jeff took his eyes off the crowds and looked at the CCTV monitors on his desk. He started following the employees in the various departments. The large team looked like a well-oiled orchestra playing harmoniously, with him as the conductor. A tremendous sense of satisfaction filled him. At that moment, he didn't have a shadow of a doubt; the business was succeeding even more than he and Eve had dared to hope in their wildest dreams.

They'd opened the store only five months ago and had been successful from day one. Eve had two business ideas. The first was to establish a construction/renovation company. "We'll start small, and in the future, we'll expand to skyscrapers, like Daddy," she said enthusiastically.

"Aren't you overestimating my skills?" Jeff laughed. "I just worked as a handyman for a few months. Window cleaning, repairing tables, and changing door hinges isn't construction."

"So tell me what kind of business you'd like. Maybe a department store?" she suggested hesitantly.

"First of all, it's important that the business be the kind we'll be able to operate without other people's help. I also prefer the business to be in one place so we won't have to run around. A small department store, for example, could be appropriate," he replied, and the more he thought about the department store, the more his enthusiasm grew.

"Okay, then. So we'll open a big department store. We'll sell everything a person needs: clothes, food, electrical appliances, household utensils, etc.," she refined the idea.

"Good idea, but I'm afraid a large shop will be too much for us. The risk is too high," Jeff said. The idea of owning a large store scared him. Just a little more than a year ago, he had been an assistant cook at a small diner in a god-forsaken town. How would he suddenly manage a large department store?

"You're right," Eve reconsidered. "It's a big risk. And also, the investment is enormous, perhaps hundreds of thousands of dollars, and possibly even more. I've already heard of similar businesses that went bankrupt. I think we can succeed only if we proceed wisely and cautiously. Every step should be calculated to the last cent. If we see that the risk increases, we'll focus on something smaller. I'm willing to risk some of my money, not all of it."

"I don't know. Calculations are your strong side, and I trust you. I think we don't have to risk a lot of money. We can purchase part of the merchandise on credit, and we'll settle our debts to the suppliers from the sales. If the shop is at a good location, I have no doubt that a lot of consumers will come."

"Let's start with the idea and see where it takes us," Eve concluded.

At first, Jeff studied their idea day and night. He trudged from location to location; asked questions and researched products and suppliers; and collected documents that included advertising, price quotations, and more. He passed on the information to Eve, who worked for days on a detailed business plan. She calculated all the possible expenses, including rent, taxes, equipment investment, and inventory costs. She examined the data from every possible angle, and the more she studied it, the more promising she thought the results looked. Nevertheless, the required initial investment was large and a bit daunting. When she finished the business plan, they started searching for an appropriate location for the store. They chose a location on 3rd Avenue, between 46th and 47th streets. The store was in a huge building in which renovations had just been completed. The entire building was owned by Eve's father. When he heard that Jeff and his daughter were planning on opening a department store, he rushed to offer them the building.

"It's an excellent location for what you're planning. I'll give you twenty-four months rent-free, and later, when the business is established, pay me eight thousand plus two percent of proceeds from sales per month. What do think, fair offer?"

"Very fair offer," Eve rejoiced, who had calculated rent would be three times more expensive.

Thus, the opportunity they hoped for opened before them.

To the disappointment of her managers, Eve took a two-month vacation and flung her entire being into the start-up stages. In the beginning, they established a company called, "Eve's Department Store."

"Eve's is a good name. There's something glamorous and prestigious about your name. What do you think?"

"I don't know," she replied self-consciously.

"I love your name...and you, too, of course," he added immediately.

"I love you, too," she replied excitedly. His suggestion, although embarrassing, flattered her. No doubt, her man loved her a lot.

During the first month, they were busy building the store. They were busy renovating and purchasing equipment and furniture, and in the end, they bought the computers and inventory. In order to finance the initial activity, Eve invested four hundred thousand dollars of her own money. Jeff contributed all of his money—

twenty-four thousand dollars. They agreed that Eve would have the right of priority to withdraw money from the initial proceeds until their investment was balanced. After that, they would divide the proceeds fifty-fifty. They also decided Jeff would work in the shop and manage it. In the beginning, he would earn a modest weekly salary of seven hundred and fifty dollars. The bank would give them the further credit of a sum similar to their investment, and they'd get the rest of their funding through credit from their suppliers. Buying inventory was done very carefully. They bought everything they needed, but in small quantities. Then, they were busy recruiting workers and placing them in the various departments. Of all the workers chosen, there was one choice that especially excited Jeff.

"The role of the Purchasing Manager is a very important one. We need someone who's hardworking, and above all, trustworthy and dedicated," Eve demanded.

"I think I have someone…"

"Who?"

"Rico."

"Who's Rico?" Eve asked.

"He worked with me at window cleaning. He's not the smartest guy in the world, but he's experienced and hardworking, loyal to his job, and last but not least, he's as honest as they come. We can trust him with our eyes closed."

"I trust you, Jeffie. And anyway, you have to get used to the idea that you're the boss, and the responsibility of managing the store is on you. For my part, in another week, the dream ends and I go back to work," she reminded him.

"That sucks."

"What sucks, that I'm going back to work? No choice, sweetie. If the business tanks, we'll need another source of income to tide us over. So we don't find ourselves on the street," she laughed.

"And can it tank?" he asked worriedly.

"I don't think so. I believe in this place. We've done recon by the book, so why shouldn't we succeed?"

The next day, Jeff invited Rico to a business meeting.

"Rico, meet Eve, my girlfriend."

"I hope he told you only good things about me," Rico chuckled, unable to tear his eyes away from Eve.

"Don't worry, only good things." She winked at him.

"I know you," he told her. "Only through the window, of course," he added and burst into laughter.

"I have an interesting offer for you," Jeff said.

"Offer?" Surprise was evident on Rico's face.

"Eve and I are opening a department store on 3rd Avenue," Jeff began.

"Department store? You? When did you become rich?" Rico couldn't believe his ears.

"It isn't me, it's her," Jeff laughed. "I'm looking for a purchasing manager. Someone to manage the entire matter of inventory. It isn't an easy role. I know it's unfamiliar territory for you, but I trust you. No more window cleaning and renovations. What do you say?"

"But I have no idea how to do the job. I know how to do the shopping for my wife in the supermarket, but a purchasing manager?" Rico joked to hide his unease.

"It's not so complicated. You have to track the inventory, find appropriate suppliers, and bargain with them on their prices. I remember you did it at Menachem's," Jeff encouraged him.

"Well, if you want to employ someone as inexperienced as me, bless you. I certainly won't refuse the offer."

"During the first year, your weekly salary will be eight-hundred dollars," Eve concluded. "If the business succeeds, your salary will increase by ten percent next year. What do you think?"

"Great. Couldn't have hoped for more. To tell you the truth, I'm not as young and strong as I used to be. It's really difficult for me to do the jobs I'm doing now. So in that sense, your timing is just perfect." Rico couldn't hide his satisfaction at the tempting offer.

"Great. Now we'll raise a toast to success. I'm sure the three of us will take the business to incredible heights," Jeff said. He opened a bottle of wine and poured the red liquid into three wine glasses.

"Cheers!" the three of them exclaimed and drank it all in one gulp. "To our success!"

When spring came, "Eve's" opened to the public.

Jeff moved the mouse to the Excel sheet. He reexamined the sales figures for the last month. The result indicated a sum that was twenty-five thousand dollars higher than the turnout required to cover all of their expenses, as calculated by Eve. Meaning an annual profit of three hundred thousand dollars before taxes, and all this in only their first year.

He rubbed his hands together in pleasure. The success of the business pleased him, yet, surprisingly, his pleasure was incomplete. He thought about Rivka, and these thoughts kept him awake at night. From time to time, he remembered the taste of her sweet tongue and the intoxicating scent of her body. He found himself yearning to catch a glimpse of her, to hear her voice. Most of the time, he was preoccupied with store matters, but when he came home, late at night, especially when he lay in bed, he would think of her and of what had become of her. Judging by the violent visit he received on his last day in Brooklyn, he understood that the helpless girl's secret had been found out. "If I'm unlucky enough to get caught, they'll find me a third-class *shidduch*," he remembered her saying. That was probably her current situation. He didn't feel guilty, yet nevertheless, he was plagued by a weird feeling that he had to help her get out of the mess she was in. He sensed the girl was in terrible despair and that there was no one to save her.

He left his office and rushed down the escalators to the ground floor, where Rico's office was located.

"I need your help," he got straight to the point. "Moishel's Mini Market. You know the place, right?"

"Who?" Rico tried to recall the name.

"You know, Moishel's grocery, where Ahron works. Ahron, who used to be my friend. Remember Ahron, who was Menachem's brother-in-law?"

"Sure! Now, I remember. What's going on?"

"It's about Rivka, Ahron's sister. I need you to check for me what's going on with her. I'd do it myself, but if I go there, they'll beat the shit out of me."

"Why?" Rico questioned. So, Jeff told him about Rivka and the violent encounter with the chastity squad.

"Boy, so many broken hearts in such a short time," Rico laughed. "Remember Laura, my cousin? She fell a bit in love with you, the poor girl."

"Stop kidding around. This is a serious matter," Jeff berated him.

The next day, Rico came in late and went straight to Jeff's office. "I checked the matter for you," he notified him.

"What did you find out?"

"According do what Bilha told me—you remember Bilha, she works for Menachem and is a relation—she's getting married."

"Married? With whom?"

"Her previous groom left her. Her parents found her another groom. A blind guy. I asked Bilha if Rivka even wants to marry this guy, and she said she didn't have a clear answer on the matter. Rumors say she's shut herself in her room and refuses to come out. Bilha said she thinks Rivka doesn't want to get married, but she isn't sure of it."

"And then?"

"And then I went to Moishel's grocery. I walked up to Ahron and asked him how his sister was doing. I introduced myself as a good friend of yours. 'Tell Jeff she's just fine,' he said uncomfortably. And then I left. But before I left, I had a feeling he wanted to say something to me, but then he changed his mind."

"That's it?" Jeff was disappointed.

"Yeah, that's it. You know what I think? Judging by what you told me, I think she doesn't want to get married. That's evident. And if she wants to leave the Hasidic community, does it make sense to you that she would marry a Hasid, and a blind one at that?"

"The thing is that the choice isn't hers to make," Jeff stated thoughtfully and then added, "So what do you suggest that I do? How can I help that poor girl?"

"Try writing to her. Offer her help. In my opinion, she doesn't know how to contact you. She doesn't know where you live now or what you're doing," Rico stated.

"But letters? Won't letters make things even worse for her?" Jeff contemplated doubtfully.

"What can be worse than marrying someone you don't want to marry?" Rico persisted.

"That makes sense. I'll write to her, and we'll see what happens."

"Do it, but don't let Eve know. So, she won't think there's something going on between you two," Rico advised and winked to a surprised Jeff.

"Don't be stupid. Everything I do, I talk it over with Eve," Jeff replied angrily.

"Okay, okay, I didn't say anything," Rico chuckled.

So, Jeff wrote to her. His letter was short. First, he sent his regards, then he asked her not to marry. "If you need any help, don't hesitate to contact me," he wrote.

Several days passed, and since his letter went unanswered, he wrote again. When his second letter didn't receive an answer, he decided to do things differently. He decided to write to Ahron. This time, his letter was long and detailed. In the letter, he appealed to his friend's compassion and urged him to help his sister. "Your sister's happiness depends on this. You can't stay indifferent. Take responsibility and do something. Don't let her life be ruined. If you don't do anything, your conscience will torture you your entire life. Faith is a positive power as long as you channel it to a positive path. Don't let it become a destructive force." In the end, he wrote that he missed Ahron and his family. "You're like a brother to me," he wrote. "I'll never forget what you did for me. My regards to Miriam and kisses to the little ones from Uncle Jeff." Then he put the letter in an envelope and added three thousand dollars. "Please give the money to Rivkel," he requested. "It'll make things easier for her in the beginning until she finds her bearings in a new place." On the back of the envelope, he wrote his phone number.

"Rico, I have another request for you. Please give this letter, in person, to Ahron. Don't leave it in the shop with anyone else. Give it only to Ahron himself. Promise?"

"Sure."

"And try, when you give him the letter, to be sure that no one else sees you do it. I'm afraid that if anyone sees it, they'll conspire against him, too. I have a feeling he'll help her. I know him well. He loves his little sister very much. He won't let her fall."

"I hope so," Rico said.

The next day, Rico entered the office and reported to Jeff about the results of his meeting with Ahron. "When I came to the store, he wasn't there, but he arrived ten minutes later. I caught him just before he entered the shop. When he saw me, he was apprehensive. 'You again,' he said. I didn't say much, just took out the envelope, put it in his hand, and told him it was important that he opened it and read it. Before he had time to react, I left so he wouldn't have any regrets."

"Good thinking. So, what do you say? Will he read it?"

"I think so. Curiosity and the money will work their magic. Will he do something for the good of his sister? About that, I'm not so sure. If he's as good a guy as you say he is, and he has some brains in his head, he'll do something."

"I actually have a good feeling about the entire matter," Jeff said.

Jeff continued with his routine. He didn't forget Rivka, but after he had done something and eased his conscience a bit, he thought of her only occasionally. The question, whether his letter had done any good, remained opened.

Until the day the phone rang.

Chapter 13

"Under no circumstance! Over my dead body! I know their son, he's completely crazy. Not slightly touched in the head, like the matchmaker said, but more like a huge hole in the head. He's a true madman. I once saw him run down the street, God help us, naked as the day he was born! His mother ran after him, holding his clothes, trying to catch up with him and put some clothes on him. He was screaming like a nutcase, and nobody understood what he was saying. You want to marry her with a man like that? No! Rivkel's life will become a nightmare. In this case, she and we are better off that she stay single," Reuven seethed after his parents confided in him of their decision to marry Rivka to the Birnbaums' son.

"If not him, then who?" Moishel asked, wringing his hands in despair.

"My friend, Yitzhak, has a brother, one or two years older than Rivkel, I think. A pleasant man and a great scholar. His name is Avner," Reuven began, as though preparing himself for a long discussion. Then, he felt silent, as if considering how to continue.

"*Nu*, so what's the problem?" Yehudit asked excitedly.

"He's...blind," he said quietly. "Actually, not completely blind. Yitzhak claims that he can see some shadows," he added in an attempt to soften their anticipated protest.

"What does that mean, 'sees some shadows'? Does that mean he can get around without assistance?" Moishel asked practically.

"I don't know, Papa! I think if that were the case, the man would already be married, with children."

"My poor Rivkel. Her entire life, she'll have to take care of him, and all because of a moment of foolishness, a moment of weakness. I don't think this man is a good match for her. *Oy*, why did this have to happen. Why?" Yehudit bemoaned.

"Mother, we can sit here all day and ask why, why? We can't change what already happened. We have to look forward."

"Look forward to what? What kind of life is waiting for her?" his mother continued mournfully.

"There's no choice, Mother. You can say of Avner that he's the best of the worst. At least Rivkel will live with a decent man who will treat her respectfully. They'll be able to raise a family. And even more importantly, he's the son of the Ziedenbaums, a well-known, wealthy family. The father is very important, a wealthy diamond merchant. He can take care of all of their needs. I'm sure the marriage will be a success. Similar things have happened. Why, look at Yoseph and Sarah, who live just down the street. Both of them are completely blind, yet they live happily, and they have eight beautiful, healthy children. *Nu*, what do you think?" Reuven asked, and waited apprehensively for his parents' answers, as though they were, in fact, discussing his future.

"I don't know. I'm filled with doubts..."

"And can you arrange a meeting?" asked Moishel, who found solace in the fact that the family was wealthy.

"Of course. Give me a few days. I'll speak with Yitzhak and get back to you with an answer," he promised, ignoring his mother's doubts.

"At least, we won't need that greedy Gietel's help," Moishel concluded, pleased to be saving a substantial amount of money.

When they told Rivka about the *shidduch*, she reacted indifferently. Her expression remained impassive, as though the entire matter didn't concern her. Even the fact that the man was blind left no impression on her. As far as she was concerned, the mere fact that he was a Hasid made him undesirable in her eyes. She remained resolute. She no longer wanted to be part of the Hasidic community!

The meeting took place ten days later. Her parents, Reuven and Yitzhak participated and, of course, the intended bride and groom. Suspicion was rife on both sides.

When the guests entered, Moishel and Yehudit looked at Avner with curiosity mixed with dread. Avner held onto his brother's arm, who helped him find his place in the armchair. As for the Ziedenbaums, they scrutinized Rivka closely, sending piercing looks, as though they could figure her out just by looking.

"What will you drink?" Yehudit asked if only to slightly ease the tense atmosphere.

"Don't bother, Mrs. Stienberg. We'll drink later," Mr. Ziedenbaum declined.

"Nevertheless, I'll get you something," Yehudit suggested when everyone sat down.

"I'll help you," Mrs. Ziedenbaum jumped at the opportunity and joined Yehudit on her way to the kitchen, where she hurried to ask curiously, "Dear Yehudit, first tell me if there's any truth in the stories about your daughter. Rumors are that she's no longer a virgin, that a Christian, God help us, had her, and it was all with her consent. Yitzhak, my son, says it's all nonsense, the figment of people's imaginations. But you must know the truth. If she's not a virgin, we should cut this short right now, and we'll go home as though nothing occurred."

"My Rivkel is as pure as the driven snow. I'm willing to swear on that, Mrs. Ziedenbaum. There wasn't even a touch of their hands," Yehudit answered, not bothering to hide her insult from the intrusive question. Anyone would think her blind son was perfect, and that all the girls of the Hasidut were chasing him!

"No need to swear, I believe you. I always knew Rivkel was a good girl from a good family, and that the rumors are just the gossip of spiteful people who have nothing to do but sit at home all day and talk nonsense."

"And your son, Avner? Reuven says he sees shadows. But when you walked in, I noticed him fumbling his way, literally unable to see a thing," Yehudit retaliated.

"Golden he is, my boy. Once, when he was little, the doctors said that maybe he saw shadows in one eye. He was born with a defect, to his bad luck. But I'll have you know, Mrs. Stienberg, that he's a very special person. Rivkel will be happy with him. He has everything a woman could wish for. Wisdom, diligence, kindness, and the most important thing, he has great knowledge of the Torah that others, who have two seeing eyes, don't have," the mother praised her son.

"If only! Hopefully, God Almighty will bless them and light their way," Yehudit concluded the exchange, gesturing with her eyes at the refreshments, a hint that the conversation was over.

An easy discussion had developed in the living room. The only ones who didn't talk were Rivkel and Avner. Rivka seemed completely disconnected from her surroundings. Most of the time she stared into space, and it looked as though the meeting didn't interest her. So indifferent was she to what was going on, that she didn't bother, not even once, to look at her intended groom. Avner was also silent, but it seemed as though his silence stemmed from shyness.

When the meeting was over, it was decided that in four months, God willing, the two would wed.

"A wedding like this never has and never will be seen in New York," Avner's father declared joyously.

After the meeting, Rivka shut herself in her room. It wasn't her family's ban that caused her to behave like this. Melancholy consumed her, and she lost the will to live. She barely ate or slept.

Reading, which she'd once loved so, was forgotten, and she stayed away from showers, which were favored by her. It wasn't long before she became thin and hunched. Her face shriveled, and her twinkling blue eyes became dull and sunken. Her golden curls, which had been her pride and joy, lost their shine and looked like a wild nest of dirty yellow yarn.

One night, she had a fleeting thought that she was losing her mind and was better off taking her own life. Yes, she'd kill herself and end her torment. But, did she have the strength to do it? And if so, then how? Would she hang herself and die gasping for air, or should she swallow pills until she lost consciousness and died? Once, she heard of a young Hasidic man who'd slit his wrists and died of blood loss. No. She couldn't hurt herself like that. In her childhood, the sight of blood, even from a tiny wound, was enough to horrify her. No! She'd find another way, one more delicate, simple, and from there, she would move on to the next world, where everything was peaceful and calm, and people were equal. Heaven would open its gates in her honor! Angels would wrap her in love! Indeed? Was there really a place in heaven for those who took the law into their own hands and took their own lives? And if she did this deed, what would become of her family then? How would they cope with the shame? How would her parents cope with the loss and the grief? They loved her so much, despite what she'd done! And Ahron, her beloved brother, he and his wife would be tormented by guilt! And besides, suicide was strictly forbidden. It was completely contrary to the Torah! No! She wouldn't find herself in heaven; she'd burn in the fires of hell! No! She wouldn't do it! Even if eventually she'd find herself under the wedding canopy, she wouldn't take her own life. She'd have to think of another way.

In the beginning, after her visit at Jeff's became common knowledge, she was still strong enough to consider running away from home. But as the days passed, she realized the task was too difficult for her, almost impossible. Slowly, thoughts of freedom were pushed away from her consciousness. Her mental and physical state didn't go unnoticed by her concerned parents.

"Come to the kitchen. I made you that kugel that you love so much," Yehudit begged.

"I'm not hungry, Mother," she could barely reply.

"Why are you behaving like this? Why are you behaving as though it's the end of the world? With your own two eyes, you saw Avner is a good man. You can't even notice the defect in his beautiful eyes. It's God's will, daughter. You must eat from now on, and a lot. Otherwise, there'll be nothing left of you at the wedding."

"Mother, leave me alone. I already told you I wasn't hungry," Rivka said impatiently.

"The wedding is in two months, and you haven't even picked out a dress. Let's go out, choose a wedding dress for you. You'll see, it'll cheer you up," Yehudit tried to coax her daughter differently.

"Mother, you know my opinion on the matter. This wedding doesn't interest me at all. You chose it, not me."

Two months before the wedding, Dvora stopped by for a brief visit and revived the idea of running away.

"*Oy vey!* Look at you! You look awful!" Dvora exclaimed the minute she arrived.

Rivka didn't answer.

"You're crazy! Look what you did to yourself!" Dvora added in alarm. Then she whispered excitedly, "Anyway, Rivkel my dear, I've come to say good-bye."

"Say good-bye?" Rivka exclaimed anxiously.

"Yes. The day after tomorrow, Adam and I are traveling to Israel. For always."

"The day after tomorrow? To Israel?" Rivka's face turned white.

"Yes, to Israel. Of course, nobody knows a thing but you. According to our plan, tomorrow evening, I'll leave the house. At night, Adam and I will sleep at a hotel, and in the morning, we'll fly to Israel. Before leaving the house, I'll leave my parents a good-bye letter. I hope they'll understand my actions. There's no choice; Adam and I are in love. He promised me that the moment we arrive at our new home, God willing, we'd get married."

"Get married? With Adam? God, you really are leaving! I always thought you were just talk, and that when the moment of truth arrived, you'd be as afraid as I am."

"Yes, dear friend, I'm leaving forever. There's no way back from the path I chose. I'm leaving without fear, and if there's sorrow in me, it's only because of you. I'll miss you so much." Dvora went to Rivka, and they fell into each other's arms.

"I'm sure we'll meet someday, sister. Our separation is temporary. When I arrive in Israel, I'll write to you. That way, you'll know where to come if you want to follow me," Dvora encouraged her weeping friend.

"I hope I can. I don't think I can just get up and leave," Rivka protested through her tears.

"You can. Of course, you can. Where there's a will, there's a way, remember? That's what we were taught! If you want something, you have to strive to achieve it! I heard about this man they're setting you up with. Don't marry him. Whatever happens, don't agree. Not that he's a bad guy, heaven forbid, but you have to marry only the man you want and love. Don't let others decide for you."

"I already said I don't want to get married, but no one's paying attention to my opinion. Everyone sees me as ruined. There's a flaw in me that can't be fixed. In their eyes, I'm a fool who doesn't understand a thing, and so, my opinion shouldn't be considered. And it's all because of what I've done..." Despair was evident in her voice.

"You haven't done a thing! I'm telling you, Rivkel, you haven't done a thing!" Dvora declared decisively.

"You know what, Dvora, when I think about it, I'm not even sorry for what I did. On the contrary, I already understand and know I don't want to live here. But what should I do? Everyone is busy with preparations, and no one pays attention to me anymore!" Rivka looked at her friend, hoping she would bring salvation.

"Rivkel, tell them you don't intend to marry and that you simply won't come to the wedding. You have to be determined. Otherwise, you're in trouble. Listen to me, and listen carefully! When I arrive in Israel, I'll write to you. All you'll need is a few hundred dollars for the plane ticket. The minute you board the plane, you won't suffer any longer. I'll wait for you in Israel. Got it?"

Rivka's eyes were wide with wonder when she nodded with difficulty.

"Now, I have to get a move on, and you must eat, understand? You must!"

Rivka stared at her friend wordlessly, only her tearful eyes indicating the storm in her soul.

"I'll see you, beloved sister." Dvora embraced Rivka and emotionally kissed her wet cheek.

After she left, Rivka started thinking again about running away. The idea instilled in her a new lease on life, but that was short-lived because fear overwhelmed her again. Later, she resumed her state of apathy and continued to shut herself in her room. She was so immersed in depression that she lost track of days, and she didn't know if it was raining outside or if the sun was shining. She wanted to tell everyone she wouldn't marry and that the preparations for the wedding were wasted, but it was as though she were paralyzed, struck mute and couldn't say a thing.

The days passed. The wedding was a month away. As promised, Mr. Ziedenbaum rented a luxurious venue, maybe the most luxurious in the city. A band and photographer were meticulously selected, and the chef of a well-known hotel was specially hired to cook the most scrumptious meal. Invitations were handed out to everybody who was somebody in the Hasidic community, and all in all, more than one thousand guests were invited, most of them residents of the borough. A wedding dress was created especially for Rivka. When she refused to leave the house, the seamstress came to her.

"God, you're so thin! How much do you weigh?" the seamstress screamed the minute she entered the house. "No more than forty-five kilo, right? You're so thin, no one will see you at the wedding. Don't you eat? Have you turned into one of those goy girls, heaven forbid, those girls called anorexics? I don't think we'll have a choice but to make you a wide dress. Maybe that way, people won't notice how thin you are," she added as she measured her hips.

After the dress had been made and Rivka had tried it on, she couldn't help but notice how pretty and glamorous the dress was. But when she looked at herself in the mirror, she saw that while the dress sparkled, her face was dull.

There were only two weeks left.

In the morning, with the help of medication the doctor prescribed for her the previous night, she managed to eat a bit. Her apathy abated some, but in the evening, she became agitated again. Her feverish mind conjured suicidal thoughts the entire night. The next morning, she snuck into her father's room while he was at the synagogue and took all of his medication. From the bathroom, she gathered all the new and old medications, of which there many. She returned to her room and locked the door behind her. Staring at the odd collections of bags and bottles she placed on her desk, she wasn't sure. Tears filled her eyes. Then she collected a handful of colorful pills, spreading them in her delicate palm. Through the tears washing her face, the colorful combination of pills looked bright and garish. This beautiful collection would put an end to her suffering. Her short life flashed before her eyes. In the beginning, it was Jeff, the handsome man who'd stormed into her life straight from the desert. Then came Avraham-David, the pleasant man whom she'd misled. Her father and mother who'd raised her with so much love and dedication. Her brothers and sisters. Yehuda, obviously, wouldn't shed a tear for her. He may even be secretly pleased. And then it was Dvora, her good friend, her soul mate. How would she react? Dvora was waiting for her in

Israel! Yes, because this was the only way this wonderful friendship could continue.

Suddenly, someone knocked on the door.

Rivka's hand jerked in alarm and the many pills fell and scattered all over the floor.

"Who is it?" she asked, while scurrying in a panic to pick up the pills.

"It's me," she heard Ahron on the other side of the door.

Lately, Ahron had been visiting a lot, and during every visit, he tried to convince her to accept her fate. "You have no choice," he kept saying. "God taught us to accept the good and the bad equally. Try to see the bright side of things and enjoy it as much as possible."

"How are you feeling?" he asked this time, as he always did, the minute she opened the door for him.

"How do you think?" she answered without raising her head.

"God, I don't know. Maybe you should go to the hospital. You don't look so good, and that's saying the least. Your eyes are dull, and you're so thin. Obviously, you've been starving yourself."

"What can I do? It's not in my hands. Yesterday, I actually ate a bit. I want to eat, but unfortunately, I have no appetite whatsoever. What would you in my place? *Nu*, let's hear you, Mr. Know-It-All, what would you do?"

"Honestly, I have no idea. ..."

"You see? It looks so easy from the side: a girl with a defect marries a boy with a defect. So simple. If you had the slightest idea what I was going through, you wouldn't wed me. Certainly not now. What's the rush?"

"The wedding date is getting closer," he reminded her, following her expression.

"Close, close. What can I do?" She stared at him indifferently. The agitation that seized her just several minutes ago disappeared as though it had never even existed.

"What, don't you care?" he poked insistently.

"No. If I have the strength, I'll come, and if not, I'll fall on the way there," she said, hinting at the difficulties she may create. *This isn't encouraging*, he thought. Once, a long time ago, he read, in a ultra-orthodox newspaper, actually, that a person suffering from depression didn't display signs of sadness or anger, for he didn't care about himself. Sadness and anger showed that he was still sensitive to his surroundings. However, the minute a person was apathetic concerning his situation, things became problematic. Rivka was apathetic in regards to her situation, of that he had no doubt. Perhaps, she was considering ending her life? He'd already read and heard about cases as such that ended in a loss of life. Was Rivka capable of that? Was she capable of doing something that went unequivocally against the Torah? Eventually, he reached the frightening conclusion that a person in depression was indeed capable of it. He wasn't thinking clearly, and he had no control over his actions.

"And if I tell you the situation can be changed?" he asked.

"How exactly?" She lifted her head. For the first time since he came in, their eyes met.

"I'll tell you how. I know I'm about to do something that will bring the wrath of the entire family on my head, but I don't care. Whatever happens, it's my obligation to help you. I'm the one who got you into this mess, and I'm the one who'll help you get out of it. If it's a sin that I'm doing, God is the one who'll settle the score with me."

"And what exactly is this thing you plan to do?" she asked skeptically, but sat straighter, narrowing her eyes at him curiously.

"Okay, the story goes like this, listen carefully. A month ago, I received a letter from Jeff. ..." He noticed the pallor of her face change the minute she heard Jeff's name. Finally, she was reacting positively.

"What does he want?" she whispered, her pale face flushing, her eyes filling with tears.

"In the letter, he asked me to help you. He said he tried to write to you twice, but unsuccessfully. I know two letters were delivered here and that Yehuda destroyed them. I also know no one read them. He tore them to pieces, and everyone agreed that he do that, including Papa and Mother," Ahron said, trying to interpret his sister's reaction.

"You see, even when I had a shred of hope, that despicable brother of mine destroyed it," she said and suddenly started hiccupping.

"Someone's thinking about you now." He smiled encouragingly.

"Probably Yehuda, who's thinking how to kick my butt," she said, hiccups mixing with laughter, as she wiped her tears. She remembered that she hadn't laughed for weeks. Ahron looked at her and laughed, too.

"Nu, go on," she said, still laughing, but no longer crying.

"Jeff wrote that he'd discovered you were going to get married against your will. He demanded that I prevent it. He said it was my moral obligation to do so. He literally ordered me to do it." Ahron paused for a long time, then took a deep breath.

"And how exactly will you help me?" she asked and anxiously waited for his answer.

"This isn't easy for me, sister. It's so hard for me. I know that with this decision, I'm causing you to desecrate the name of God, heaven help us. You know that Papa can perform *kriah* on you. I haven't slept for nights because of this, and I've even consulted with rabbis outside of our sect. In the end, after consulting with Miriam, I've decided to do as Jeff suggested."

"And what did he suggest?"

Ahron shoved his hand into his pocket and pulled out an envelope stuffed with dollar bills.

"There are three thousand dollars here. Would you believe it? He asked me to give you this money and said it would help you. He wrote his phone number on the envelope and also added his address. He asked that you call whenever you need help."

"So much money! Why did he give so much?"

"So you'd be able to get out of here."

"Get out? Me?" Rivka panicked.

Ahron nodded.

"And you think I can take this money?"

"Not only can you take it, you must. He did it out of his own free will. You mustn't refuse charity."

"And where would I go?"

"It's all arranged. I'll explain everything. But first, promise me something."

"What?"

"Promise me you won't go to him. I know he's a good man, don't forget he was my friend. But he's a Christian, and you mustn't forget that. If you go to him, my sin will be too heavy to bear, and I won't be able to live with myself. Can you promise me that?"

"I promise. It's actually quite simple for me. The last time I left his place, I saw a woman get out of a big car and go into his apartment. I'm sure she's the reason he didn't want me. What's important for me now is that I leave this place and go live somewhere else, living the way I want to. I'm no longer interested in him, even though I think of him frequently…" she said sadly.

"Then let's continue. To make it easy for you, make an Aliyah."

"Aliyah? Me? How exactly do you make Aliyah?"

"I checked it all for you. This evening pack a small suitcase, the smallest you can pack. Tomorrow at dawn, while Papa will be praying the morning prayer and Mother will be sleeping in her room, I'll come to take you. We'll travel together to the Jewish Agency."

"The Jewish Agency?"

"Yes, the Jewish Agency. I checked everything. The Jewish Agency is an organization that brings Jews to Israel. They have branches all over the world. They also have one on 3rd Avenue. You and I will go there and ask them to help you."

"Israel! I'm shocked! But where will I go there?" she asked and then her eyes filled with light. "I know! I'll go to my friend Dvora." "Dvora? What's Dvora doing in Israel?" Ahron asked in bemusement.

"She's been in Israel for a couple of months."

"Dvora in Israel? I didn't know. Whatever. But don't go to her! Go to Aunt Rachel. I've already spoken to her the day before yesterday and told her to expect you. She was so happy. Said she'd treat you like a queen. You'll live in her house, on the kibbutz, until you get settled. The agency people will take care of all the rest."

"You spoke with Aunt Rachel? I can't believe what I'm hearing. Can I kiss you, brother?" she asked earnestly.

"Yes!" he surprised her and gave her his cheek.

"How will we tell Papa and Mother?" she asked after kissing him.

"Write them a letter. Give me the letter tomorrow morning. I'll give it to them after you leave America. The most important thing is that you apologize and ask for their forgiveness. Write to them that you're traveling to Israel to Aunt Rachel. Promise them that you'll continue observing the mitzvoth. That's what is most important to them. I know you're going to change your lifestyle, but always remember, Rivkel, where you came from, that there's only one God and that He's guarding you. You mustn't, under any circumstance, turn your back on Him. Do you promise?"

"No chance that will happen. Without Him, none of us are worth a thing," she replied, her voice choked with tears.

"I'll leave now, and you go eat before you faint," he said and left the room.

The minute he left, Rivka snuck out of the room and put all the medications back in place. Then, she went to the kitchen and ate. First, she ate a little, as much as she could. Two hours later, she returned to the kitchen and ate again. She ate everything within reach. She hadn't eaten like that even during the meal before the Yom Kippur and Tisha Be'Av fasts combined. Then, she took a long, leisurely shower. When she came out, she wore her pajamas and combed her hair painstakingly. After that, she took her backpack, packed a few items of clothes, a notebook, a pen, and a book. When she finished, she sat down to write. She wrote, and as she wrote, tears streamed down her face. She filled four pages full of small, crowded writing. Pages on which the ink mixed with her tears. When she finished, she climbed into bed, yet sleep eluded her. She was awake until dawn. Even the stomach pains that were caused by nervousness and binging couldn't prevent the happiness that washed over her. In the morning, Ahron arrived as promised, and together, they snuck out of the house.

Outside for the first time in months, Rivka noticed that both winter and spring had passed, and a warm, caressing sun, heralding the beginning of summer, welcomed her pale, thin face.

Chapter 14

Ahron and Rivka walked quietly along the hall. Nevertheless, the echo of their footsteps on the laminated floor was loud. From the rooms along the corridor, the gazes of curious officials followed them in the early morning hours, causing them discomfort. On the walls, they noticed pictures of the founding fathers: Hertzel and Ben Gurion. Definitely not pictures they were used to seeing until now.

"Not even one picture of a rabbi," Ahron whispered in complaint.

"Why would there be a picture of a rabbi? We're not in a yeshiva or a synagogue," Rivka whispered back.

"In order to highlight the common dominator. Show the Jewish connection between the Satmars' Rabbi Teitelbaum, of blessed memory, to Shimon Peres, for example."

"This is a stronghold of Zionism. The rabbi didn't acknowledge the Zionist movement. In our establishments, I haven't seen pictures of Zionist leaders, only pictures of rabbis," Rivka protested, and Ahron was silent.

"Can you direct us to Morris's room?" he asked one of the secretaries after despairing of finding the room they were looking for.

"End of the hall, right," she replied and studied them curiously.

They continued walking until they reached the required room. Ahron knocked on a fancy wooden door. In the middle of the door, was a big sign that announced "Morris Ben-Dahan; Senior Aliyah Official."

"Come in," they heard a voice on the other side.

They entered quickly, happy to find shelter from the inquisitive eyes of the officials.

The official suspiciously scrutinized the unexpected guests. In all his years of work, he'd never been visited by radical ultra-orthodox Jews, who renounced the Zionist state and had no desire to immigrate to it.

"Hello, are you Mr. Morris?" Ahron asked.

"Yes, I'm Morris. How can I help you?"

"We're here regarding matters of Aliyah. The receptionist sent us to you. She said you're in charge of Aliyah," Ahron continued.

"That's correct. I'm the person you're looking for. Do you want to make Aliyah?" he asked in surprise.

"Not me. She does." Ahron pointed at Rivka.

"Welcome. First of all, fill out the request forms. Then, we'll conduct a personal interview." He took out a bundle of forms and put them on the table next to Rivka.

"I thought you were husband and wife," he said apologetically when Rivka started filling out forms.

"No, God forbid! She's my little sister."

"Did something unusual happen, or is her Aliyah planned?" The appearance of the odd couple in his office was uncommon and instilled some life in the sleepy official.

"She's got this crazy idea in her head that she wants to immigrate to Israel," Ahron lied. The questions addressed to him made him uncomfortable.

"When your sister finishes filling out the forms, we'll interview her, and then we'll know everything," Morris said.

Rivka continued filling out the forms. First, she filled in her personal details, then she answered the questions regarding the reason she was applying for Aliyah. In the end, she was required to mention her destination in Israel. When she was finished, Morris led them to an adjacent room, where an older, maternal-looking secretary sat. She took the forms, went through them for a long time, then lifted her eyes and said in a cordial voice, "Pleased to meet you. I'm Rochelle, the social worker. I'm here to make sure the process occurs without any hitches. I see only your request in the documents, Rivka. What about you?" She turned her piercing stare to Ahron.

"God forbid, I'm not making an Aliyah. I'm her brother. She had some misgivings about coming alone, so I came with her," he explained.

"I understand. Well, according to the accepted process, we tend to meet several times with the applicants. So, you'll have to come here for a week, every morning for four hours. The purpose of the meetings is to prepare you for the encounter with your new country, explain the anticipated acclimation hardships, as well as your rights as a new *olah*—that means a new immigrant— regarding work, studies, and financial aid. Go home now, and come back in two days for the first meeting," she concluded.

"I don't think you understand my situation. There's no way I can return home. I have no place to go back to," Rivka said in fright.

"Why? Have you run away from home?" Morris tried to confirm what he'd already realized.

"Yes, I ran away. Or more accurately, I left," Rivka replied. She was afraid her answer would impede matters.

"Why did you leave?" Rochelle insisted on asking difficult questions.

"It's a long story. Not something I can explain briefly," Rivka replied uncomfortably.

"And do you have a passport?" Morris asked suddenly.

Rivka shook her head and paled. Another obstacle had arisen.

"Okay, never mind. Don't stress yourself. We're accustomed to these situations, and we have a solution," Morris soothed her.

"If she isn't going back with you, you'd better go. But don't worry, we'll take good care of her and do everything that has to be done. We have a building in the city that belongs to the agency. She'll stay there during the following week. During that time, we'll procure a passport for her. Then, we'll put her on the plane, and viola, Israel," Rochelle said to Ahron, and then addressed Rivka, "Do have some place to go to in Israel, Rivka?"

"Yes, I have an aunt in Kibbutz Ayelet HaShachar. I'll stay with her until I find a place to stay."

"Great. Beautiful kibbutz, Ayelet HaShachar," Rochelle said. Then she turned to Ahron and said, "You can say good-bye to your sister."

"Good-bye, Rivkel. Take care of yourself. Don't forget to tell me the time and number of your flight. And when you get to Aunt Rachel, call me right away. I also expect you to write a lot." He wanted to hug his sister tightly, hold her close, but chose to maintain rules of modesty. He was deeply sorry that he couldn't even embrace his own sister. *Without a doubt, the rules we live by are too harsh*, he thought painfully.

"Good-bye, brother. I love you. Thank you for everything you did for me. Send a special thanks to Miriam from me and many kisses to the little ones." By then, Rivka could no longer help herself. She burst into tears.

"Don't cry, Rivkel. You're following your dream. You wanted to leave, right? So, here, you're leaving, and may God help you," Ahron soothed her.

"Before you go, promise me something," she requested amid her tears.

"What?"

"Thank Jeff for the money. I probably won't see him again, and you're the only one who can thank him for me."

"I promise," he said, without thinking too deeply about his answer. Then, he turned around and hastily left the room, before Rivkel could see him shed tears as he left behind his weeping sister.

"Don't cry, child. Everything will be fine," Rochelle said soothingly and rushed to embrace her.

"Well, I think you'll manage without me. I'll go and take care of the necessary arrangements for the Aliyah," said Morris, who felt unneeded.

"That's it. Now, I'm okay. Saying good-bye to my brother was a little hard for me. I'm sorry, I didn't mean to make a fuss," Rivka apologized, drying her tears.

"Rivka, sweetheart, you have nothing to be sorry about. I feel for you and understand what you're going through. I've come across desperate young people whose parents didn't want them to immigrate to Israel, who ran away from home and came here. You'll get to meet your brother, and a lot. Nowadays, distances have shortened. It's just a matter of seven hundred dollars and a ten-hour flight," Rochelle calmed her.

"Call me Rivkel, like everyone else does. I feel strange when you call me Rivka," Rivka noted.

"Rivkel is a little girl's name, not a young woman's. Until now, everyone called you Rivkel because they treated you like a child. Rivka is a lovely name, very mature, and it suits you tremendously. Imagine Yitzhak calling his wife Rivkel," Rochelle said, and to ease the tension, added in a deep voice, "And now, Rivkel, I want to bless Easue and Jacob. Bring them to me." When she finished, she burst into laughter.

"You're right. I never thought of that," Rivka also laughed in relief. "Force of habit. Ever since I can remember myself, I've been called Rivkel. At home, at school, everywhere."

"You must be hungry, Rivka. Am I right? Let's go to the cafeteria and eat something until Yehudit comes."

"Yehudit? Who's Yehudit?"

"The house mother. Remember I told you we have a building close by? Yehudit is in charge. She'll take care of you this week," Rochelle explained as they waited for the elevator.

When they arrived at the cafeteria, Rivka studied the food to find something she could eat. "Do you have a sandwich only with vegetables?" she anxiously questioned the cafeteria worker. Even though she was going to leave her entire life behind her, deeply ingrained habits forced her to fear the food's kashrut. Who knew what kind of kashrut certification they had here, she thought. Certainly not mehadrin, which was the most stringent.

"We don't have only vegetable, my dear," the cafeteria lady said. "We have vegetables and cheese. Very good," she offered her wares proudly. Rivka hesitated several seconds before she weakly said, "Yes." If she had to get used to secular Israeli food, she might as well start here, she decided. When she ate, she tried to distract herself whether the cheese was kosher by thinking of her parents. Did they find the letter? And her mother, how would she handle her leaving? At this very moment, she was probably weeping. And her old father, would he have the strength to cope? She was the apple of his eye, his youngest, born when he was no longer young, his most beloved child.

"What are you thinking of?" Rochelle interrupted her thoughts.

"My mother and father. My mother's name is also Yehudit. When you talked about Yehudit, I remembered my mother. Is Yehudit like a kind of mother?"

"Yehudit is an amazing woman. She isn't as old as you must imagine. Barely thirty. I promise you, she'll get you on your feet. A week with her will help you fix your head. She has experience and wisdom that a lot of people, twice as old as her, don't have."

"And when is she arriving?"

"About an hour," Rochelle answered, glancing at her watch.

An hour later, Yehudit arrived. Rivka was glad to see she was a smiling, vivacious woman. She took Rivka to the agency's building, a large building in the middle of Manhattan, with many empty apartments. Rivka settled into one of them. Since there were few tenants in the building, Yehudit was free to help Rivka as much as possible.

Every day at noon, when Rivka returned from the agency's lessons, Yehudit welcomed her with a warm smile. They'd eat lunch together, and had many heart-to-hearts.

"I don't want to be ultra-orthodox anymore. I'm sick and tired of that way of life. I want to broaden my horizons, and study in the university. I want to wear sandals and shorts and go to the beach like other girls. It doesn't mean I'll stop believing in God; I just think there's no contradiction between the two. God created the world for us to enjoy, didn't he?" Rivka concluded.

"I agree with you one hundred percent! I'll tell you something that might astonish you. I left Bnei-Brak for the exact same reason that you're now leaving New York," Yehudit surprised her.

"What, you used to be ultra-orthodox like me?" Rivka asked, amazed.

"Yes, just like you."

"And what happened?"

"I fell in love."

"With whom?"

"With a secular man, an employee of the Foreign Ministry. After he proposed to me, I left home. My family went ballistic and cut off all contact with me. Someone told me that some of them even mourned me and sat *shiva*. Two years ago, Ron, my husband, got a job here, at the consulate, and I came here to work at the agency," she smiled.

"And children? Do you have any children?"

"Of course. Two girls and a boy."

"And now you have no contact with your family?" Rivka asked apprehensively.

"Only with my youngest brother, who calls and writes in secret."

Thus, the two of them would sit, thirstily drinking in each other's words. But they did most of their activity in the early afternoon hours. After a short rest at noon, they'd go out to a shopping center. Yehudit was happy to help Rivka achieve her dream to get rid of her conservative clothes and dress like a secular girl. "These pants look great on you, Rivka. In a week, if you continue eating like you're eating now, they'll sit on you perfectly," Yehudit said with satisfaction when she studied Rivka wearing the latest jeans in style.

Rivka hurried to study herself in the mirror and couldn't take her eyes off herself, as though she were hypnotized. She felt the jeans cling to her legs and thighs, as though part of her body. An indescribable feeling of pleasure surrounded her. She felt that in a minute, she'd reach the seventh heaven. No more dresses that fell from her waist and dragged on the floor, no more thick, long stockings that covered her feet and legs, even in the summer, but tight shirts and pants that would make the most of her curves.

"Now, let's match a jacket to the shirt and pants, so you'll be able to wear it for the flight tomorrow."

"This jacket is gorgeous. Try it on," the saleslady said and handed Rivka a green jacket.

"Wow!" an exclamation of admiration came out of the mouths of the two women. Rivka rushed back to the mirror to study herself, bursting with happiness.

"Can I leave these clothes on?" she asked the saleslady shyly.

"You know what? I have a suggestion. Leave these clothes on and we'll buy another pair of jeans and a shirt," Yehudit said without waiting for the saleslady's answer.

"No, no we shouldn't. I've already wasted too much money today," Rivka hesitated.

"If not another pair of jeans, at least buy a nice bathing suit. It's very hot in Israel now. The pools and sea are full of bathers. Here, try this on," Yehudit said, holding a colorful bathing suit.

"Not a bathing suit. Please! I'm shy," Rivka replied, and suddenly surprised everyone present when she burst into uncontrollable laughter.

"Why are you laughing?" Yehudit asked, miffed.

"Sorry! I'm really sorry. About a year ago, I came into the city with a friend of mine, and she went into the dressing room to try on a dress in one of the stores. I remembered how she looked with a plunging neckline, her entire chest hanging out, and it made me laugh. The bathing suit you're holding reminded me of that," she explained while taking the bathing suit from Yehudit.

"If you're shy, try it on in the dressing room and stay inside," the saleslady suggested.

"You're a real beauty. Your legs might be thin and pale, but you have a beautiful body," Yehudit said in surprise when she peeked into the dressing room and looked at Rivka wearing the bathing suit.

"How did you want my body to be tan? It's constantly covered with clothes. It hasn't seen a ray of the sun even once in my life," Rivka smiled.

"Never mind. Israel is so sunny. A few days at the pool or on the beach, and you'll be as brown as all the other girls."

At the end of the evening, after they bought a bag, shoes, underwear, makeup, and a bottle of perfume that Rivka thought was stunning, they returned to the agency building, and Rivka rushed to her room. The next day, she had to get up early and arrive at the airport at dawn. She was better off resting before the long flight. She was sure she'd be too excited to sleep, but no more than several minutes passed and she fell asleep easily, with a smile on her lips.

In the morning, she got up early and showered. Yehudit came by and combed her golden curls, fixing them into a modern hairdo. Then, she wore her new clothes, and finally, she put on makeup and sprayed some perfume on herself. When she looked at herself, she couldn't believe her eyes. She'd gathered some of her hair with a pink rubber band, leaving the rest of her shoulder-length curls loose, which gave her a new and glamorous look. The eyeshadow she'd applied made her eyes stand out, while the foundation and blusher concealed her paleness. She put on fire-engine-red lipstick that made her lips look soft and sensual. Her elegant clothes made her look more mature, no longer a girl, but a woman. Now, even she, who disregarded herself most of the time, held her breath at her reflection. The tremendous change caused her both joy and fear.

"You're so beautiful! You're absolutely stunning, Rivka. Watch out that they don't kidnap you in Israel," Yehudit laughed as she looked at Rivka with pleasure. Rivka lowered her head self-consciously, as though she'd done something wrong. Pride and coquetry were frowned upon among Hasidic girls.

"Are you nervous?" Yehudit asked.

"Very! You know, a new country, a new language…I do know a few words in Hebrew, words from prayers and what I learned here…but I believe in myself and in my strength," she replied with a forced smile.

"Don't worry. Two months in an Ulpan will settle the language issue," Rochelle, who'd come to say good-bye, assured her.

"Thank you for everything you've done for me. I hope we'll meet again," Rivka said, and lightly kissed the two women's cheeks so she wouldn't smear their faces with her new lipstick.

"Good luck," they wished her.

Rivka took her bag and a little suitcase in her thin hand and hurried to the taxi waiting for her at the building's entrance. She sat in the back, and when the taxi pulled away, she closed her eyes and devotedly said the Traveler's Prayer, a prayer for a safe journey. Before she boarded the plane, she called Ahron and said good-bye.

"*Nu*, did everything work out?" Miriam asked in concern when Aaron returned home in the evening.

"I think so. I hope Rivkel is all right now. The Jewish Agency has an organized mechanism that will take care of her and accompany her until she settles in Israel. Concerning that, I'm calm. I respect those people. Many of us disdain Israel and the people who act for the country's benefit. I think it's a wrong approach. These people do important work."

"And your parents, how did they react?"

"I told my father this was better than Rivkel marrying someone she didn't want. At first, he was confused; he almost fainted. He called my mother, and from their conversation, I understood that what bothered them most was canceling the wedding. The fact that Rivkel left for Israel and was with Aunt Rachel eased their minds slightly. I think that deep down, they expected it and were relieved. Anyway, they hadn't come to terms with that wedding, which had been forced upon them. The main problem was with Yehuda. That man is a fanatic. We have to keep an eye on him. He's lawless."

"What did he do?"

"Screamed like a maniac, cursed her and me, and if he could, he would have gone after her and forced her back home. With me, of course, he didn't want to talk. He thinks I'm to blame for all the troubles of the family."

"Let him think whatever he wants; it's his problem. Although I think that he's so hot-headed that it's difficult for him to think logically. Also, he's connected to the most fanatical rabbis, who never stop inciting him and driving him crazy," Miriam dismissed Yehuda's opinion.

"Sometimes, I feel like he hates me."

"You mustn't think that way, even though, sometimes, I think he's jealous of you…jealous because your father chose you to work with him at the store. Don't be upset," she added, approaching her husband and caressing him softly.

"What do you say, my wife, did I do the right thing? From the day I was born, I was raised to believe in one way and one way only, and now I've helped my sister abandon that way. I feel confused by this entire situation," Aaron said and entwined his fingers with those of the wife of his youth.

"A person chooses their own path and will be the one accountable before the Creator. We just helped her to follow the path she has chosen," Miriam stated surprisingly, and after an awkward pause added sadly, "I must tell you, my love, that I yearn for my hair that was taken from me after the wedding, and sometimes I ask myself if a headscarf isn't enough. Is the headscarf not modest enough? If I were brave enough, I would grow my hair and cover it in the way of other modest women."

"So, you're saying I did the right thing?" Aaron persisted, surprised by her words and wishing to steer the conversation to where it began. He wondered whether a new wind was blowing, even with his own wife.

"You were fine. All your brothers, either they're too extreme or they are too soft and unable to act. Without you, Rivkel would be marrying someone she didn't want to marry and would ruin her life. And then, there would've been no going back. We would have been extremely remorseful. Don't torture yourself, my love, you did well! You saved her! You'll see, she'll be happy in her new life. The day will come, God willing, and you'll be the guest of honor at her wedding. I'm sure of it. And when that day arrives, I'll remind you of this."

"I hope you're right, my wife. I want you to know that I trust you more than I trust myself."

"I'm your helpmate, isn't it like that?" Miriam said, and added with a wink, "By the way, an hour ago I returned from the *mikveh*…"

"And the girls?" Aaron asked.

"Sleeping soundly," she replied with a mischievous smile.

"Well then, in that case, I'll go take a shower," he said with a wink.

Chapter 15

"*All my loving,* ..." Jeff's ringtone blared from his shirt pocket. Usually, it was Eve, occasionally it was his mother, and in the not-so-distant past, it was Ahron.

However, since the incident, they'd lost touch. Jeff took out the phone and glanced at the screen. To his surprise, it was Ahron.

"Yes?" Jeff answered as though he didn't know who was calling him.

"Jeff, hello! It's me, Ahron," Ahron said, his voice calm. Then he was silent, as though waiting to see where the conversation would go.

"I saw your name on the screen. How are you, buddy?" Jeff asked as though they talked on the phone every day.

"I'm fine. And you?"

"I'm fine, too," Jeff said and fell silent.

"You must be asking yourself why I'm calling..."

"Yeah, I'm surprised. But to tell you the truth, I was hoping you'd call eventually."

"I called to say thank you," Ahron said.

"Thank you? For what?" Jeff said oh so innocently.

"First of all, I promised Rivkel I'd send you her thanks for the money you sent her. Second, thanks from me, for that letter you sent me. It influenced me greatly."

"I'm glad to hear that."

"I also wanted you to know that…"

"What?"

"That Rivkel is in Israel. Your help wasn't for nothing. Your money, plus another small sum that I'd added, funded her trip to Israel," Ahron notified him.

"How?" Jeff asked, hiding his excitement with difficulty.

"I did exactly what you asked me to. A month after I received your letter, I went to my parents' house and took Rivkel out of there. I gave her the money you sent her and took her to the Jewish Agency. Are you familiar with it?"

"Not really."

"It's an organization that helps Jews immigrate to Israel. They have branches in the USA, and one is in New York. I brought her there, and they took care of her. A week later, she called me from Aunt Rachel's house. Remember, I told you about Rachel?"

"Of course, I remember. One of the three sisters I saw in the picture. Your Grandma Gittel and Hannah's sister, I think."

"Right. Good for you! Good of you to remember!" Ahron praised him.

"Listen, Ahron, this call has really made my day. I feel we have so much to talk about, and I'd love for us to meet." Jeff suddenly felt as free as he had before, before the incident.

"I don't know if that's a good idea. You understand, right? After what you and Rivkel went through, …" Ahron hesitated.

"Me? What do you mean?"

"You know, you meeting with Rivkel, my brother's violence, the way he ran you out of the basement apartment. I felt bad about that."

"Enough of that, Ahron. I've already forgotten. And really, nothing happened between Rivkel and me. We just talked, like we talked many times in your house."

"I know, but I'd already told you that we measure things differently," Ahron said.

"No one knows that better than me after what I experienced on my flesh. Honestly, I didn't know your brother was the one who beat me up. I thought it was a gang of punks, you know, those guys you call the chastity squad."

"They really were the chastity squad, but my brother, Yehuda, was their leader. He's such a hothead. First, he acts, then he thinks. Truthfully, when I'd heard she'd come to visit you, I was mad at you both, but especially at you," Ahron said.

"*Me?*"

"Anger was my initial reaction because I thought you'd initiated the meeting. Then I spoke with Rivkel, and I realized it wasn't your fault," Ahron softened his words.

"Leave it, it really isn't important now. Forget about it…we're all human beings, and we all make mistakes sometimes. Let's meet. I have so much to tell you."

"We'll see. Maybe sometime in the future…"Ahron declined politely.

"Listen, buddy, I'd really love to come over. I really miss Miriam and the girls. But unfortunately, I understand that it isn't possible. But you can come over here. To 3rd Avenue. Between 46th and 47th streets. There's this department store, Eve's. Do you know it?"

"No."

"I work there. Come and visit me whenever you want, and I hope it'll happen soon." He hoped his new vocation would tempt Ahron to come.

"We'll see. I don't want to promise," Ahron said disappointingly. "Anyway, I'll call you."

Jeff laid his phone on the desk, and thought about what he'd just heard. Rivka was in Israel! Good news! The girl, whose fate seemed entwined with his, realized her dreams, broke free from her parents' chains, and immigrated to the land of the Jews. It had worked. His correspondence with Ahron had succeeded. When he passed him the letter via Rico, he was convinced he'd receive an answer but wasn't sure the money would be used for the purpose he'd sent it for. He'd feared Ahron would find a way to return the money. He knew that his integrity and honor wouldn't allow him to hold on to someone else's money, not even for a brief period. When he didn't receive an answer, he assumed the money had reached its destination. But lately, his confidence had been shaken, and he wished to know what had happened to Rivka. He had already seriously considering sending Rico on another surveillance mission. When Ahron called, he felt as though a heavy burden had been lifted from his heart.

Now, he was wondering about the tiny country Rivka had traveled to. First, he googled "map of Israel" and clicked on one of the sites Google had found for him. To his surprise, Israel was a tiny dot on the globe. After an hour of visiting endless sites, he learned a bit about the little country and its difficulties. *One day, I'll visit there*, he decided. *Maybe I'll even suggest to Eve a holiday in the birth country of Jesus Christ.*

He felt that all that he had to do now was meet his friend and settle matters between them. It was important to him to maintain the warm relationship with the kind man who had helped him out when things were rough for him, when he'd just arrived in the city. He was convinced they would come full circle and that his friend would arrive some day for a visit. But his heart told him it wouldn't happen soon.

Spring, summer, and autumn passed and winter stood at the city's gates. A cold wind started blowing, dragging yellowing leaves of autumn that fell, one by one, from the trees. Rays of sun disappeared, and the top floors of the skyscrapers were covered with heavy clouds that brought about a gloomy atmosphere. The many tourists swarming the streets in the summer evenings had disappeared, as though the wind had carried them off to a secret place. The city lights, which glowed at night, illuminating the skyline with a vast light, suddenly looked dim and weak. Wintry New York wrapped up warmly, preparing itself for a long, hard winter.

At "Eve's," things continued as usual. Masses of consumers continued visiting the store, and the sales increased and with them, the partners' profits. The lively store became a kind of home for Jeff, where he spent most of his day. He didn't hide the pleasure he derived from the successful business. He dedicated most of his energy to it. To Eve's displeasure, his loyalty upset their evenings together. In order to lawfully employ workers without burdening them too much, work was divided into two shifts. At the end of the shift, all the employees were replaced. Jeff worked both shifts, and if that wasn't enough, at the end of the day, he stayed to count the till and lock up the store. Eve, on the other hand, if there weren't any unusual events, arrived home hours before he did, right after the stock market closed. During those hours, she'd expectantly wait for his return. To her disappointment, Jeff would come home exhausted, take a quick shower, and go to bed. On the one hand, she was pleased by his hard work and loyalty to the business, which proved to her that she was right when she gambled with her money on her successful man. On the other hand, he, like her father, like all the other men she knew, had become a workaholic. She laughed when she recalled that not so long ago, she was exactly the same way. There was no doubt that her man had changed her completely.

"I think you're overdoing it," she told him more than once. "Nothing will happen if you let Rico take charge once in a while or bring in a store manager who'll manage the store in your place during one of the shifts."

"The main reason for the business's success is because I'm there all the time. A business managed by remote control is destined for failure. That's what you want, for the business to fail?" he insisted stubbornly.

"You know very well that I don't. The investment and profits are mine, too. But I love you, and I want us to be together. I feel like we're wasting away our most beautiful years on work," she said sadly and seemed to grow smaller as she sat on the sofa.

"I love you, too, beautiful. But you have to understand that the company is a new one, and we have no choice but to dedicate most of our attention to it. As far as I'm concerned, work with me in the store. That way, we'll be together all day long," he said, stroking her hair.

"You know what? I'm game. Really. I'm willing to give up everything so we'll be together," she replied, and for one fleeting moment, she felt she really meant it. She even imagined them making love clandestinely in his office, addicted to each other while listening to the tumult of the crowd.

"Are you out of your mind? I was just kidding. Working together can ruin a couples' relationship. I've heard stories of fights and divorces that started as work disputes." Jeff regretted his words and hoped Eve would forget about her weird decision. The great Eve Klein leaving Wall Street in order to work at a department store. Really!

"You may have forgotten, but we aren't married, so there's no fear we'll get divorced," she scoffed, pleased by his reaction. Finally, the conversation was focusing on a subject that had been bothering her so much lately.

"Eve, be serious. Your entire life, you've worked hard to get to where you are. Don't turn your back on that success. Take advantage of these years to make money. Soon, you'll have kids. Taking care of children is a job in itself. Then, you'll be able to retire from your job," he tried a different tack.

"Before you have kids, you have to get married. That's the correct order, right?" she pressed the issue, happy that the conversation was going in the desired direction.

"Of course, I wasn't thinking differently," he replied uncomfortably.

"And when will that happen?" she asked, resting her head on his stomach, staring at the ceiling, her entire being attentive to what he would say next.

"Whenever you want," he answered, bemused, and hurried to hug and kiss her on her lips.

"Wait, I don't understand. Are you proposing to me?" she asked in surprise and tore herself away from him.

"Sounds like it, doesn't it?"

"Ah," she murmured. This wasn't how she'd hoped he'd propose.

"This isn't good. This wasn't how I planned to propose to you. Let's start over, and do it right this time," he said, as though he'd read her thoughts.

"You're right. I'm waiting." She sat up, stretched, and stared at him curiously.

Jeff sat up, looked straight at her, and began in a serious voice. "Eve, the most beautiful, smartest woman in the world. I, Jeff, confess to you that I love you deeply and profoundly, and I'm asking you to be my partner until the end of our days. Will you agree?"

"Yes, my love," she said amid tears of joy. His proposal had made her very happy because it had been bothering her for quite a while. More than a year had passed since Jeff had moved into her house, their love had flourished, and they got along great. Yet, he never said a word on the matter. Why hadn't he raised the topic of a wedding or even hinted slightly about it? Was it because of the thriving business that had most of his attention and that had caused him to forget how love should eventually be realized? Or perhaps it was something else?

After that evening, Jeff decided to put more of an effort into his love for her. He felt compassion for his sad beloved, who would soon be his wife.

Occasionally, he'd emerge from among piles of inventory and customers and surprise her. On her birthday, he came home early and cooked dinner himself. They had a candlelight dinner, accompanied by a bottle of champagne. He even went as far as to write her a love poem to which he added a gift, an expensive watch that had her name carved on it. The poem had thrilled her so that she read it three times out loud. Then, she stuck it to the refrigerator door.

"Every time I open the door, I'll read first what you wrote to me," she said excitedly, and Jeff was happy that his love was as thrilled as a little girl from his gesture.

"You'll do it once or twice, tops," he chuckled. "But I'm not seeing you standing a year from now before the fridge, reading that poem, and only then taking out a beer or ice cream. But don't worry, darlin', next year, I'll write you a new love poem."

"To tell you the truth, you surprised me. I didn't know you knew how to write so beautifully," she praised him at the end of the evening.

"When you love someone, things become easier and simpler," he smiled, pleased from the success of his poem.

But love tends to become routine, and despite the many gestures of love he lavished on her, with time, the subject of the wedding slipped his mind.

However, it didn't slip Eve's mind. After Jeff's proposal, she told her parents about the upcoming nuptials. Her parents received the news joyfully, even though they'd only met their future son-in-law a handful of times. But they became fond of the handsome southern man, who was rugged yet honest. Jeff, in contrast to her, decided to postpone the conversation with his mother to a future date.

"What do you think about a spring wedding?" Eve suggested several days later. "The flowers blooming always make me feel good. April or May seems fitting. I've always dreamed of getting married in April."

And Jeff agreed. Despite his apprehensions regarding the upcoming wedding, he loved her very much and enjoyed doing various things for her. He even did as she asked and appointed a foreman to take his place on the evening shift. And how unsurprising that this time, like the last, he also knew exactly who he wanted for the job.

The next day, he called Ahron, who immediately apologized for not visiting the shop.

"Never mind. Now, you have an opportunity to visit. I have an offer that might interest you."

"What is it?"

"I prefer you come here, and then I'll tell you. Since it's about my place of work, it's better that you'll come here and see with your own eyes."

A week later, Ahron arrived at the shop. The meeting was emotional. To someone viewing from the side, the connection between the two might seem puzzling and odd. Yet, that's not how the two friends felt.

"Come into my office," Jeff invited Ahron respectfully.

"Wow! This is your office?" Ahron said with admiration and made himself comfortable in a cushiony armchair facing Jeff, who sat in a manager's armchair.

"Yes, this is my office."

"Well then, the beating my brother gave you was worthwhile." Ahron burst into laughter.

"Someone already said that there's good in every bad." Jeff joined his friend's laughter.

"True. We say, 'out of the strong, something sweet.' Now, tell me what this is about," Ahron said, after he'd calmed down from his incessant laughter.

"Okay." Jeff took a deep breath. "The thing is, after I left the basement apartment, I moved in with Eve."

"Eve?" Ahron cut him off.

"Eve is my girlfriend and my future wife. The last time I'd visited you, we had just met, so I didn't have time to tell you about her."

"Mazel tov!" Ahron instantly remembered the woman Rivka had told him about.

"Thanks," Jeff grinned.

"*Nu*, go on," Ahron prompted him, in suspense.

"Eve is a successful broker in the stock market. She earns an excellent salary. She has a big apartment in the heart if the city. After what happened with your brother, I had no choice but to move in with her. After several months of unemployment, I felt as though I was losing my mind. I couldn't stand the fact that I was financially dependent on her. You know, I've been working since I was a boy. Eve saw my distress and suggested we found a business as partners. This is how this amazing department store was created."

"Business? You're talking as though you opened a grocery store or vegetable stand. This is a huge business that requires enormous investment!" Ahron was impressed, curious to learn more.

"Eve brought most of the money, and the rest, we received credit from the bank. The inventory is funded by suppliers," he explained, happy to show his friend that he, Jeff, understood money management.

"Bravo to her for taking that significant risk. If she did that for you, she must love you very much."

"Yes, she does love me very much, that is…" Jeff replied thoughtfully. "Now, to the case in question. Several days ago, she complained I was working too hard. She claimed, rightfully, that we barely had time to spend together. She suggested I appoint a store manager so I'll have a bit more free time."

"She's right. That's why Papa and I employ people, so we'll have enough time for family and Torah lessons," Ahron agreed.

"And I think you're just the man for the job. You have a developed marketing sense, and you have experience running a business. I have no doubt you'll succeed." Jeff followed his friend's reaction tensely.

Ahron looked at him in surprise. His fingers drummed on the desk restlessly, and it was obvious that his brain was working feverishly in order to find the right answer.

"I'm really surprised. I wasn't expecting this kind of offer. … You know, this is a place where women walk around dressed inappropriately. I don't know. I'll have to think it over, maybe even consult with my rabbi," Ahron replied, and deep inside, he already knew he couldn't accept the offer, as tempting as it was.

"If you're going to consult with the rabbi, chances you'll take the job are nonexistent. That's a polite way of telling me no," Jeff replied understandingly. Once again, he had read his friend's life incorrectly. Ahron was shackled by the chains of tradition. How could he forget how different Ahron was from him?

"You're right," Ahron apologized. "Chances are small, mostly because of my parents. After what they went through with Rivka, I can't give them another blow. But I want you to know that I appreciate your offer. There's nothing to do, we can't always get what we want."

"That's a pity," Jeff said. He understood that both of them had missed an opportunity here for professional success, which would greatly help their business and friendship. Jeff thought of Rivka and hoped that at least she'd found her freedom.

Chapter 16

"Ten minutes to landing," the captain notified the passengers, and the huge Jumbo Jet began its descent. The lower it flew, the greater the pressure in Rivka's ears. The odd symptom frightened her, and she covered her ears with her hands in an attempt to stop it, but without much success.

"Here, honey, chew. It'll help you get over the pain." The old lady who sat next to her saw her distress and handed her some chewing gum, while addressing her in Hebrew.

"Thanks," Rivka answered in English. Even though she didn't understand a word, she took the chewing gum and hurriedly shoved it in her mouth. While she chewed, she felt the pressure in her ears lessen gradually. She heaved a sigh of relief.

Feeling better, she leaned her head on the window and curiously studied the approaching ground. Between the sparse clouds, she could clearly see the sea and the people frolicking on its shores. Several minutes later, the sea disappeared, and only the ground remained. She was surprised to see a very small number of skyscrapers. Most of the buildings, unlike those in New York, were small. From above, they looked even smaller. From her seat on the plane, she could see and hear the wheels of the plane unfold. The plane listed sharply to the left and then leveled itself for landing. The passengers burst into raucous applause when the plane landed, and its wheels rolled deafeningly on the tarmac. The plane continued forward and gradually slowed down, until it stopped. Several minutes later, the doors opened, and Rivka, like the rest of the passengers, rushed outside. The exhausting, almost twelve-hour flight had come to an end. For Rivka, who had never been on a plane before, it hadn't been easy. She had a difficult time falling asleep, and unlike the rest of the passengers, was awake the entire flight. During those long hours, she berated herself for forgetting her only book at the agency building. She tried to concentrate on the movie projected on the little screen before her seat, but she was too tense and excited and, in the end, she gave up on that activity. At the beginning of the trip, she'd managed to keep herself busy. She read the Traveler's Prayer again and even added a few chapters from Psalms. *New clothes and makeup can't change my inner world. I still believe in God,* she coached herself. When the flight ended, she immediately prayed, "*Our praise to You, Eternal our God, Sovereign of all: for giving us life, sustaining us, and enabling us to reach this season.*"

After she had gone through passport control, she collected her suitcase, put it on a trolley, and ran to the Arrival's Hall, where she searched with frightened eyes for her aunt. When she didn't see her, a terrible fear snuck into her heart that her aunt might've forgotten her. For a second, she regretted declining Morris's offer, that someone from the agency would wait for her at the airport and help her make her way to the kibbutz.

"That's unnecessary," she replied decisively. "My brother Ahron sent my aunt my flight number and the time of landing. He said that it's better she wait for me in the airport, and not someone I don't know."

Now, she continued worriedly scanning the people waiting for the arrival of their dear ones. Then she saw her. An old woman standing at the side, waving to her frantically with her thin hands until their eyes met. Rivka abandoned her trolley and luggage, ran to her aunt, and fell into her arms. The old lady and young girl embraced and kissed each other for several long minutes, and it was only after Rivka pulled back from her aunt's arms, that she noticed she wasn't alone. One step behind her, following them with bemusement, stood a tall, beautiful young man.

"Rivkel, my sweet, I'm so happy to see you," her aunt said in Yiddish. When she noticed Rivka glance at the young man at her side, she added proudly, "Rivkel, meet Amir, my lovely grandson, Abigail, my youngest daughter's son. He accompanies me whenever I need him to."

"Nice to meet you. Grandma told me so much about you," the young man said in English, ducking his head bashfully.

"Good things, I hope," Rivka said quietly, but her heart was pounding. *As beautiful as Jeff,* she thought.

"Amir, sweetheart, go get her suitcase," her aunt instructed and Amir complied immediately.

They walked slowly to the car park: Amir leading the way with the trolley, Rivka and her aunt following. The entire time, Rachel couldn't stop scrutinizing Rivka, wondering about her clothes.

"Where did the long dresses and thick pantyhose go?" she finally asked, when they settled in the back seat of the car.

"Why, aren't I dressed nicely?" Rivka was almost offended.

"You're dressed beautifully, my lovely. I just didn't expect to see you wearing these clothes as well as makeup. When I saw you come out, it took me a while to recognize you. I did recognize your face immediately, but the clothes and makeup confused me."

"Didn't Ahron explain to you why I'm here?"

"No. He just said you're doing Aliyah, and you'll come to the kibbutz for a while. He said that, in the beginning, you should spend time with people you know so things will be easier for you, and it sounded logical to me. At a certain stage, I thought it odd that you were coming to a kibbutz, but then I realized something must've happened. To tell you the truth, I didn't think too much about it." Her aunt insisted on speaking Yiddish, even though she was fluent in English as well.

"I'm fed up with the life I lived there, Aunt Rachel. I couldn't stay there anymore, so I came here," Rivka answered in English.

"For always?"

"Yes. I want to say in Israel forever."

"That's wonderful, *maideleh*. You take me back fifty years, to the day I first wore pants. *Oy*, it was so exciting and hard. I'll never forget that day," her aunt reminisced. Then, she leaned toward Rivka with tear-filled eyes and kissed her again.

"Grandma! Stop with the Yiddish. It's a ghetto language. I know Rivka doesn't understand Hebrew, but what's wrong with English?" Amir intervened.

"It's okay. I understand Yiddish, and I also know how to speak it," Rivka assured him.

"That's not it. Every time Grandma meets someone from the family, she won't stop speaking in Yiddish, even though she's fluent in English and Hebrew. It's as though she insists on going back to her childhood." Amir glanced at Rivka through the rear-view mirror.

"What's so bad about that?" Aunt Rachel asked.

"This is Israel, not Poland, Grandma. If you want to go back to your childhood, travel to Poland for a visit. I'm willing to accompany both you and Rivka if you want. As a matter of fact, why not? Let's go, the three of us," Amir said, pleased with the idea. "Traveling to find your roots is all the rage now in Israel," he explained to Rivka.

"No, dear. I can't. Even though many years have passed, I can't. Just the thought of that cursed place—where my parents' and brothers' and sister Hannah's ashes are scattered—kills me. No, no. Yiddish is sufficient for me." This time, she spoke in English, and when she finished, she began to sob. Rivka hurried to stroke her hair.

"Look, girls, look how beautiful it is outside," Amir tried to distract them, and they obliged.

For the first time since she came to Israel, Rivka noticed the sun washing the green fields on both sides of the road. The open fields and birds gliding above instilled a sense of freedom in her. She felt like one of those birds. She could also fly anywhere she wanted. For the rest of the drive, and until they reached the kibbutz, she couldn't tear her eyes away from the magical vista. Only when they arrived at the kibbutz, did she look again at Amir. When she did, her thoughts wandered to Jeff. She felt a sudden and powerful yearning for the man who'd influenced her life more than anyone. She wanted him to see her now, with her new clothes, at her best, determined and full of confidence. Perhaps, if he saw her like this, he'd treat her differently, and who knows, maybe he'd prefer her over that woman. Just then, she felt as though she'd made the right choice and that the future held more, even better, surprises.

"Home sweet home," Aunt Rachel declared when Amir pulled over next to a small house surrounded by a large yard. Rivka surveyed her home for the near future with wide eyes. She liked everything she saw: the grass glistening under the sun, the dogs napping in the shade, the cats wandering to and fro, the caretakers pushing children in their carriages, and more than anything, the freedom of love. Next to a large, impressive building, which she later learned was the dining room, she saw a girl and guy kissing openly. For a moment, she felt as though all her dreams had come true.

Within a short while, she became a real kibbutznik, as though born one. Wearing shorts and sandals, she worked on the dairy farm, milking the cows. She watched in fascination as the thick white liquid poured into a large tank. She worked at the dairy for two months. With Tzvika and Noa, who were more or less her age, they milked by hand the cows that couldn't be milked by machines and had to be milked manually. Her first week on the kibbutz, right after she arrived, she was recruited to work in the kitchen. She set tables, waitressed, but mostly washed dishes. She worked morning, noon, and evening, three shifts a day, with just short breaks in between. Very quickly, the delicate, spoiled girl, who'd never worked a day in her life—not even to do the household chores—felt as though she was on the verge of exhaustion.

"It's really hard for me in the kitchen," she complained to her aunt at the end of the first week.

"You have no choice, sweetheart. That's just how it is over here. All the new arrivals work in the kitchen or the dairy, and they work around the clock. Do you prefer the diary? It's hard work there, as well. But if you want, I'll ask that you be transferred to the dairy. I still have a say in this place," Aunt Rachel suggested with joking self-importance.

"Yes, I prefer the dairy. At least there, I'll work with cute cows."

It wasn't less hard at the dairy. Milking demanded that she kneel for long periods of time. Her thin body, which wasn't used to any kind of work, ached. But since milking the cows started very early in the morning and ended at noon, she managed to grab a few hours of rest before she traveled to the Ulpan in Zephath, where she learned Hebrew.

On the days she didn't study, she kept her old aunt company. Sometimes, she spent time with Amir. They drove up to nearby Zephath to see a movie or frequent a café or a restaurant. He taught her how to "wipe" hummus, eat falafel, and even though she wasn't especially enthusiastic, she ate those unfamiliar foods so he wouldn't consider her an old-fashioned religious girl, confined to her habits. To her surprise, she became involved in kibbutz life faster than she thought possible. She became friendly with many kibbutzniks, and they grew fond of her. She even learned how to folk dance. Life with secular people enchanted her. Nevertheless, she didn't completely abandon the religious laws. She always prayed before eating or drinking, washed her hands as prescribed by Jewish religious laws, blessed the candles on Shabbat night, and occasionally read Psalms. When she lit the candles, tears filled her eyes. She no longer ate *kosher lemehadrin* and, worse than that, she desecrated the Shabbat. Rivka would never forget the first time she traveled on that holy day. Her distress was seared in her memory. During the first Shabbats in Israel, she bravely withstood Amir's cajoling. "I feel it's not time yet," she politely declined his entreaty to take a short drive in the area.

"You don't understand the views you're missing," he said and added a whistle of admiration. To his grandmother, he complained, "You get that, Grandma? She works at the dairy on Shabbat, peeks at the television on the Shabbat, eats at a restaurant with dubious kosher certificates, but the lady won't travel on the Shabbat."

"Leave her be. I totally understand her. It took me a while until I traveled for the first time. Traveling has a different significance. You always fear that because you're desecrating the Shabbat, an accident will happen," Rachel defended Rivka.

And then, on Saturday morning in the spring, she finally agreed to travel to the Golan Heights. The entire drive up the winding road, she cringed in her seat, gripping the handle over the window, as though the little plastic handle had the power to save her from impending disaster. She was positive that, eventually, the car would slip over the edge of the road into the gaping abyss, to the kingdom of darkness and the underworld, and Amir and herself would come to a horrifying end.

"Why are you so nervous?" Amir inquired with a smile.

"You know very well why…Shabbat," she could barely reply.

When Amir stopped the car, she ran out of it as though she were a lion in a cage. She started breathing quickly, as though suffering from hyperventilation, her heart pounded, sweat ran down her body, and she felt as though she was going to die. Amir noticed her distress and rushed to her, hugged her with a strong arm, and they sat on a bench, from which they had a view of the Sea of the Galilee.

"Have some water. It'll help you calm down." He handed her a bottle of mineral water, and she gulped from it eagerly, as though she'd just finished a trek in the desert beneath the scorching sun. When she finally looked forward, she encountered magical views that she'd never come across before, which helped her regain her equilibrium. Her curls flew in the wind, stroking her neck, and it reminded her how she'd managed to escape the terrible slaughtering knife that threatened to destroy her hair and leave her bald. When she thought of those awful days, she hurried to crush the golden strands between her fingers, brought them to her nose, and inhaled their perfumed scent. The fragrance permeated her nostrils and filled her lungs. A supreme feeling of freedom encompassed her and caused her indescribable pleasure.

Between one Saturday and another, which she devoted to exploring her new country, she found herself missing her parents and especially Ahron and his daughters. She managed to subdue those feelings through weekly phone calls to her mother and Ahron. The first time she called her mother, she expected her mother to yell at her, but to her surprise, her mother wasn't angry at her at all.

"How are you, daughter? Are you eating properly?" her mother asked in concern.

"I feel great, Mother! I've never felt so good. I live with Aunt Rachel on the kibbutz, eat all the time, and I'm enjoying every minute. The only thing that saddens me is that I'm far from you."

"That's wonderful, daughter. I'm so glad to hear that. But I hope you haven't entirely abandoned the way of the Torah and the commandments..." she continued in concern.

"No, Mother. Don't worry. How can I turn my back on everything you taught me?" she replied without specifying. Then she inquired after their health.

"Papa and I are fine. At first, it was difficult, especially when people wouldn't stop slandering and gossiping about you and us. Some even boycotted the mini-market and sales decreased, but don't worry, Papa had savings that helped us through that difficult time. Canceling the wedding was very difficult. The Ziedenbaums were furious, and Papa had to reimburse them for the expenses they claimed to have. Yehuda and Margalit wanted to sit *shiva* for you, but Papa explicitly forbid it. Just so you know, Ahron did a wonderful job regarding the matter and calmed them and us. Now, when I hear you, I'm very relieved."

When Rivka heard all that, she also was relieved. Now, with her soul at peace, she could focus on her Hebrew studies. Because of her burning desire to learn, the words she remembered from the prayers and Psalm chapters and conversing with Amir, who insisted on talking to her in Hebrew, after a year, she spoke Hebrew fluently.

Amir was very supportive during those days. He frequently drove her to the Ulpan, spent his free time with her and, several times, got up early and helped her milk the cows. They were both well aware of the fact that their family ties prevented anything romantic from happening between them, but their friendship grew stronger. Sometimes, she wanted to tell him how beautiful she thought he was and how his beauty reminded her of Jeff, but she feared Amir would interpret it as though she were trying to hint she was interested in more than pure friendship. Once, she let her thoughts wander and asked herself if there was anything wrong in a marriage with the grandson of her grandmother's sister. Yet, even though she knew there was nothing wrong about it, she never felt a true desire to change the status of her relationship with Amir.

"What brings a girl like you to make such a drastic change in life? Obviously, something must have happened to you if you made such an extreme decision…" Amir said curiously during one of the times he offered to drive her to the Ulpan.

"My life started to go wrong when I fell in love for the first time. I'm not really sure, but I think it was love. Otherwise, it's hard for me to explain the madness that consumed me at the time. I think it's a miracle I stayed sane," she admitted to him.

"What does that have to do with *Yetzia bish'eila*?"

"*Yetzia bish'eila*?" Rivka didn't understand.

"*Yetzia bish'eila* is when a religious person becomes secular," he explained with a smile.

"I see," she murmured thoughtfully.

"*Nu*, so what happened then?" he prompted.

And she told him about Jeff and her desperate love for him, about her attempt to be with him and how she got caught in his house.

"And now? Do you still think of him?"

"To tell you the truth, I think about him quite a lot, but, thank God, it's not with that same madness that consumed me and made me do endlessly foolish things." Her expression turned sad when she remembered what she had done.

"I'm sorry. I didn't mean to make you sad," he apologized.

"Never mind. Let's change the subject. Tell me about yourself," she requested.

"I have nothing special to tell you. I've never had a real love," he laughed.

"So, tell me about your service in the army. You were in the army, right?"

"In the Artillery Corps. I was a gunner. My army service wasn't very interesting. Why do you ask?"

"In New York, when I was at the agency, they told us about the IDF and gave us the opportunity to enlist. Since I arrived, I've thought about it a lot. I think I want to be a soldier. What do you think?"

Her eyes gleamed as she spoke.

"I think it's a great idea. The army will do you good. Your Hebrew will improve immeasurably, and the army will instill in you the sabra mentality. And more importantly, after the army, you'll be able to sustain yourself without being dependent on others. You'll be independent. If you want to stay in Israel, I really recommend that you enlist. And you're at the right age," he added. Rivka was pleased someone was encouraging her to take this dramatic step because as much as she wanted it, she also feared it terribly. What would her parents and siblings say now that she'd completely abandoned their ways?

Rivka took the olive-green uniform that the stock-keeper gave her and wore it before the scrutinizing gazes of the other recruits. Doing so, she felt frighteningly naked. How would she endure this scrutiny during her entire service? The terrifying commanders that screamed at them endlessly didn't add to her desire to stay in this frightening place, all fear and discipline, which she'd tried to run away from when she left the Hasidic community. Just then, she regretted her decision to join the army.

"From now on, when a ranked soldier addresses you, you answer every request with 'yes, sir,' or 'yes, ma'am,' is that clear?" the sergeant screamed at the group of girl soldiers standing in line.

"Yes!" all the soldiers answered as one.

"Yes what?" the sergeant hollered in fury.

"Yes, ma'am!" they all screamed back, and some started giggling.

"Glad that's clear, girls. I'm glad you're not slow-witted. Pay attention! From now on, you're in the army, under strict discipline. Don't even think of refusing your commanders' orders. Disobeying an order means insubordination. Insubordination means grave punishments. Punishment may be military confinement and, sometimes, even military prison. Get it, girls? Prison, as in under lock and key. Am I being clear enough?"

"Yes, ma'am! All clear!" the recruits answered as one.

"Good. Now you're free to go until tomorrow. At six a.m., report to lineup, and then transportation will take you to a different base, where you'll go through basic training. And God help anyone who's late," she warned them. The girls grabbed their duffle bags and ran to the communal tent. Later on, Rivka would remember the warmth and fondness with which the girls who shared her tent treated her. That warmth reminded her of her friend Dvora. The two girls spoke on the phone frequently, and she found out that Dvora had a little baby girl and lived in the center of Israel. Did she do the right thing by joining the army? She could've also been a wife and mother now. ... However, she wasn't sorry. She was happy with the new way she'd chosen.

After basic training, she went through classification tests and was stationed at a two-month course for secretaries at air force operational squadrons. "If you finish this course successfully, you have a good chance of serving in a combat squadron," the classification officer told her. And Rivka, who yearned to serve in a combat squadron, invested all her energies in the course in order to succeed. Despite the difficulties that she still experienced regarding reading comprehension in Hebrew, her success was amazing. Even her commanders said they hadn't seen achievements and motivation like hers before. Her joy knew no limits when she was informed that she was stationed at an air force base in the north. The squadron chosen for her was one of the best, the F-16 squadron.

After completing basic training and the course, she felt wise in the ways of the military. She quickly realized what was required of her and did her job meticulously and dedicatedly. The pilots were fond of her and praised her work endlessly. Two weeks before the High Holidays, the squadron commander invited her to his office. "The commanders here have decided to give you a certificate of merit," he notified her. Rivka was stunned silent, only the tears streaming down her cheeks disclosing her emotions. The sweet, fragile girl, always willing to help, about whom no one in the squadron knew her difficult past in the Hasidic court in Brooklyn, was liked by all. She had heart-to-hearts with the girls, joked with the boys, and only the soldiers who tried their luck and asked her out were rejected. Even the most desired pilots in the squadron were politely rejected. The reason for that was simple: Captain Yoav Sadeh.

She'd heard of him the moment she arrived at the squadron. Even though he was lean and not especially tall, his reputation preceded him as a fearless pilot. She immediately liked his pleasant face. His brown eyes reflected calm, restraint, and wisdom. Unlike others, he always dropped by before and after every flight, interested in her well-being, discussing matters of the day with her at length. Mostly, she enjoyed it when he shared his flying experiences with her. He visited her office at every opportunity or free moment, holding two fresh bread rolls filled with cottage cheese and two cups of cappuccino that he brought from the top floor. Sometimes, he pampered her with candies from the canteen or treats his mother sent him. Unbelievably, despite spending so much time with her—almost every free moment—he didn't ask, not even once, that she meet him for a date in the evening. Even when there was a movie at the base movie theater, he went with his friends and didn't ask her to join them. She also liked that very much, that he didn't make overtures to her like all the other guys. With Yoav, she always felt protected, and his empowering, embracing presence dimmed somewhat her memories of Jeff.

One day, when he returned from flight practice, he sat next to her, and said sadly, "I don't understand how it happened…"

"What?"

"Eitan screwed me over. We had an aerial battle for almost half an hour, and in the end, the bastard got me. Sat on my tail and I couldn't escape. I made endless maneuvers, and I couldn't escape that fox. And now that fucker went to tell all the guys. …"

"Nonsense. You can't win all the time. Now, you know you're human and vulnerable. During the next flights, you'll have to be more careful," she said sensibly and stroked his gloomy face.

"Rivka'le…" he suddenly said quietly. "If you'll agree to go out with me tonight, I'll score at least one victory. …"

"How important is that victory to you?" she asked, not making it easy for him. But her twinkling eyes and palm, still stroking his cheek, said differently.

"Very important. You have no idea how much…maybe even more important than my victory over Eitan," he replied and pressed her caressing hand to his heart, and Rivka consented immediately. She noticed how his smile carved an adorable dimple into his right cheek.

In the evening, before he came to pick her up from the kibbutz, she told Amir about the budding relationship between Yoav and herself.

"Do you love him?" he asked.

"I don't know. But I really enjoy his company. We have a good time together," she replied.

"So, have a great time tonight." She noticed his voice had become sour.

"Amir, we're family. I didn't think you thought about me that way," she said, surprised.

"I know, Rivka. But I still feel that this is a missed opportunity. Maybe because we're cousins, even though cousins also get married, even more so second-degree cousins. But don't worry about me. I never thought the relationship between us would go any differently…but, you know, I've become attached," he said glumly.

"Me, too," she said and hurriedly ended the conversation. Yoav's car was waiting for her outside.

Chapter 17

The first rays of sunlight flickered through the overcast horizon. Only the early birds populated the streets, as silent as shadows. The silence was absolute until the sounding of lowing cows from the town's outskirts broke the silence. After that, there was the roar of the bus, which collected the few people waiting at the station. Lazily, the bus embarked on its journey from Eloy to Phoenix.

Jeff and his mother were among the passengers. Jeff took a window seat and stared indifferently at the desert vista. His mother preferred the seat facing him, so they could see each other and talk. Occasionally, Jeff took his eyes off the window and looked at his mother. He was sad to see that during his few years of absence, she'd aged greatly. Her hair was completely white, and many wrinkles creased her face and forehead. Her mouth was missing several teeth, which made her jaw shrink and made her look older than her years.

Despite the short distance from Eloy to Phoenix, the bus journey was long because the bus driver stopped in every town to let passengers off and collect new ones. Jeff bit his nails impatiently. The prolonged journey was starting to make him uncomfortable. The awakening desert view, which used to fascinate him, seemed now monotonous and boring. Even the towering cacti displaying their amazing flowers didn't improve his mood. He chose to focus on the thorny branches, which seemed to him more aggressive and threatening than usual. From time to time, his thoughts wandered to his sister and her illness.

"The doctors say she's depressed," his mother had said when they spoke on the phone several days previously.

"Do I need to come?" he asked hesitantly.

"I think it'll help her if you come. You always were a supportive figure for her," she urged him to visit.

Jeff didn't hesitate. The next day, he packed a small bag and flew out to Eloy. It was strange, he thought when he packed. He was going back almost the same way he'd left less than three years ago. His bag was the same bag, and the jeans he was wearing were the same jeans he'd worn when he'd arrived at New York.

"Should I come with you?" Eve offered.

"The situation there is really delicate…" he hesitated. "I think it's better I go alone. Besides, the stock market's on fire now. It's better that you stay."

And Eve respected his request, was even glad for it. The stock market was indeed rocky in the past several days, and she was better off preparing herself for the next days of trade, which might be critical. A week before, one of the companies announced that it was expecting heavy losses. The announcement elicited shock in the capital market and, as a result, all the share's quotations plummeted. Then came other disappointing announcements from other companies, which exacerbated the situation. Even though Eve was expecting the change, and even though she reduced her investments significantly, the damage done to her investment portfolios amounted to millions of dollars. A similar day of decrease, and a significant chunk of the profits accumulated in her investment portfolios was lost. The frightened investors lost faith in the market and sold indiscriminately. Even her personal charm wasn't enough to convince them to stay. In a special television speech, the president tried to assure the investors, but even his speech couldn't ease the panic. Another trading day ended in a downward trend.

But it wasn't the stock market's difficult situation that made her want to stay in New York. Jeff didn't know yet, but her period, that was usually regular, was two weeks late. Her gynecologist made an appointment for her in two days. Deep inside, she already knew she was pregnant, but since she wasn't sure, she preferred to keep quiet and wait for the results of the checkup. Furthermore, judging by Jeff's conversations with his mother, she understood that it wasn't a good time to meet his mother and sister. Let him go alone. She wouldn't be another burden on him.

"Tell me exactly what happened to her," Jeff prompted his mother when he arrived at his childhood home.

"It all started several days after you left. She became quiet and sad, barely said a word. Several months later, these strange symptoms started. Little inconsequential things that a normal person doesn't pay attention to, really scared her. She'd get seizures, had a hard time breathing, and could barely speak. Then her situation deteriorated even more; she stopped bathing and changing clothes. She simply neglected herself awfully and spent most of her time in bed without doing a thing. I took her to a doctor, and she gave Pam sedatives. In the beginning, there was an improvement, and she looked as though she was snapping out of it, but a week later, her situation deteriorated again. She stopped talking and barely ate. Her situation was so bad that the doctor was forced to hospitalize her."

"Why didn't you tell me earlier?" he asked.

"I was afraid to worry you," his mother said. "I know how hard you work."

"So, how long has she been in the hospital?"

"About two months."

"And what do the doctors say?"

"They hope that, with the help of medication and treatment, her condition will improve. They claim she has fears that are related to her childhood. One doctor told me, unequivocally, that these fears will disappear when she gets better."

"So the situation isn't dire?"

"Not dire, but not good. That's why I wanted you to come. She isn't getting better."

Jeff continued staring at the desert view, allowing his thoughts to take him back in time to the day he left Eloy. He recalled Pam's reaction when he told her he was leaving for New York. All these years, he'd sensed his sister was suffering a mental crisis. The way she'd talked with him in the beginning, her heavy stammer, and more than anything her endless tears were more than a sign of what would happen. His main fear was that she would try to kill herself, but he hoped the situation wasn't as bad as that, and that this disease wasn't endangering her life. Could it be that all of this would've never happened had he stayed?

"I shouldn't have left," he said. He took his eyes off the window and looked at his mother.

"What?" she asked absentmindedly.

"I said, I never should've left when Pam was so vulnerable. I should've waited a bit," he clarified.

"You did what you had to do. You had to think of your future," his mother said with dry practicality.

Jeff didn't hide his surprise at her answer. "When I left… according to your reaction, I thought you were the one who wasn't happy. …"

"Maybe I was selfish at first. The way you left also bothered me. Then, I realized it was best for you. Don't forget your father was alive at the time, and the thought that Pam and I would be alone with him scared me."

"Did he hurt you?"

"No. He was very sick by then. He barely got out of bed. He'd go to the toilet, and that's it. Sometimes, he would cuss…you know, his regular cussing."

"Say, Mom…with all the mess going on at home, I never understood why he picked on you being a Christian. As far as I remember, he never even went to church. What right did he have to upset you about it?"

His mother turned to look at the window, as though wishing to avoid his eyes. "It's a complicated story," she said quietly.

"Tell me," he demanded.

"I don't know. ..."

"What do you mean 'you don't know'? If it has anything to do with Pam or me, we have a right to know! You have no right to hide it from us." His angry exclamation attracted the attention of the other passengers.

"Well?" he prompted.

"Maybe it *is* time you knew. When we return from visiting Pam, I'll tell you." Tears filled her eyes, and her lips quivered. And Jeff, paying mind to her distress, didn't push her. He went back to staring sadly out the window.

"I'm so happy you found your place and that you're successful. By the way, how's your wife?" she asked suddenly.

When he told her over the phone he was getting married and asked her to come to New York to attend the wedding, she refused because of Pam's situation. But what troubled him more than anything, was that she showed no interest in his intended bride. For two whole years, ever since he got married, she hadn't asked a thing about her. Not even her name.

"My wife? An amazing woman. I couldn't have asked for a better spouse. Here's a picture of her. Her name's Eve." Jeff took a picture out of his wallet and gave it to his mother.

"Pretty woman," she said. When she finished looking at the picture, she handed it back without a word.

"And children?" she asked, unexpectedly.

"Kids? Oh, do you mean is she pregnant? No. Not yet, but we'll get there, too."

The bus continued its journey and a tense silence settled between Jeff and his mother.

"The rates fell sharply yesterday on Wall Street and Nasdaq. Dow Jones fell 3.5 percent, and the Nasdaq shed 4.3 percent." The newscaster's voice broke the silence. "Commentators claim that the source of the crisis lies in investors' fears that the companies they've invested in will collapse as a result of large losses they've accumulated and widespread downsizing. Tension is discernable in the market in preparation for the day of trading in just another hour. Many think that there's no escape but to involve the government in market activity in order to prevent its complete collapse."

Jeff looked around. The dramatic announcement didn't impress any of the passengers, who all looked like hardworking people that never even considered investing in the stock market. Jeff took his phone out of his pocket and called Eve in a panic, but all he got was voicemail. Then he called her office. Jessica, her secretary, told him Eve hadn't arrived yet. Weird, he thought. Usually, even during trading, they talked. She always found time to talk to him, even about random stuff. It seemed as though she looked forward to their light-hearted conversations, the jokes that helped her take a break from her difficult job. So, why wasn't she answering? He felt another burden settle heavily on him.

The bus continued its tedious journey, red dunes rolling stubbornly behind the windows. Once in a while, especially when they reached a town, the primordial views were replaced with thick vegetation protruding from the ground, bringing with it a real change, until the bus returned to the asphalt roads. Damn, Jeff was mad at himself. Why had he agreed to his mother's request to take the bus when his financial situation allowed him to easily rent a car? After visiting Pam, that's exactly what he'd do, he promised himself. After a two-hour ride, they finally reached the center of Phoenix, where they took the subway to the hospital.

When Jeff saw the white building, he felt his legs grow weak. Cold sweat covered him. The sign in front left no place for doubt. This was a well-known mental facility. A real nuthouse.

"If you continue acting this way, you'll get carted away to Stone-Wall," he remembered the sentence with which his father used to threaten his mother.

"What's Stone-Wall?" he once asked the woman he worked with at the diner at Eloy.

"A mental hospital that also has closed wards. Some of the patients are even tied to their beds so they won't harm themselves or others," she explained, and innocent, young Jeff was horrified to the depths of his soul. Now, he was entering the infamous facility. From the entrance hall, he saw a closed yard. Many patients, most of them wearing white, shuffled around, looking like ghosts. The odd sounds and desperate cries they made reached his ears, even through the sealed glass. He knew that, in most of the closed wards, visiting was complicated and required scheduling in advance.

"Don't worry; Pam's in the open ward," his mother assured him, as though reading his thoughts.

When he entered the room, he saw his beloved sister lying in bed, staring at a certain spot on the ceiling. He approached her, calling her name. Pam turned her head slowly, sent him a bemused look, and after what seemed like an eternity, sat up, reaching for him, sobbing and calling his name.

Jeff leaned into her, gently kissed her forehead and cheeks, and held her for a long time.

The nurse who was in the room was stunned. "Goodness, she's talking! I swear, she hasn't said a word since she arrived, and now she's saying your name."

But Pam wasn't speaking. She might've called his name, but all her other efforts to talk failed. It was as though she had no air in her lungs. She expressed her emotions by writing them down, telling him she missed him very much and that she loved him.

"I love you, too," he said softly, stroking her hand. Then he sat by her side for hours, telling her about Eve and New York. He noticed that his stories made her emotional and improved her situation. When he finished, she gestured with her hand that she wanted to come with him.

"When you're healthy, I'll take you away from this place," he promised.

"No, now!" she wrote, and Jeff calmed her down, explaining to her that first she had to get better and, only then, would he take her wherever she wanted. He told her about a magical spot in Central Park where he and Eve loved to go to be alone, and promised he'd take her there. Then he went to talk with the doctor.

"Your presence here is important. Obviously, you're a good influence. You have to visit more often," the doctor ordered.

"I'll come," he promised seriously.

"Don't worry, Pammy. I'll stay in Eloy at least for a week, so I'll be able to visit you every day. You'll see, everything will work out, and you'll get out of here soon," he promised cheerfully.

When they returned from the hospital, Jeff was concerned. He thought about Pam and her future. How could he help her rehabilitation? Would New York would be good for her, or should she stay in Eloy? Then he thought about Eve and the crashing stock market. He wanted to call her but postponed the call because just then, his mother served dinner.

"Don't worry about Pam. I believe she'll be home in a couple of weeks. At least, that's what the doctor promised. When she comes home, I'll make sure she lacks for nothing," Jeff promised.

"And then what? She'll come back here…and then?"

"Let's hope things will work out," he replied laconically.

"Thinks won't work out! Nothing just works out by itself in this place! If you want to help her, you have to get her out of here."

"And what about you? Are you going to stay here alone?" he persisted.

"Don't worry about me, I'll manage. If I know Pammy's in a good place, things will be much easier for me."

Jeff was silent. Perhaps, the first stage was finding her a place with people in her situation, a kind of home were men and women her age lived together and took care of themselves. If only he could find a place like that in New York, and even find some light work for her in the department store. Spending time with him would do her good, work would help her return to life, and she'd regain her confidence and speech. And when her condition stabilized, he'd rent her an apartment next to his and Eve's apartment, and who knows, maybe she'd get lucky and meet someone nice and raise her own little family.

"Don't worry, Mom, if that's what you want, I'll get her out of here," he promised.

But his mother looked at him doubtfully and didn't say anything.

"How're you managing without him?" he asked, in order to change the subject.

"Managing. The bastard wasn't any use when he was alive, so in that sense, his absence hardly makes a difference."

"And in other ways?"

"You know…I'd gotten used to him," she said curtly.

"What had you gotten used to, his fists and cussing?" he asked ruefully.

His mother was silent.

"You promised me an answer," he reminded her, restless again.

"Yeah, I remember," she said, as though considering how to continue.

"I remember, to this day, his words. He'd tell me that Pammy and I were born in sin. What did he mean?" he asked, determined not to let her avoid the subject this time.

As a response, his mother got up and went into her room. After some time, she returned with a big stack of pictures.

"Take a look at these pictures. Maybe you'll understand," she said.

"I don't understand what these pictures have to do with the bullshit Dad spewed." He looked at the pictures, which didn't mean a thing to him.

"Keep looking," she urged him, and Jeff looked at the old pictures.

"Here, this one." She gripped his wrist. "Take a good look at this one. What do you see?" she asked, overcome with emotion.

Jeff brought the picture close—a picture of a large, old structure.

"I don't understand what this means," he despaired.

"Look at the front. There's a Star of David there. This is the symbol Jews place before their synagogues. What you see is Warsaw's main synagogue."

"Yeah, so?" Jeff recalled the pictures he saw at Ahron's house. They were almost similar.

"That's where my grandfather prayed. ..."

"Your grandfather? He was a Jew?"

"Yes. My grandparents were Jews. So were their children, one of whom was my mother. According to the Jewish religion, my children and I are also Jews. Your father never accepted that. He couldn't accept the fact you had Jewish blood," she said.

"Even though I was young," he said with difficulty, "as far as I remember, Grandma went to church with you. She was an even more devoted Christian than you were. Something's not falling into place here," he said, agitated and confused.

"Your grandmother, my mother, may she rest in peace, was born a Jew. The daughter of a respected Jewish orthodox family in Warsaw. When the Nazis invaded Warsaw, they gathered all the Jews and put them in the ghetto. You must've heard of that, right?" she asked, but continued talking without waiting for an answer.

"Most of her family died in the death camps, but my mother hid in the ghetto and managed to avoid deportation. Several months later, she was captured when she wandered outside of the ghetto walls and was sent to Auschwitz. On the way, with another Polish youth, she jumped from the train and found shelter in the woods, with Polish partisans. That's how her life was saved. After the war, she immigrated to the USA without knowing what had happened to the rest of her family. Without knowing she was the only one who'd survived. A year after she arrived here, she met my father, your grandfather. They fell in love, and she chose to convert to Christianity and change her name to Susan. Shortly after, they got married. After she got married, she stopped showing interest in her past. It was only after my father passed away that she told me everything." At this stage, his mother was emotionally tearful. Jeff handed her a tissue, and she wiped her tears promptly.

"But why? Why convert to Christianity? Nowadays, Jews and Christians get married, and no one converts their religion? So, why did she do it?" he insisted stubbornly. He remembered Rivka's words when she offered herself to him.

"My mother told me that my grandfather, my father's father, agreed to the wedding on the condition that she convert to Christianity. But if you ask me, I think that after everything she went through during the Holocaust, she wanted to deny her Judaism. It's understandable, right?"

"And Dad knew about this story before you got married?" Jeff inquired as he continued to study the rest of the pictures.

"Yes, your father knew, and he didn't care. He was okay with it until you turned six, I think. And then one of his screwed-up friends in the bar taunted him that you were a Jew, and you had to be circumcised like all the Jews. Everyone there burst into laughter, and your father became a laughing stock. Instead of leaving that goddamn bar, he got drunker and drunker until he went completely crazy. And then he made our lives a living hell."

"Bastard! That man was a bastard! How can a man ignore his kids like that? How? I don't get it," Jeff said between clenched teeth and continued to study the pictures angrily.

Suddenly, he stopped. His face, which had burned with anger, became cold and pale. Cold sweat covered his forehead and face. He started breathing quickly, and the strong hand holding one of the pictures started trembling. Desperately, he tried to steady his rebellious hand, but to no avail. Then, he tried to focus on the picture, but it shook in his hand like a pendulum. When he tried to say something, his throat closed, and the only thing that emerged from his mouth was white foam. It looked as though he was a second away from suffering a heart attack and collapsing.

"What happened, Jeffie?" His mother panicked, not understanding what was going on. She ran to the kitchen to fetch a glass of water.

"Drink and calm down," she ordered, still holding the glass of water.

"It's... it's..." Jeff thrashed in his chair, trying to speak but unable to say a word. In the end, he threw up his hands in despair, pointed at the picture he was still staring at. Then, he started shuffling through the pictures frantically, until he reached the last one.

"I asked what happened...you're scaring me, Jeffie! Why are you looking at the pictures that way?" his mother asked fearfully.

Jeff raised his eyes and looked at her as though she were a stranger. His body trembled, and with quivering lips, he managed to whisper, "What was Grandma's name? I mean before she converted to Christianity?"

"Hannah," his mother replied.

"Tell Grandma Hannah I found her family," he whispered weakly. His body curled into himself as though he was a newborn babe, and he burst into heartbreaking tears. After a long time, he told his mother about Gittel and Rachel, and about Ahron and Rivka. They talked until the small hours of the night. He told her, and she sat there and cried. Sometimes, she shed tears of grief for her lost past and the many family members she'd never met and, sometimes, her tears were tears of joy, full of hope for the future.

"Mom, do you know," he said just before he went to sleep. "I think I've also found a place for Pam."

"Where?" she asked curiously.

"For the time being, it's a secret. When I'm sure it'll work out, I'll tell you," he said and refused to add another word.

When he climbed into the bed of his youth, sniffing the old sheets that seemed as though they hadn't been laundered since he left three years previously, he called Eve immediately. He knew the conversation would be a long one. He also knew what he'd tell her. But this strange day had rules of its own. It held another surprise, one Jeff wouldn't know about until he'd return to New York.

Chapter 18

Yoav sat alert in his seat, ready for whatever came his way. With a sure hand, he grasped the steering stick and navigated the plane after Number 1. After the planes had gained a bit of altitude, they leveled and stabilized for a peaceful vertical flight. Outside, the sun was shining, and the rays permeating the bubble canopy brightened the crowded cockpit. Beneath sprawled the green fields of the Jezreel Valley. But no more than several minutes passed before scenes of green vegetation were replaced with the blue waters of the Sea of the Galilee. After crossing the small lake, the planes gradually broke right and glided to the practice range. The tranquil view changed steadily and became dry and intimidating.

In the beginning, Yoav thought of the briefing they received before the flight and the possible risks in practice flights, which were destined for a special, complex operation. But very quickly, his thoughts wandered to her, to Rivka. What would happen to her if his plane were intercepted? How would she cope if he were taken into captivity? Would she wait for his return? This wasn't the first time he thought of her when he flew. Ever since she arrived at the base, he'd thought of her every time he went up in the air. But until now, these thoughts hadn't bothered him during practice. During drills, he was alert and focused, not allowing himself to be distracted. Only later, did he allow himself to imagine her and derive pleasure from her beauty and immense charm. Mostly, he imagined her wearing the Air Forces light-blue uniform, which went well with her creamy complexion and blue eyes. But sometimes, he went as far as envisioning her under the wedding canopy, with him, Yoav, standing by her side, taking off her veil and kissing her.

During the first months of her arrival, their relationship entailed no more than conversations about this and that in her office at the squadron. Every time he saw her, he felt his heart beat faster, but only after their first date, which he'd remember until his dying day. Did he feel he truly loved her? He wanted to spend every second with her. One time, he found himself jealous of one of the pilots who'd spent time in her office, chatting with her. Sometimes, the fact that he knew nothing of her past bothered him. He knew she'd come from America and lived with her aunt on a kibbutz, but apart from that, nothing. When their relationship became more serious, he tried to find out, but she avoided answering. Who were her parents? Why did she leave her country of birth? Since when had she lived with her aunt? Was she kicked out of her home, or did she leave of her own free will? Perhaps, she was an orphan, and she had no home or family? And why did he sometimes find her reading chapters from Psalms or whispering a prayer over her food? When he asked if she was religious, she denied it. And even if she were, why would she be ashamed of it? Why wouldn't she admit it? This bothered him a lot, but didn't detract from his powerful love for her, maybe even increased it. She was as beautiful as she was mysterious. In his eyes, she was an unapproachable goddess, unattainable, even though she initiated most of their make-out sessions. He wasn't the conqueror. She initiated, she conquered, she set the pace to their lovemaking. And perhaps, that's why his desire for her only grew more powerful. One time, when they kissed, he tried, in the heat of the moment, to rid her of her clothes. However, she rejected him sternly.

"Don't try that again," she instructed. "I'm not ready yet."

"Sorry," he said briefly, a bit offended. But he obeyed immediately and reeled in his invasive hands.

And there was that time that she sent her hands to his intimate parts, and he, naively, thought that the moment had finally arrived, she was finally ready, but to his disappointment, she changed her mind and retreated. Sometimes, he found it hard to understand her indecisive behavior.

Now, with his plane hovering in the sky— he, its only ruler—he felt as though his love for her knew no boundaries. He tried to put into words what he felt for her, but couldn't. Right there and then, he decided that when he landed, he'd go straight to the operations room, and before everyone, he'd propose. He'd confess, and tell her the truth: that without her, his life wasn't a life. And she'd probably accept his proposal, and become his wife, his eternal beloved. And when she'd smile at him and accept his proposal, he'd gather her in his arms and kiss her to the cheers and applause of everyone else.

But what if she refused? Was it the time to propose? She was so young. A child really. What if she rejected him not because she didn't want him, but because of her age? If she said no in front of everyone, he'd suffer another defeat—one even bigger than the one he experienced during that aerial battle against Eitan. Wasn't it better to do it privately, during one of their dates, far from anyone's scrutiny? Perhaps, he should postpone the matter for a few months? Yesterday, before he kissed her good-bye, she looked at him and smiled, as though waiting for him to say something.

"If you don't have anything special to say to me, I'd better go to sleep," she teased him, and he wasn't sure if that was disappointment he heard in her voice.

Now, he saw her again, her beautiful face reflected through the plane's canopy, her blue eyes looking only at him. Now, her lips were pressing against the canopy, trying to reach his lips. In a second, he'd feel the sweetness of her lips and the heat of her burning body. Suddenly, he started sweating. The cockpit, where he'd always felt as though he was sitting in an armchair at home, became crowded and airless. He checked the AC and saw it was working without a hitch. He took a deep breath, trying to get rid of the thoughts of the one and only, his unattainable goddess.

"Everyone ready?" Number 1 radioed and cut off his thoughts.

"Affirmative," was the answer.

"What about you, Number 2? What are you daydreaming about?" Number 1 asked.

"I'm ready." Yoav snapped out of it, and the planes opened their afterburners, ascended, gathering altitude, and then dove down to the target. The practice was one hour long. Yoav tried to concentrate but failed to do so.

His concentration was so shot, that he screwed up the final practice.

"What's wrong with you?" the commander reprimanded him the minute he landed.

"I'm sorry." Yoav lowered his eyes.

"We won't have a choice but to replace you. You've become really sloppy lately," the commander said succinctly, and Yoav knew he was right and accepted his words in resignation.

In the evening, he told Rivka about practice and its dire conclusion.

"I don't believe it!" Rivka's jaw dropped.

"Believe it," he replied morosely.

"But why did this happen?" she asked.

Yoav was silent. He didn't want to blame her, not even slightly, for his failure.

"What happened? Tell me or I'll go to your commander," she persisted.

"I couldn't concentrate on practice. I was so out of it that I failed to perform the simplest actions."

"You couldn't concentrate? *You*? Why couldn't you concentrate? What were you thinking about?" she wondered.

"You…I was thinking of you…" he said quietly.

"*Me?* Yoav, that's not like you!" she scolded him. Then, she added contritely, "So…what were you thinking about?"

"What will happen to us if something, God forbid, goes wrong, and if I should propose to you now. …" He squirmed in embarrassment.

"And did you reach any conclusion?" she asked with shining eyes.

Yoav was silent for a second. Then he mustered his courage and looked at her imploringly while holding her hand. "I fell in love with you at first sight. My life isn't a life without you, Rivka. Will you marry me?"

Rivka looked at him with tender eyes. Her smile seemed to shine on him. She gathered his head to her breast, kissed his curls, and didn't say a word.

Chapter 19

"Mrs. Farmer, you're pregnant!" her gynecologist announced. When Eve heard the news, her happiness knew no bounds. She was so excited, that tears ran down her face, choking her.

"Why are you crying, sweetheart? You're going to be a mother!" the doctor smiled, swept away in her young, beautiful patient's excitement.

Eve had been trying, unsuccessfully, to conceive for two whole years. She was starting to fear something was wrong with her. Her fears grew as the months passed. At a certain stage, her doctor suggested that she and Jeff undergo tests and that she, Eve, may even have to go through fertility treatments.

When she told Jeff, it seemed as though he wasn't concerned at all. "It'll happen, love, it'll happen," he soothed her. Yet, as the days passed, her desire to conceive grew stronger. Her love for Jeff was so all-consuming that she yearned to perfect their bond. In her eyes, children were the missing link in their relationship.

When she left the clinic, the first thing she thought of doing was calling him and sharing the news. Only then, did she notice the many messages he left for her while she was undergoing the tests. She called him back and, as if to spite her, she got his voicemail. She tried to call him all day long, but to no avail. It was late, when he finally called her back. She heaved a sigh of relief. She was dying to tell him about the pregnancy, but he was so excited and confused, that she couldn't get a word in edgewise. She immediately realized something had happened. In the beginning, he told her about his meeting with Pam. Then he told her about his grandmother, Hannah, who'd survived the Holocaust and who was, in her past, a Jew. When he was done, she started telling him about her doctor's appointment, but he cut her off, proclaiming he was confused and didn't know what to do. After she despaired of telling him the news, she simply listened patiently and tried to give his confused ramblings all her attention, but she didn't understand everything. Nevertheless, she asked many questions in an attempt to be part of the experience that had shaken him so. In the end, he asked about the stock market, and she told him that, at the end of the day of trading, there was a change, which tempered the sharp declines. Before they said good-bye, she still considered sharing the news with him, but his exhausted voice and the cool distance he showed her, made her reconsider her timing.

The next day, the stock market declines were stopped. Eve thought how lucky she was, and how things were going just as she wished them to. Now, she could decide, without any distractions, on the date of her retirement. After all, that was what Jeff told her during one of their conversations. "Retire when you have kids." It was time to retire from her extremely stressful job and just relax. Granted, in the past she'd been addicted to her job—everyone had said that about her—but marriage had softened her. Jeff's love had moderated her eagerness for more and more professional successes and, now, all she wanted was to nest in her house. Money was no obstacle; she had more than enough. Her investments were secure, the department store was flourishing, so they could rely on their livelihood. And if she got bored, she could always help Jeff manage the store or work from home. She knew quite a few brokers who became freelancers after they became mothers and reaped even more success than they had on Wall Street. She agreed with her boss that she would stop working in October when she'd be six months pregnant.

At noon, Jeff called. This time, he did it from Pam's room in the hospital. Once again, he was excited and, this time, he told her about his sister's dramatic improvement and that she might go home soon. The doctors had told him that if her condition continued to improve at this rate, she would no longer have to stay at the hospital. Then he told her about his plan regarding Pam's future. Even though the plan seemed a bit strange to her, she didn't say anything on the matter. In the end, he told her that he'd be back in New York this upcoming Friday, and he'd take the red-eye. As he talked, she decided to surprise him when she saw him.

On Friday, she waited for him impatiently at the airport.

"No trading today?" he laughed when he brushed a light kiss over her lips.

"Of course, there is! But you'll be surprised to hear that trading isn't my top priority today," she beamed at him.

"How's that? Since when is the stock market not your top priority?" He winked at her beaming face.

"The day I saw you cleaning my office window was the day the stock market became secondary in my life," she said, while rubbing her stomach in circles.

"Are you pregnant?" he guessed at once.

"Uh huh." She nodded, flushing.

"See! I told you there was no reason for worry!" he scolded tenderly and couldn't contain his joy. He rushed to embrace her and scatter kisses all over her face. As he kissed her, he kept telling her how much he loved her and how happy he was about the surprising news. She could see by his reaction that he was excited, so excited that he was confused.

In the car, he fell silent and withdrew into himself. It seemed as though all the recent events and discoveries had left their mark, and he had a difficult time taking everything in.

"Since when have you known?" he asked.

"The day you left, I went to the doctor. That's why I didn't insist on coming with you," she explained.

"And why didn't you tell me?"

"I wanted to! You have no idea how much I wanted to! But that first evening, you wouldn't stop talking. You were so excited by your discoveries that day, you wouldn't let me get a word in edgewise. Then, the following days, the only thing that interested you was your grandmother, Hannah, and Pam. I didn't want to burden you."

"Okay," he said thoughtlessly and remained quiet and thoughtful for long minutes.

"What are you thinking about?" she inquired after a while.

"It's not normal!"

"What?"

"Everything that's happened to me these past days. It's unbelievable. First, I find out my sister is hospitalized in a mental facility and her condition is so bad that she's lost the ability to speak. She just stopped talking after I left, and the minute she saw me, she opened her mouth to talk again. Then I find out my grandmother was Jewish. You know, when my mother told me my grandma was born Jewish, I almost passed out. But when I realized my grandmother was Ahron's grandmother's twin sister, I almost had a heart attack...and I kid you not. Do you realize what's happening? It's crazy! A Christian meets a Jew, randomly, and finds out they're related. How's that possible? Then, I come home to you and discover I'm going to be a father, and instead of losing my mind from happiness, I feel insanely confused."

"But these are great things!" Eve enthused.

"A wise man once told me, when good things happen, start worrying, because the bad is close behind," he dismissed her optimism.

"The man who told you that doesn't sound too wise to me. Go to him and tell him that there's good in every bad. We shouldn't search for the bad, but when it comes, we can make the best out of it. For example, that unpleasant incident you had with that girl in Brooklyn. Eventually, it brought you to me," she smiled mischievously.

"But sometimes, there are bad things that can't be repaired. For instance, when someone close to you dies. Then what? What's good about that?" He looked at her triumphantly.

"Or you find out the guy who beat the crap out of you, is actually a relative," she continued laughingly.

"Yeah, I'd love to see the look on Yehuda's face when he gets the news that I'm Hannah's grandson, which means we're cousins," he chuckled.

"You see? Think positive, and things will be positive. Think negative, and bad things will happen. It's a self-fulfilling prophecy. Nothing bad is close behind; on the contrary," she said and resumed stroking her stomach soothingly. He followed her hands stroking her stomach, which suddenly seemed a bit swollen.

"By the way, starting in October, I'll no longer be at work."

"Great," he answered absentmindedly, without giving much thought to her words.

"Shall we go home or do you want to go to work?" she asked.

"Work! I have to clear my head," he answered, and Eve instructed the driver to go to the department store.

But even there, Jeff couldn't focus. The paperwork that had accumulated on his desk continued lying there uselessly. Many times, he considered calling Ahron, but changed his mind, rejecting the idea.

At night, he couldn't sleep. Like a caged lion, he paced the house, his thoughts frantic. He realized that according to Jewish law, if his grandmother was Jewish, his mother was Jewish, as well. Thus, he was Jewish, too. But was his grandmother really considered Jewish? Could a converted Jew still be considered Jewish? The matter required clarification. Maybe Ahron could check with his rabbi. However, his father and grandfather were Christians, so he was also a Christian. In the end, he decided that if he was baptized as a Christian, he might as well stay a Christian until the end of his days. On the other hand, Jesus was also an observant Jew from Nazareth, and all of Christianity was founded on his doctrine. So, what did it matter anyway? In fact, according to the Law of Return, which he learned from Ahron, if he wanted, he could even do Aliyah. Maybe even meet Rivka. He smiled for the first time in days. Who would believe he and Rivka were cousins? And maybe it was believable, and that was the exact reason he was sent to her.

But how could he tell Ahron? And how would Ahron react when he learned that his beloved aunt converted to Christianity for reasons of convenience, or worse, heresy? He was an ultra-orthodox Jew, among those willing to sacrifice their lives in order to sanctify their religion. He would be unbearably disappointed by Aunt Hannah. Shouldn't he just keep it a secret in order to avoid hurting his friend? Wasn't it better that Ahron, whom as a gesture of respect and appreciation named his daughter after his aunt, never find out about her conversion? As he pondered the matter, he thought there might be another possibility, a slim one. Perhaps, Ahron would accept the news understandingly. Why not? Maybe the news about his long-lost aunt would please him. Shouldn't he be happy to discover that she didn't die in the gas chambers like he originally thought? Perhaps, when Ahron found out that he, his good friend, was actually his second cousin, it would make him happy? Yet, what if Ahron refused to believe him?

He decided it wouldn't be hard to convince Ahron of the truth of his words, if and when he ever brought the story to his knowledge. He did, after all, have proof. Actual proof. Many pictures in which Hannah was documented standing by her family, with whom Ahron was closely familiar. If necessary, he'd take Ahron to Eloy to meet his mother.

And Rivka? What about their strange relationship now? He remembered the beautiful girl who visited his house and kissed him passionately. He remembered the lust filling his body, and how close he was to doing the forbidden deed. He concluded that the goddess of luck had been on their sides that night. How would

Rivka have felt had she'd known she'd been prepared to give her virginity to her cousin?

After methodically considering all the options, he decided that for the time being, he wouldn't share his discoveries with Ahron and Rivka. The time would come, and then he'd reveal to them the wonderful story.

When he reached his decision, he felt slightly relieved and climbed into bed next to Eve, who slumbered peacefully. He hoped sleep would no longer elude him, but to his surprise, discovered that it wasn't meant to be. His thoughts continued plaguing and bothering him. He imagined a youthful Hannah, and tried to find similarities between her and Rivka, but had difficulty comparing skinny Rivka to the girl from the faded picture. When he tried to compare himself to Ahron, a shudder wracked his body. When he mentally removed Ahron's clothes and long sideburns, he realized they were significantly similar. The same blue eyes, the same small, upturned nose, the same strong chin, and even the same small ears. Under the different clothes, the family ties were glaringly obvious.

Then he started thinking about the third side—the sister living on a kibbutz in Israel. He decided Aunt Rachel would serve as the bridge between the grandchildren. She, more than anyone, would understand the meaning of the painful decision her sister Hannah made. After all, she'd also changed her way of life after her family's tragic demise in the Holocaust and had abandoned religion. She also went through Hannah's agonizing ordeal. Therefore, she was the only one who could judge her. And if Ahron considered Rachel his aunt, even though she abandoned their way of life, why should he treat Hannah differently? The more he thought about it, the more he was convinced that eventually, Ahron would accept the fact he had a Christian relative, just like he resigned himself to the fact his grandmother's sister and his own sister abandoned religion.

Now, all that was left to do was locate Rachel. To do that, he needed information he didn't have. He'd have to find out her last name or at least the name of her kibbutz. Her last name had been mentioned in his presence, but he'd forgotten it. All night long, he unsuccessfully tried to remember her name.

With dawn, he finally fell asleep, but before that, he decided that the next days would be dedicated to finding Aunt Rachel. He knew where to start. He'd go to the Jewish Agency.

The next day, he walked to the building that was located not far from the department store. He carried a large envelope with priceless pictures. He knew the pictures wouldn't help him locate Aunt Rachel; nevertheless, he decided to bring them. Maybe to verify his story in case someone decided not to believe him. After all, he was having a hard time believing the odd story himself.

After going from room to room, and after several conversations with several officials, he found out it was impossible to locate the aunt by first name only. It seemed his naïve attempt had reached a dead-end. Apparently, he'd have no choice but to ask Ahron.

When he walked back to the store, he kept thinking of Rachel's forgotten last name. Suddenly, he stopped dead in his tracks, his face lighting up as though he'd found a treasure. He whirled around and ran back to the agency building.

"Two years ago, a girl named Rivka Steinberg came here," he said to one of the officials. "I know she wished to immigrate to Israel. She's living now with my aunt, the aunt I'm searching for. Perhaps, she left details regarding my aunt's name or the kibbutz she lives in."

"Go to the second floor. At the end of the hall, is the manager of the Aliyah department, his name is Morris," instructed the bored official.

"Of course! Of course, I remember the girl. But before I disclose any information about her, you have to prove you're a relative," Morris insisted.

"Take these pictures, call Rachel, Rivka's aunt, and ask her if she knows anything about them. If she does, it'll prove the family ties between us." Jeff spread the yellowing pictures on the table.

"Makes sense," Morris replied, and Jeff sighed in relief. The old pictures were proving to be really useful.

"It's very late now in Israel. Come back tomorrow and by then, I hope I'll have an answer for you. Anyway, call before you come, so you won't make an unnecessary journey," Morris concluded.

"My aunt is convinced her sister died in the Holocaust. You have to relay the information carefully," Jeff explained. He feared his old aunt's strength would fail her when she discovered the truth.

"Don't worry. For the time being, we won't tell her a thing. We'll describe the pictures and ask her if they sound familiar. If her answer is affirmative, we'll stop at that. Later, we'll send someone on our behalf to the kibbutz, and he'll show her the pictures and tell her about her sister."

Jeff relaxed, thanked Morris, and rushed back to work.

Chapter 20

The black horse galloped lightly and circled the ranch over and over, its strong legs pounding the ground, raising clouds of dust. After several circles, it started slowing down, until it stood by a wooden fence. Then it shuffled its legs, threw back its glorious mane, and swished its long-haired tail. The horse's big black eyes were wide open, its ears pricked, alert to every sound.

Pam sat in the saddle, as straight and handsome as the noble Arabian. Her hands held the reins firmly, her legs urging the horse to follow her lead. As a child, she'd ridden horses. Her father, before becoming addicted to alcohol, taught her and Jeff how to ride. Every evening, he drove them to the nearby ranch, where they enjoyed riding the horses. They became excellent riders, as a cowboy's kids should. After that, she didn't ride for a long time, but it was a skill she hadn't forgotten. Therefore, when she applied for a job at the ranch, she got the job easily. She'd been working on the ranch for three months as a riding instructor and coach for the young riders. She was talking again, although she still stuttered. Her stammer didn't impede her work. On the contrary, it helped her better understand some of her students' disabilities. Some of them were youths at risk, some were handicapped, and some—those with whom she'd bonded most of all—came from an abusive home. Her joy knew no bounds when she saw them connect with the strong, muscular animal, deriving confidence from riding that they would otherwise never receive.

During her first month in Israel, she stayed with Aunt Rachel, as planned. But after a month, Pam felt she wanted to move forward with her life. Despite the love she felt for her aunt, she decided to embark on a life of independence. She was thirty years old. When would she start living if not now? Ever since, she'd lived on the ranch, leading the horses with a firm hand, to the satisfaction of her employers. The new place had been so good for her that her vivacity had returned. The disease that had plagued her just a short while ago hadn't left its mark on her and, in fact, no one apart from her aunt knew of it.

Aunt Rachel sat and looked at her wonderingly. How did the girl lead the horses so firmly? From her blue eyes, which had faded through the years, one could see only her pupils, which danced with joy. Her beautiful, wrinkled face beamed. Even her thin, trembling hands were temporarily steady. It seemed as though her soul had finally found peace. As far as she was concerned, she was prepared to return to her Maker.

She looked at her niece again and thought how she didn't resemble her sister. Pam was short and chubby, while Hannah had been tall and thin. Nevertheless, she was glad that she'd received the wonderful opportunity to meet the granddaughter of her beloved, lost sister. Who could've guessed that fragile, submissive Hannah, the weakest one in the family, would escape that hell? Who could've guessed that Hannah, who'd been so honest, would live a life of lies, far from her family? Who could've guessed that the girl of such strong faith, who never stopped murmuring, "With God's help, with God's help," would convert and marry a goy?

And to think that everything had begun only several months ago. A man from America had called her and asked about pictures from many years ago. Then, there was a visit from the Jewish Agency, and they asked questions about Hannah. Where had they lived? Where had they gone to school? What was the name of the synagogue where their father had prayed? At first, she'd thought it was one of the Holocaust researchers from "Yad Vashem" Museum, or maybe those people who recorded old Holocaust survivors from the Spielberg Archive. But when the man asked when she'd last seen Hannah, she started getting suspicious. Why would a man from the agency ask when she'd last seen her sister? What kind of cruel question was that? It had been years since her sister had died. Did he know something she didn't? Perhaps, he thought she knew something and wasn't telling him? And then he told her that her sister had indeed passed away, but not in the Holocaust. She'd died a natural death, he'd told her. When she died, she'd left behind one daughter and a granddaughter and grandson. Rachel almost fainted when she received the news.

"Hannah? Alive?" Her jaw went slack with astonishment, and she didn't know whether to laugh or cry.

"No, no, she isn't alive," the man repeated. "She passed. But she didn't die in the war; she died a natural death of old age."

When the shock wore off, she started crying. Right in front of that strange man, she'd sobbed without shame until she ran out of the few tears she still had left. Then, the man gave her a note with the grandson's name and phone number, left her confused and torn, without any idea what to do. The entire day, she couldn't decide what to do. Should she contact Hannah's grandchildren, or should she just leave things as they were? Perhaps, she should wait until the mysterious grandson made the first move and called her? She looked again at the note the man gave her. So, this was her long-lost nephew. Who would've believed she had a nephew called Jeff Farmer? It was a nice name, Jeff Farmer, but more suited to a Hollywood actor than a Jewish guy. She remembered "Baruch from Magentza" by Shaul Tchernichovsky, which she'd studied at school. She still remembered how horrified she was when Baruch chose to kill his daughters with his own two hands, and all for the sanctity of God, *Kiddush Hashem*. And now, she found out that her beloved sister had chosen to convert for nothing! Nothing!

How could she understand why she did it? She had no idea what Hannah had been through since they'd been separated. She had no idea how she'd managed to save herself from death. She'd also been in the ghetto, but she was given up for adoption to a gentile woman, which was what saved her. But her sister had been in the camps, and who knows, perhaps the horrifying ordeal she'd gone through had driven her so mad that she'd done the worst thing possible. She shouldn't judge her sister. Who was she to judge her, by God? She had to respect her decision, like others had respected Rachel's decision to leave her religious way of life. But with all due respect, that didn't mean that now she had to meet Hannah's Christian grandchildren. That was too much for her. Not only did her sister not even try to find her, but she also had to go and convert to Christianity and had severed all ties to her Jewish roots. So why should Rachel now, as old as she was, cope with the consequences? On the other hand, how could she leave this earth without meeting Hanna's offspring—Hannah, whom she hadn't seen in sixty years? How could she deny the only possible tie left with her sister? What would she say to Hannah when she met her in the next world. How would she explain her decision to ignore Hannah's offspring? *Oy* God, this is too much for me, she screamed silently at an obscure point on the ceiling. Did God hear her? Was her sister watching from above?

When evening fell, she started feeling sick to her stomach. When she took her temperature, she saw she had a fever. She made herself a cup of tea, adding a sprig of rosemary to it to ease the pain. When that didn't help, she called Amir.

When her grandson came, he saw her in bed, shaking with cold despite the heavy heat. He called a doctor right away, who assured them it was nothing but a light flu. No need to panic.

After he had left, she told Amir everything that had happened in the course of that strange day. Amir was wise; he'd definitely find an answer to her questions and deliberations. But the news didn't excite Amir, as though he had new aunts revealing themselves every day.

"I'll call Jeff," he suggested. "But I think that first we should share the information with your other sister's son. The one who lives in Brooklyn."

Was her grandson out of his mind? What had happened to his wisdom? He always had good advice to give. But now, she was willing to swear he was insane. Tell Moishel that his aunt converted to Christianity? What a joke. The poor man would have a heart attack. It was bad enough that his daughter had abandoned his way of life, now to tell him that his mother's sister converted? God forbid. No, the timing wasn't right. But she would tell Rivka. Rivka was strong and mature enough. The next time she came home from the army and visited, Rachel would tell her.

"What do you say we tell Rivka first? Then, we'll think, together, how and when to tell Moishel."

"I thought of calling her anyway," Amir said. "We'll ask her to sleep over tonight. You shouldn't be alone, and I can't stay. I have to go study for an exam I have tomorrow."

Rivka arrived immediately. She asked her commander for special leave, gave up on an outing with Yoav, and arrived bursting with curiosity. Amir left the minute she came. Said he was sorry, he had to go and left the two of them alone.

"That man from the Jewish Agency drove me completely crazy," Rachel mumbled, and Rivka noticed her shaking hands. She'd been noticing for a while that her aunt's hands trembled uncontrollably.

"What man from the agency? What are you talking about, Aunt Rachel?" She stroked her aunt's hands in an attempt to stop the bothersome tremors, which looked as though any second they would drive her aunt mad.

Rachel rose from her sickbed wordlessly, shuffled to the dining room table, and took a note out of the drawer.

"Here, read it." She shoved the note into her niece's hand and returned to bed to wrap herself in the thick blanket.

If her aunt's hand shook, if her heart plummeted when she heard about her lost sister, there was no describing what happened to Rivka when she saw the name written on the paper. His name! She felt as though the vertebrae of her spine had become weak, as though she'd become a rag doll. A strange pain, one she'd never experienced before, spread along her back.

"This is the grandson of your grandmother's sister. He lives in New York. A Christian through and through," Rachel explained. She couldn't understand Rivka's horror. Was it just because he was a Christian? Didn't the years she spent in Israel help her? Was she still stuck in that Hasidic neighborhood in Brooklyn? Perhaps, Rachel was wrong to tell her. Now, she'd tell her father, Moishel, and who knew how he'd react. If she was so shocked that Hannah had converted, what would happen to the religious faction of the family?

"My grandmother's sister's grandson? I don't understand, Aunt Rachel. Could you explain what's going on?" Rivka asked, her voice conveying her distress. But before she received an answer, she felt an awful dizziness come over her, as though the ground was shaking beneath her. Her arms and legs started trembling, and she felt as though she were on a carousel. When she felt slightly better, she looked at the piece of paper again. No, it couldn't be that same Jeff Farmer, she calmed herself. For sure, there were many Christian Jeff Farmers in New York. It was just a coincidence meant to drive her out of her mind.

"And not only a grandson. There's also a granddaughter," Aunt Rachel added. "Remember my sister, Hannah?"

"Yes, Grandma's twin," Rivka replied shakily.

"She didn't die in the Holocaust like we all thought. The official I told you about said Hannah escaped from that hell, immigrated to America, and got married. She had one daughter, and that daughter had two children, a son and a daughter."

Rivka's heart continued pounding.

"He said that a young man named Jeff came to their offices

in New York. He claimed to be Hannah's grandson. He had old pictures of us as young girls in Warsaw. Judging by those pictures, there's no doubt that he's the grandson of my sister, Hannah."

"And where did she disappear to all those years ago? Why didn't she try to contact you?" Rivka's voice was steadier now.

"She had good reason, Rivkel. She'd converted to Christianity and didn't want us to find out."

"Converted to Christianity?" Rivka's voice was shaking again.

Was it possible that "her" Jeff, whom Aunt Rachel was talking about, was the long-lost grandson? If so, she'd almost committed the act of the devil by giving her virginity to a relative. What would she do now?

"I was shocked, too, when the man from the agency told me she'd converted," Rachel identified with Rivka.

"And did you call him, this Jeff?" Rivka managed to ask after she'd regrouped some.

"No! I didn't think it was the right thing to do," Rachel said, and after a thoughtful pause, added, "maybe I didn't have the necessary courage."

"What's wrong, child? Why aren't you saying anything?" Rachel asked after they both sat silently for some time.

"I'm thinking," Rivka said, and wondered whether she should tell her aunt what had happened to her in New York.

"What are you thinking of, child?"

"Nothing special." When she said that, she ducked her head so that her aunt wouldn't see the tears filling her eyes.

"Rivkel, don't try to pull my leg. You're hiding something from me. It's all right if you prefer to keep it to yourself, but don't say it's nothing special. Judging by your eyes and shaking hands, I can see you're going through something. Tell me, child, and I'm sure you'll feel relieved."

Rivka looked at the wise old lady. Her face was tear-streaked when she whispered, "Do you know why I came here?"

"Of course, I know! You didn't want to remain ultra-orthodox, so you had to leave. That's also the reason I came to the kibbutz. It was the only way to break away from my old life."

"That's true, Aunt Rachel. You have no idea how right you are, but it's only partially true."

"I can guess, child. Is this the reason you're crying now?"

"Y-yes."

"Well then. Go on. I'm all ears."

"It all started when I met a man who wasn't Jewish, a friend of my brother, Ahron. He lived in our basement apartment and worked for Menachem, my brother-in-law. At the time, I was engaged, but this man captivated my heart from the first moment. Aunt Rachel, you won't believe how beautiful he is..." Rivka gave in to her memories. "You should've seen him, sitting on the sofa, Hannah'le on his lap as he read her a story. That day, I stayed at Ahron's place until late. I was so happy I couldn't leave. When I left, it was as though I were hypnotized, insanely charmed by him, impatiently waiting for the day I'd see him again. The temptation to go to his apartment was huge. I struggled with myself every single day. One day, I broke. I couldn't help myself, so I went. I was very conflicted with myself before I went, but in the end, I couldn't stand it any longer...I went to his place twice." Rivka took a deep breath and thought how to continue.

"And then what happened?" Rachel urged her. She felt vastly relieved that, for the time being, they were taking a break from the grave discussion about her converted sister. Young love always thrilled her, but she still didn't understand why her niece was telling her about her unrequited love in New York.

"And then, my secret was discovered. Someone, saw me go in, and everything went to hell. You can't even imagine. There were some crazy rumors about me, and I didn't do anything. ..."

"Oh, my poor child."

"The rumor that I'd been at his place spread like wildfire. People said I gave my virginity to a Christian. But that's not what happened, Aunt Rachel. I swore it never happened. But it didn't help."

"And what did happen?" Rachel asked with curiosity mixed with horror.

"A kiss, Aunt Rachel. A kiss so sweet that its taste stuck to my lips as though I were possessed. A kiss that gave me no peace for days, and maybe...who knows? Maybe it still doesn't." Rivka held her breath. Her thoughts took her back to those days.

"Then what?"

"Then Mother and Papa wanted to marry me off to a blind man."

"Blind? Are they crazy?"

"Believe me, Aunt Rachel, I didn't think about his blindness for one second. What drove me crazy was the thought of remaining orthodox. That was something I just couldn't cope with. Suddenly, the world I lived in seemed so disconnected from me, so unsuitable for me."

"And what happened to the boy?"

"My brother, Yehuda, and his gang beat him up, Papa kicked him out of the apartment, and I haven't seen him since." Her eyes filled with tears again. "And I wanted to see him so. I loved him so much...but Jeff didn't want me. ..."

"Jeff? Did you say, Jeff? God help us, what's going here? You don't want to tell me it's the same Jeff, right? Jeff Farmer?" Rachel was horrified.

"I don't know, but I think so..." Rivka said, almost soundlessly.

"God help us!" Rachel mumbled. "What kind of God is playing tricks on us?"

"You know, Aunt Rachel, when we met at the airport and I saw Amir the first time, I almost fainted. He looks so much like him that, for a minute, I thought fate had brought us together again. Now I understand why. That's why I thought it was him, Jeff. ..."

Rachel sighed. "Wondrous are the ways of fate. ..." she mumbled. "*Nu*...and do you still love him?"

"I don't know, Aunt Rachel. Even now, I don't know. I think Yoav is enough for me...although everyone says first love is special," she added sadly.

"That's true."

"How do you know, Aunt? Did you have a love like that, too?"

"Indeed, I did," Rachel sighed. "All loves are both beautiful and sad. Come sit next to me, my lovely, and I'll tell you." Rivka did as her aunt requested, sat next to her, and they hugged each other.

"Your fever's down, Aunt. I guess stories are good for you. I'll make us something to drink, and then we'll continue talking."

Rivka straightened, took a tissue, and wiped her tears. She'd regained her good mood. She decided God had saved her from a fatal mistake.

Chapter 21

Rivka was so exhausted, she almost decided to skip her shower. In the end, she took a towel and a change of lingerie, went to the shower, and with her remaining energy, forced herself to bathe. The warm water was pleasant. She swayed under the pounding water that washed every part of her body. She felt her blood accelerate in her veins and revive her. Then she soaped her entire body, first delicately, then more vigorously. Closing her eyes, she let her mind wander back to that forbidden kiss. The memory of Jeff's tongue against hers surfaced as though they'd just kissed. Its taste was so sweet that she imagined herself a bee, sucking the nectar of a flower. He'd intoxicated her to a point that he'd completely paralyzed her and befogged her senses. The sponge caressing her skin and her forbidden thoughts made her nipples hard. Forbidden lust consumed her. She dropped the sponge and recalled the moment she'd almost submitted to him and how an unknown force tore her away from him, preventing an encounter with someone who may very well be her cousin. Granted, he wasn't the only Jeff Farmer in New York, but deep inside, she knew that the man she'd fallen in love with and her new cousin were one and the same.

If so, she had to speak with Ahron as soon as possible. If Jeff was their cousin, Ahron probably already knew it. He'd already told her that they'd renewed their friendship. He also told her that he'd visited Jeff, who was the owner of a successful department store, and that he was happily married. Tomorrow, she'd call Ahron and see what was what.

The water continued running, steam filling the room, to a point that she could barely see. She breathed heavily and started thinking of Yoav and absentmindedly found herself comparing him to Jeff. Although they didn't look alike at all, she decided she'd chosen well. Yoav wasn't as beautiful and exciting as Jeff, but his pleasant face, his calm nature, his emotional fortitude, and the peacefulness he instilled in her compensated for everything. She still felt she wasn't ready for marriage. Therefore, she told him they'd get married only after her army service when she turned twenty-two. Would she be ready then? She wasn't really sure. On the other hand, Dvora, her friend from New York, had been ready enough to marry at a young age, raise children, and manage a household.

And what would happen at the wedding? She saw what had happened to Dvora. She'd been present at her friend's wedding. Only the groom's family had honored the occasion. Dvora's family had refused to attend. Both Dvora and Adam's pleas had fallen on deaf ears. As a result, she'd cut off all ties with her family and hadn't even told them about the birth of her child. Did a similar fate await Rivka?

The next evening—morning in New York—she called Ahron. They talked about this and that and, all the while, she kept expecting him to mention Jeff. When he didn't, she started talking about their grandmother, Gittel, and their Aunt Hannah, but even then, Ahron didn't say a word implying he knew anything about the matter. She started thinking her feelings had misled her and that the Jeff she knew wasn't, in fact, her second cousin. In the end, she decided to tell him everything Aunt Rachel had told her.

Ahron was shocked. He was silent for a long time, and after what seemed like an eternity, he said in a shaking voice, "Yes, it's the same Jeff. It must be. I feel it in my entire being. It also makes sense that he found Aunt Rachel through the Jewish Agency. I was the one who told him that you came to her through them. I'll call him tonight and ask him, then I'll let you know," he promised.

Ahron called the next day. Way before he'd told her what he'd found out, she'd realized Jeff was her cousin—one and the same.

"Don't ask," Ahron told her. "In order to check his reaction, I told him we'd found out Hannah had survived and immigrated to America at the end of the war. I told him she'd married and had children. When I told him Hannah had a grandson named Jeff, he confessed immediately and said he was that grandson. Then he invited me to come over. 'If you don't come over right now, I'll go crazy,' he begged. I went to him at once. When I arrived, he fell into my arms and then took out the pictures he found at his house in Eloy, pictures his mother had hidden from him all those years. When I saw the pictures, I immediately realized our grandmothers had been sisters."

"What did you see in the pictures?"

"Aunt Hannah and Aunt Rachel and Grandma Gittel. Some of the pictures were completely identical to those we had at home. Aunt Rachel probably has copies of those."

"Amazing. This is just unbelievable. How did they manage to keep hold of those pictures in the chaos surrounding them?" Rivka wondered.

"What are you talking about? Keeping hold of the pictures, that's what surprises you? The question I keep asking myself since yesterday is how Jeff and I met. Out of all the millions of people who live in the USA, how did he find me? I have no doubt that the hand of God is involved! Regarding the pictures, as far as I'm concerned, it's very simple: pictures keep, and that's that. That's what they do, right? Endure. Anyway, if it really bothers you, you can ask Aunt Rachel how she kept them."

"I will," Rivka said and started calculating, statistically, the odds of that fateful meeting between Jeff and her brother. One to three hundred million, that was the probability, the number of American residents. Maybe even less? Jeff had met Ahron by chance. He could've met Reuben, Yehuda, Rivka herself, or any of the other siblings.

"You know what surprises me about this entire matter?" Ahron cut off her calculations.

"What?" she asked when she finally reached the conclusion that the odds of this encounter were lower than the odds of winning the lottery, for example.

"When I first saw him, I felt close to him without knowing why. Now, I know that the hand of God was involved. God guided me to approach him and help him. I have to confess that I love him now, more than ever."

She loved him, too. She had no doubt about it. He'd done so much for her. Thanks to him, she was now at a place that was so good for her. But she mustn't love him like she had. She mustn't. She had to think how to untie the old knot, while tying a new one. A healthy, strong bond between relatives. A phone call wouldn't be sufficient. Therefore, she wouldn't call him. She would wait patiently to see what happened.

But barely an hour had passed, and he'd called—though he didn't call her, but her Aunt Rachel. For several long minutes, Aunt Rachel listened to him, although she understood but a little. Finally, he said, "Ms. Rachel, I'd like to visit you with my wife and sister. Is that okay?"

When she asked when they'd come, he said next month. He wanted to visit as soon as possible, as though to make up for the lost years. How could she refuse? How could she say "no" to Hannah's grandson? Of course, she couldn't. "Welcome," she said simply.

When the conversation ended, she realized that the entire time, he hadn't called her, not even once, "Aunt." When she told Rivka about that, her niece simply said, "Aunt Rachel, don't take it personally. He still hasn't accepted the fact that he has a new aunt. Give him time. It's difficult for him...just like it is for us."

The next day, her aunt started preparing for the new relatives' visit. First, she took her childhood pictures out of the attic. Then she gathered her children and grandchildren, showed them the pictures, and told them about Hannah, her big sister. In the end, she surprised them all and said Hannah's grandchildren, Jeff and Pam, would arrive for a visit in a month.

"Aunt Rachel, I have to ask," Rachel persisted. "How did you manage to keep those pictures all these years? How did you save them from destruction? And how do all of you have the exact same pictures?"

"It's very simple," her aunt explained willingly. "A few days before Papa was taken, he took pictures of all of us. He duplicated them, and each of us received copies. He told us to take good care of them because they may help us reunite at the end of the war. I had a little backpack where I saved all my documents and the pictures Papa gave me. I took good care of them all through the war. I know Gittel also managed to save them, and now I know Hannah did, too. I know that for sure. The man from the agency showed them to me. The exact same pictures I have. ..."

"If so, your father was right," Amir said, and looked at his grandmother with admiration mixed with compassion. "Because of the pictures, Hannah's grandchildren got in touch with us. If not, we wouldn't have known about her and her family."

"*Ach*," Rachel sighed. "Yes, my father was a wise man. If not for the war..." Rachel's lips started to tremble.

"Don't be sad, *Ima*. Fate summoned us a meeting with Hannah's grandchildren. I think there's a certain compensation in it," one of her daughters consoled her. And indeed, for Rachel, it was a consolation that her family couldn't even imagine.

The excitement toward the visit of the long-lost family from America was contagious and didn't skip over a single family member in Israel. The excitement grew the closer came the date of their arrival. Rivka was more excited than everyone else. Two days before they arrived, she asked for Rachel's advice. "Do you think I should come with you and Amir to the airport?"

"I don't know, child. Do what your heart tells you to do," her aunt replied, and Rivka noticed her aunt was excited and confused. So confused that the tremors in her hands returned, and with increased force. The only one who kept his cool was Amir.

"Don't you girls think you're exaggerating a bit?" he joked with them. "These things have happened. Just several months ago there was an item on the news about two sisters who survived the Holocaust and met after years of separation. From what I saw on TV, they didn't seem so enthusiastic when they finally met. ..."

Rachel stared at him in astonishment and said angrily, "You youngsters don't understand a thing!"

"I do, too," Rivka said, insulted.

"I didn't mean you, sweetheart. It's my grandson who always sees things only from his point of view and thinks he's the only one who knows everything. 'Don't talk Yiddish,' 'Don't get too excited', and all these things that only he understands, of course."

And Rivka realized that everyone was excited, and agitated, and even slightly scared by the meeting. Just…everyone was reacting in his own way. Even Amir, the eternal cynic.

A day before the guests arrived, Rachel's house was in a tizzy. The children decorated the house with balloons and colorful ribbons, prepared posters with drawings of flowers and greetings in English and Hebrew. The men traveled to the city to buy stuff, and Rachel's daughters cooked their best dishes. Even the kibbutz administration pitched in and, at Rachel's request, provided an apartment for the guests. In the evening, Rachel went to bed with a good feeling. Everything was ready for the guests from New York.

"I can't believe I'm going to meet Hannah's grandchildren," she told Amir on the way to the airport. As always, she talked in Yiddish, as though to prove to him that she had no intention of changing her ways.

"Grandma, don't get confused. They don't speak Yiddish. Don't forget they're Christians," he stated sharply.

When she got out of the car, her entire body trembled so that Amir had to hold her tightly, fearing she would fall. All his attempts to calm her failed. Through tear-filled eyes, she saw three blurry figures approaching her: a tall, painfully handsome man; a tall, beautiful, clearly pregnant woman; and a sweet, chubby young woman, with a round, childish face. The tears clogged her throat, and she couldn't even talk. The tall man was moved to tears, which made it easier for her. Hannah's grandchildren were as excited as she was. God help her make it through this meeting without collapsing, God forbid.

"Hello, Auntie," were the only words Jeff managed to get out of his mouth. Then he fell silent for a long time. Luckily, Eve and Pam filled the silence. They quickly found common ground with Rachel and Amir and a free-flowing conversation got going between the four of them. Jeff just stood there, staring at them in astonishment, at his four family members, as though from the sidelines.

For several seconds, it seemed like a delusion.

Only in the car, did he finally manage to talk. "Auntie, you look exactly like I imagined," he said, and Rachel was pleased that he was finally calling her his aunt.

"I also imagined you easily. You look just like Amir," she laughed, and her eyes twinkled when they passed between him and her grandson.

"How did you know he'd look like Amir?" Eve asked, noticing the surprising resemblance.

"Because of Rivka. When she told me about Jeff, she said he looks a lot like Amir," she explained to Eve, while examining her swollen belly.

"Rivka? Where is she? Why didn't she come?" Jeff asked, his voice strangled. He was afraid that someone would hear his heart pounding.

"She's in the army," Rachel explained immediately. "She can't go home whenever she wants. She'll go out on a short leave in the evening and come visit you. At least, that's what she promised me." But Rachel wasn't sure Rivka would arrive. She sensed her niece's many deliberations and fears.

As their visit drew closer, Rivka became more and more confused and absent-minded. She didn't say anything to Yoav apart from that she was going on leave and traveling to the kibbutz to meet a relative who'd arrived from America. When he immediately offered to join her, she didn't know what to say. She couldn't refuse, because he'd get suspicious. On the other hand, it was entirely impossible that he be present during her first meeting with Jeff after so much time had passed. She desperately regretted not traveling to the airport with her aunt and Amir. She was better off embarrassing herself in front of everyone, even in front of Jeff's wife, just not in front of Yoav. Although after he'd proposed, she'd told him she came from an ultra-orthodox home and even revealed the circumstances that forced her to leave her community. She also told him about her love for Jeff and made sure to constantly mention (even though she wasn't entirely positive about it) that it was a love long gone and that, now, he was the only one she loved. So, how could she explain to him that, now, her long-lost cousin from America was none other than that guy from Brooklyn, whom she'd told him about? He would definitely follow her reactions during the entire reunion, and if she blushed or, even worse, cried, how would he accept it? He may think, rightfully so, that she was still in love with her first love, and then what would become of their relationship? If she could prevent him from coming to their first meeting, things would calm down with time. At least, that's what she hoped. The initial excitement would pass, and then she would be able to introduce the two men.

As the hours passed, Rivka's anxiety increased. In the end, luck was on her side. An hour before they were supposed to leave for the kibbutz, Yoav came and said that, unfortunately, he wouldn't be able to join her because he was required to stay at the base because of a certain state of emergency. Rivka heaved a sigh of relief.

Wearing the light-blue uniform that flattered her so, she ran toward Jeff, and fell into his arms, burying her face in his shoulder, afraid that the others would notice her tearful face.

"Stop crying, kiddo," he said softly and nudged her back gently. "Let me take a look at you."

"Sorry, I'm so sorry," she apologized and buried her face in his shoulder again. They stood like that for long minutes, until she managed to tear herself away from him.

"You look great," he said admiringly. "I told you things would work out. Come meet my wife and sister. This is Pam, my sister, and Eve, my wife."

"Pleased to meet you," she said quietly while kissing the cheeks of the two women who'd been following her entire meeting with Jeff in bemusement and excitement.

Chapter 22

The fog covering the early morning horizon had dissipated, and the sky was clear. The sun shone brightly on the city, and visibility was so good that one could notice the flocks of birds flying among the skyscrapers. Once in a while, the birds changed direction abruptly, landing on the roof of one of the buildings, before they flew off again. Golden foliage, gloriously beautiful, started drifting off the trees, heralding the arrival of autumn. It seemed as though the pleasant weather, the bright sun, and the wonderful visibility, had lured everyone outside. Hordes of passengers filled the train stations. Yellow taxis and blue-and-white buses flooded the roads. Bridges and tunnels filled with vehicles that created heavy traffic jams at the entrance of Manhattan. Businesses had already opened their gates, and hordes of consumers were at their doors. The cafes were crowded with people who had stopped for a cup of coffee before beginning their work day. Another day had commenced in the big city.

"Can I catch a ride with you today?" Jeff asked. "My car is stuck in the shop; I'd appreciate a lift."

"Gladly, honey." Eve took one of the morning papers and sat down to read it. She browsed the papers every morning and read the financial section carefully. However, in the past months, even though the stock market was profitable again, she had become sick and tired of her job. She was nearing the end of her sixth month, her face had become round, her stomach grew, and she waddled heavily. The fact that the rest of her body had remained thin gave her an amusing look, like a clown.

"Why are you torturing yourself this way? You only have a few more days left on the job, and then it'll all be behind you," Jeff tried to cheer her up.

"I don't know. I'm so sick of work that it's become a nightmare. Every day is harder than the last." She had a hard time smiling back at him. "Why are you looking at me like that? Do you notice anything new in me?"

"Yes," he said and continued to study her tenderly.

"What?"

"You're prettier than you were yesterday."

He'd noticed for quite a while how beautiful Eve had become. Pregnancy suited her. Her face had become round and her skin tight, her skin flushed and her lips swollen and as sensual as ever. He thought her face so beautiful that he took advantage of every opportunity to press his lips to her cheek or mouth. That morning, he felt, more than ever, the profound love he felt for this woman, who sat on the chair in the kitchen, drank coffee, and read the papers. This was his woman, his love, who soon would be the mother of his children. It seemed that the more they lived together, the more he loved her. Even more than he had in the beginning. There was no doubt, ever since he'd abandoned his hometown, God had blessed him.

"I'm ready to go," Eve said after a while, collected her car keys, and waddled heavily to the elevator. Jeff rushed after her, following every step she took, worried that she'd fall.

On their way to the elevator and parking lot, they met most of their neighbors, something that had never happened before. Meeting a neighbor or two was routine. It was unusual that they'd encounter three, but that day, Jeff noticed that, strangely, they'd met almost everyone. He did a quick calculation and saw that the neighbor from the top floor and the one who lived across the hall were the only ones missing. All of them were interested in Eve's welfare and asked about her due date, and Eve had a smile for every one of them as she answered them patiently. Some of them ignored him. Even though he'd lived in the building for several years, they still considered him a passerby. But maybe it was just his imagination, and she really did attract attention because of her pregnancy.

"Way to go, my angel," he said as he sat next to her in the car.

"For what?" she asked in bemusement.

"For your amazing patience with all these people, who for some reason, all left for work at the same time. Did you notice that?"

"No. But now that you mention it, I do. ... Anyway, it's just a coincidence."

Jeff continued thinking about it, and finally reached the conclusion that Eve was right, and even if she weren't, it held no significance.

When they arrived at the department store, she kissed him and said, "Good-bye, my love."

"Good-bye, sweetheart. Call me when you get to work," he demanded, and she smiled. "And drive carefully!" he called after her when she started driving away, smiling at him mischievously.

"I'm always careful, baby. Careful is my middle name," she yelled and giggled.

Before he entered the shop, he followed her car as it drove away. To his surprise, she took the turn at a nearby street instead of driving along the avenue, as she always did on her way to work. He wondered about the strange change of course she took. Where was she going? Where was she headed, the woman who was his life's purpose, who carried his offspring in her womb? The most important thing was that she drive carefully. During her last ultrasound scan, they discovered she was carrying twins. She had to be more cautious than usual. Their doctor had said that twins were a high-risk pregnancy.

"Do you want to know the sex of your babies?" she asked.
"What do you think, Jeff, should we find out?" Eve conferred with him.

"No, let's leave it as a surprise," he replied decisively.

Thoughts about Eve and the twins were stressing him out to a point he forgot to say good morning to his employees—even the Puerto-Rican cleaner he was very fond of and made it a habit to ask after her and her children's welfare. During the holidays, he always gave her a beautiful present, as well as the bonus all the employees received, but today she was kicked rudely out of his office. The surprised cleaning lady left with her tail between her legs.

It was ten past eight. The store would open in another fifty minutes—enough time to read the paper. Occasionally, he sipped from the coffee placed on his table. Managing the store had become easier and simpler lately and, sometimes, it was downright boring. Most of the work was done by the staff and junior managers, so that he, himself, remained almost idle. Apart from the important decisions discussed in his room from time to time, and keeping track of the business's expenses, he didn't do a thing. At noon, he'd lunch with Eve or Rico. Eve loved fancy, expensive restaurants, and every time she heard about a new, recommended restaurant, he would book a place in advance to make her happy. With Rico, he liked eating at greasy workers' restaurants or crowded diners. It reminded them of their previous life as laborers. Even though they could now afford any restaurant, they stuck with street food. Twice, he'd even crossed the Brooklyn bridge and met Ahron for lunch at a kosher restaurant. These were their only meetings as cousins. Naturally, they discussed Aunt Rachel, Pam, Rivka, and the miracle that had brought them together. They reminisced about Jeff's first day in the city and, once, Jeff took advantage of the opportunity and asked Ahron what had compelled him to approach Jeff in the mini-market, and offer him help.

"The finger of God. A strange, unexplainable urge. I can't explain it. Perhaps, who knows, something about the way you looked or walked reminded me of our family."

"My laugh," Jeff joked.

"What about it?" Ahron asked in puzzlement.

"You were the one who said my laughter reminded you of Rivka's laughter," Jeff reminded him.

"Oh! You're right! On the other hand, when I approached you, you weren't laughing at all. You were down in the dumps. I think I just felt sorry for you," Ahron summarized with a smile.

Thus, Jeff found himself, for the first time, pondering the long, strange journey he'd made since leaving Eloy. In hindsight, he admitted that he'd been especially lucky. His situation couldn't have been better. Even his mother, after endless wheedling and cajoling, had agreed to leave Eloy and now lived next to him in protected accommodation. And Pam—who would've believed—had fallen under Israel's spell and made Aliyah. She was so happy there, that during their last conversation, she told him she was seriously considering studying Judaism and registering as a Jew. He remembered their visit to Israel.

"Why don't you move to Israel?" Rachel suggested, only half joking.

"I don't think so, Aunt Rachel," he declined gently.

"Why?" she insisted.

"Our livelihood is in New York," Eve answered, instead of him. "Besides, I don't understand why people would leave a safe place for a dangerous one, rife with war and terror attacks."

"She's right," Jeff agreed. "Aunt Rachel, times are different than they used to be."

"The land of Israel is the land of the Jews. This is where they should live, for better or for worse. Things aren't better in the diaspora. What, there weren't terror attacks in New York? Is there a place safe from attacks? There's no safer place for Jews than

Israel. And I know what I'm talking about," Rachel declared firmly, ignoring the fact that Eve and Jeff were Christians.

"I'm willing to seriously consider it, on condition that I find work," Pam surprised everyone by saying.

"Work? That's not a problem at all. You can work on the kibbutz. Even if you don't have a profession, you can work in the kitchen or dairy farm," Amir enthused.

"No way! I worked there, and it was awful. We have to find her a good job, a job that she can enjoy and that will support her financially," Rivka interfered.

"The question is if there's something else she knows how to do," Amir said defensively.

"I-I, ..." Pam hesitated. "I know how to ride horses."

"Great!" Amir exclaimed. "There's a ranch a half hour away by car. I'm sure if you're a good enough rider, they'll hire you."

When Pam found her place, Jeff was vastly relieved. The road to her recovery hadn't been easy, for both of them. For months, as per her doctor's instructions, he spent his weekends traveling to see her, sitting for hours by her bed, and taking care of her. Slowly, she regained her confidence; her mood improved; and finally, she started talking again. When she recovered, she came with him to New York and stayed at his place for several weeks. At the time, they'd spent a lot of time with each other, and she'd even helped him manage the store. He was so happy to see her so relaxed, focused, and full of life. When she heard about their Jewish aunt who lived in Israel, she was thrilled and asked to go visit her. Who would've believed that his Pammy now lived in Israel?

His phone rang, cutting off his thoughts. It was Eve.

"Hey, hubby," she joked.

"Hey, yourself, my love. How's work?" he asked.

"Just got here. Why do you ask?"

"No reason," he replied without adding a thing.

"You sound tense."

"Just a weird feeling. But now that you've called, I'm okay."

"Okay, love. Have a lovely day. I have to hang up. Everyone's waiting for me to start a meeting. I'll call when it's over."

"When?" he asked insistently, glancing at his watch. It was half past eight.

"About an hour, maybe a bit more."

When he ended the call, he noticed that Eve had called him from her mobile phone. Usually, she called him from the office landline. Which meant her meeting was out of the office, a meeting she hadn't told him about. He thought that strange but chose not to overthink it. Ever since they'd left home, he'd been plagued by a bad feeling and he couldn't stop worrying. Random things drew his attention and bothered him. The heavy feeling made his thoughts run wild: what would happen if she got hurt during the last months of her pregnancy? The doctor did mention something about a high-risk pregnancy. And what if something went wrong when she gave birth? This was a twin birth; no doubt it increased the risk during childbirth. And a difficult birth could risk the mother's life. …

He returned to the paper in an attempt to shove aside his negative thoughts, which Eve, the eternal optimist, couldn't abide. However, after some time, he dropped the paper uninterested. He wouldn't have felt the difference had he read yesterday's paper. All the items seemed equally boring and tedious, as though repeating themselves. When he put down the paper, he thought about his new family. His relationship with his aunt and Rivka had grown stronger. So much so, that they regularly spoke on the phone or emailed. Yesterday, Rivka wrote to him that she was getting married. When he read her email, he was happy and extremely excited. He remembered what he'd promised her then, in the basement apartment. One day, you'll realize your beauty and worth. On that day, you'll find love.

That day had arrived. Rivka was getting married. The wedding would take place next spring, which meant he and Eve would once again board an El-Al plane, and go to Israel. But by then, they'd have two little souls, two weepy toddlers. Oh, the joy! How happy he'd be to show the little ones to his new family. How happy Rachel would be that her sister Hannah had been blessed with two great-grandchildren, and soon, great-great-grandchildren. She'd told him that the family she'd raised in Israel was her revenge on the Nazis, God curse them and their memories. Now, she had gotten to know that Hannah, her beloved sister, had also had her revenge and had left her large familial mark on this world.

When he thought of Rivka's wedding, he wondered if her family would push their pride aside and arrive from Brooklyn. If so, how would they plan a wedding, in which both parties came from such different worlds? Even during their visit to Israel, they'd talked about it in detail. Rivka was afraid that her wedding would be like Dvora's wedding—that only the groom's side would attend. But Rachel assured her immediately, "Don't worry, Rivkel. Your family will arrive. There's no other option. Even if I have to fly to New York and bring them myself. They'll come to your wedding!"

Jeff opened his inbox and sent Rivka an email.

Hi, Rivka. How are you? I was happy to hear that you and Yoav were getting married. Being married is great fun. You'll find that out yourself very soon. You've made a very good choice. Yoav is a great guy. Have you told the family? If not, I'd like to tell Ahron myself. See you, Jeff.

"Good morning!" he heard Rico sing just as he shot off the email.

"Morning, Rico." He raised his head.

"What's the matter? What's having you so preoccupied?"

"Nothing special," Jeff said.

"Doesn't look that way. I heard you scolding Clara and realized you were a bit antsy this morning. Something happen?"

"Nothing. Don't be a pain in the ass. I'm a bit stressed out. I'm allowed, right?"

"Sure you are. But don't take your anger out on the cleaning lady. The poor girl came to my office in tears. She didn't understand what had happened to Mr. Jeff."

"I'm sorry. I didn't mean to hurt her feelings. I'll call her soon and apologize. Come on in, in the meantime. Why are you standing? You need something?"

"Nope. Just passing by to see if everything's okay with you. No harm, right?"

"No harm at all! Can I order you a coffee?"

"No thanks. Already had one."

"You remember Rivka?" Jeff changed the subject.

"Sure."

"Yesterday, she sent me an email telling me she was getting married."

"Great! Congratulations! You see? Things have a way of working out. I remember how worried you were about her," Rico said enthusiastically.

"You're right. Things do work out," Jeff said, but his expression remained thoughtful and worried.

"So, why do you look so bad, brother? That's not like you," Rico stated.

"I don't know. ... Something's bothering me, and I don't know what. Did that ever happen to you, that something bothered you, and you didn't know what?"

"Sure."

"I've had a bad feeling since this morning. A heaviness. I can't explain it. A feeling that something bad is going to happen...."

"Let's try to find out what's bothering you, brother. Your mother is safe, your sister is happy, your wife is about to give birth to twins. You've found your lost family, you've built a glorious business, and, now, Rivka is getting married.... All you need now is to win the lottery!" Rico guffawed, causing Jeff to smile for the first time that morning.

"If I win the lottery, I promise you a fair share," Jeff promised.

"But, boss, you don't buy lottery tickets…so a fair share of nothing is nothing." Rico laughed again.

"What are you talking about?" Jeff huffed. "I bought a ticket a month ago, and you know—"

Jeff never finished the sentence. Deafening explosions, the likes of which he'd never heard, cut him off. The earth shook beneath their feet. They had no doubt that the explosions and thundering noise came from nearby. The employees of the store, which hadn't opened yet, immediately ran out to the street. Rico and Jeff also leaped up and frantically ran outside. The streets were already swarming with frightened people. Jeff surveyed the sidewalk at length but didn't notice anything that indicated something had happened.

"Here, it's there, look!" someone yelled, pointing at the sky.

Thick, black smoke billowed toward the sky.

"Where is it?" someone else asked.

"I think it's the World Trade Center!"

Thick, black smoke rose from the Twin Towers. From every direction, they heard the wailing of the rescue vehicle sirens, which had started rushing toward the buildings. Something terrible had happened. But what…

"It's already on the news!" yelled one of the cashiers, and all of the employees rushed back to the store. They couldn't believe their eyes. A passenger plane had flown straight into one of the buildings, crashing into it and splitting it in two. A huge flame burst from the building. The plane smashed to pieces, and its fragments, which flew in every direction, looked like gigantic fireworks. Looking at the footage, which was broadcasted repeatedly, it didn't look like an accident, but a plane aimed at the heart of the building.

"This can't be," Jeff whispered, his face as white as a ghost's. He had to call Eve, he had to call Eve. …

"This is crazy!" Rico exclaimed in panic.

All of the employees panicked. One employee started screaming and crying, and when she finally fell silent, she started trembling.

"Calm down, there's nothing to be afraid of. We're far away from there," Rico tried to reassure her.

"My brother, my brother's there," her voice shook. "My brother works there, in the building that was hit."

"Rico, calm her down, and then send everyone home. There's no point in them staying here. I don't think we'll be able to open the shop today," Jeff instructed with what little strength he had left.

Several minutes passed, and only the explosions echoing from the television broke the silence in the empty store. Jeff tried to call Eve. There was no answer at her office. He tried her cellphone but kept getting voicemail.

"Don't stress, brother," Rico tried to calm him. "All the communication systems must've collapsed. Don't go putting crazy stuff in your head. Eve works far away from the towers. I don't think you have any reason to worry."

"But she's not at the office," Jeff replied, choking up. "In the morning, when she dropped me off, she turned at 47th Street, which means she didn't go to the office. Then she called me from her cell phone. When she's in the office, she always calls from her landline."

"That still doesn't mean anything. I think you're stressing yourself over nothing. Everything's such a mess now, and everyone probably left their offices to see what happened. She must be down somewhere. She probably forgot to grab her phone, from the shock."

"If you had to drive from here to the World Trade Center, where would you turn?" Jeff inquired.

"I don't know," Rico answered, although he knew that he'd probably turn where Eve had turned.

"I'd take 47th Street," Jeff thought out loud. Then he added, "I think I'll go to her. I have to know she's okay."

"Are you crazy? The streets are jammed with rescue vehicles. You'll just bother them. It'll take you hours to get to her."

"Take me as far as you can, and I'll walk from there," Jeff ordered, and Rico was left with no other choice.

In the end, the drive to Eve's office took only minutes. But it seemed like an eternity to Jeff. The roads were empty. It seemed as though traffic had frozen in place.

When they arrived, Rico stopped with a screech of brakes at the building's entrance. Jeff ran out of the car, ignoring the security officer's protests. He entered the elevator panting. When the elevator reached the sixty-second floor, he discovered all the employees in the hallway, watching the impending drama on the television. Among them, he found Jessica.

"Where's Eve?" he asked.

"I…don't know," she stammered.

"What do you mean, you don't know? You're her secretary, aren't you?" Jeff grasped her shoulders and shook her.

"She had a meeting out of the office this morning, and hasn't arrived since…" The secretary's body trembled.

"Where was the meeting?"

"At the Twin Towers…" she mumbled in terror, her face white as a ghost's.

Chapter 23

A freezing autumn wind whispered against the silence of the cemetery, carrying dry leaves to the mute headstones. The whisper of the wind sounded like silent weeping, as though wishing to share the sorrow of the mourners in the funeral process, who, like the wind, wept. When they gathered and stood as one over the open grave, the weeping stopped and the eulogy began.

"Don't cry for me, don't cry. No more tears! Why cry? Why shed even one tear if I was happy in my life and peaceful in my death? I know you stand, surrounding me and wondering, how? How is it possible that after what I've been through, I use the words 'happy and peaceful'? Indeed, you're right! There's room for your question.

"I had a life filled with ups and downs. Bad people, people of injustice, threatened to cut them off at their start. They set a large fire, and it threatened to consume everything. The flame didn't skip almost anyone. Big and small, man and woman, the fire wished to burn them all in its flames. True, I was fortunate and didn't have to witness the horrors that occurred in the camps. Nevertheless, I carry within me the sights of black smoke rising above, and, with it, rise the broken screams of my family. I've kept in my heart the sight of the tortured faces of those burned at the stake. They've followed me everywhere I went, and every minute of the day. At night, when I rested my head on my pillow, in the morning, when I opened my eyes.

"Indeed, those days were filled with sorrow. Indescribable sorrow was my lot in life, and yet, at the end of the day, my life has been a good one. Fate, surprisingly, was kind to me. It plucked me out of the valley of death and gave me a lively family life—many children and grandchildren. God sent me a gentile woman, a Polish peasant, who in her mercy, saved me from the devil's butcher knife and gave me my life back. Then, fate came and surprised me again, when it sent to my home two charming, lovely girls, the daughters of my sisters, Gittel and Hannah. They didn't come alone but were accompanied by an angel, an angel who saved me from the agonizing yearning for my sister.

"I will shamelessly admit, Jeff, that when the man from the agency came, I was confused. I didn't know whether it was good or bad. Yet, when I first saw you, my heart sang. It was as though I'd met my sister herself.

"Now, as you all stand united, my soul is calm. Because what more can a person ask for? Indeed, my life has been good, and I have no complaints. But even good things, especially good things, must end. I feel my time approaching, the hourglass running out of time. I feel, with all my heart and soul, the moment of truth approaching. In several days, or weeks, or months, I will follow the path of man, and I will do so gladly. So, don't cry for me, because I've been happy in my life and peaceful in my death. Yours with love, Rachel."

Amir put down the page he was reading from and took a deep breath. The emotion was evident in his face. In a moment, he'd start sobbing, but he screwed up his face with all his might and kept the tears in check. He wanted to fulfill his grandmother's instructions to the T. Rivka, who stood facing him, could no longer handle it. She laid her head on Yoav's shoulder and wept silently. Pam, who stood on the other side of Yoav, started crying, too, even though she didn't understand what Amir had read. She'd also become very attached to the kind old lady.

"No wonder Grandma asked us not to cry," Amir continued, while sending the two of them a semi-rebuking look. "She was an amazing woman. Somehow, she'd given me this letter sealed in the envelope, and asked me to read it after she died. I knew she'd ask us not to be too sorry for her. That's how Grandma was. She always wanted to make us happy. Now, even though only several hours have passed since she died, I already miss her. I'll miss our heart-to-hearts, our traveling together, I'll even miss the Yiddish, which really annoyed me."

Amir smiled, and the rest of them smiled with him. After a short pause, he added, while looking directly at the small body wrapped in a sheet laid before him, "Yes, Grandma, we'll miss you terribly. May you rest in peace."

Amir finished his eulogy and got off the little podium. Slowly, he walked back until he took his place at his mother's side, who rushed to hug and kiss him. After the short funeral procession, Rachel was buried in the small kibbutz cemetery. Her children said kaddish, and then the quiet funeral ended.

Rachel returned to her fathers. She died of natural causes. On Thursday, she went to sleep and didn't wake up the next day. Every morning, a member of the family would accompany her to the dining room. On Friday, Osnat, Amir's younger sister, came to her house and found her dead. The doctor who was summoned immediately pronounced her dead.

"At night, when she slept, her heart stopped beating," he stated assuredly.

The minute she was notified of Rachel's death, Rivka hurried to notify Ahron and Jeff, despite the late hour in New York.

"God gives, and God takes. Let the name of the Lord be praised, both now and forevermore," Ahron murmured after he heard the news. Ahron wasn't too sad. Not that he didn't love the aunt from Israel, God forbid, on the contrary. However, the way he saw it, his aunt had passed from an empty, unimportant world to a world full of good.

On the other hand, the sad news hit Jeff hard. A heavy sadness descended upon him. During the days they spent together, a special bond formed between him and his young-at-heart aunt. The bond had grown stronger, and the two would talk on the phone almost every day, as though they were lovers. He felt that Rachel was the perfect grandmother and mother figure, which were so missing in his life. The minute he returned to New York after visiting her, he started planning his next visit. He would've found the time to go visit her again, but Eve's advanced pregnancy cut the plan short. Now that he heard of her death, he had a difficult time coming to terms with the fact that he wouldn't see her again.

But that wasn't the only reason her death had landed on him out of the blue. The terrible attacks of 9/11 and the ordeal he suffered after them, had made him more vulnerable and fragile than ever. Jeff would never forget the terror of those days until the day he died. He recalled the terror that gripped him when Jessica told him that Eve had attended a meeting at the Twin Towers. Before he'd discovered what had happened to her, he felt the loneliness, the yawning abyss that had opened it jaws, threatening to suck him in. He realized the chances of Eve escaping the inferno were slight.

"Where exactly was the meeting? Tell me!" he urged Jessica, trying to grasp at straws of hope.

"The meeting was in the north building, at the Hodgson's law firm. The firm is on the twenty-first floor," she said, following his expression worriedly.

"And the building hit was the north one, right?" Jeff tried to reconstruct in his mind the sights broadcast over and over again on television.

"What, didn't you know?" she asked in surprise and stopped crying.

"What?"

"The south building was also hit. Ten minutes ago, another plane hit it, and they said on the news that another plane hit the Pentagon."

"Then, the first building hit was the north one, and then the south?" Jeff wanted to be sure of the information.

"Yes." She nodded and looked at him in terror.

"God save us!" Jeff buried his face in his hands. "The twenty-first floor," he mumbled, calculating that if the plane hit the higher stories, there was a chance that the people in the lower ones could escape without a scratch. Ten minutes had passed between one attack and the next, enough time to get out of the building and run far away, without the fragments of the second plane hitting the fleeing people. Was it possible that Eve had survived the inferno and escaped the building? If so, how could she have escaped while so heavily pregnant? And even if she had escaped from the burning building, had she emerged unscathed? Did the toxic black smoke, which must have spread through the entire building, reach her lungs and cause damage to her or one of the babies?

"I have to find out what happened to her," Jeff said.

"How are you going to do that?" Jessica posed the difficult question.

"I'll try to go wherever I can. I'll search the hospitals. Whatever it takes. I can't just sit around doing nothing," he explained and turned to go.

"I'm coming with you," Jessica stated, grabbing her bag and following him hurriedly.

For hours, Jeff, Rico, and Jessica searched the streets of New York for Eve. First, they tried to get close to the buildings, but the rescue forces spread in a wide radius around the area prevented them from doing so.

"It's too dangerous to go close. The buildings are burning, and we're afraid they'll collapse," one of the police officers explained to him. No more than several minutes passed when they realized the man had been right.

The buildings collapsed as though they were a tower of cards. Like a volcano vomiting its loathsome content, the building spat humongous clouds of dust, containing stones, metal rods, various objects, dirt, and black toxic ash. When the deadly mass met the ground, tsunamis of destruction rose from the street, as though they were a fountain, and rose to a tremendous height, then fell with a deafening crash, and galloped in dizzying speed along adjacent streets, destroying in their rage everything in their way. Panicked people fled frantically in an attempt to escape the dust tsunamis chasing them, and when they realized they wouldn't be able to escape, they found shelter in houses and behind trees and parked cars. It didn't help some of them. The enormous gusts of dust reached the hiding places; trees were uprooted; and cars, with their passengers, were lifted in the air as though they were nothing more than pieces of paper.

Even though the three of them were very far from the towers, one of those clouds reached them. Luckily, it lost momentum and sank slowly, covering their bodies with a thick layer of dust that made it difficult for them to see and breathe.

"Let's get out of here quickly!" Rico yelled. The dust that infiltrated his mouth choked him, and he started coughing. Jessica also started coughing incessantly, and Jeff hurried to cover her face with a handkerchief in order to ease her breathing.

After despairing from searching the vicinity of the towers, they went to the information center set up in the municipality offices but had to admit defeat as the place was full of hysterical crowds. They started scanning the hospitals to which the casualties were admitted, but there also, their searches were in vain. In most of the hospitals, there was utter confusion and chaos, to a point that they couldn't even reach those injured or find out their names. As they searched, Jeff tried calling Eve's cell phone again and again, but in vain. No sign of life came from Eve. The only phone call he made that day was to Eve's worried parents, and he managed to talk to them only after calling them repeatedly. He updated them lengthily regarding the day's events. Eve's frantic father promised to do everything he could to find out what had happened to his daughter.

"Update me regarding any development whatsoever. Don't hesitate to call me at any hour," he demanded of Jeff just before they ended the conversation.

Evening fell on an exhausted New York, which was suddenly empty of people. The stunned residents that had filled the streets only hours before started to slowly absorb the events of that horrible day. They went home and left the huge streets orphaned. The few that still remained outside were relatives of the people missing, who continued frantically searching the many hospitals, vacillating between hope and despair. The rescue vehicles that tirelessly continued with their rescue attempts, continued driving along the abandoned streets. Their sirens were a shrill testament to the terrible tragedy that landed suddenly on the effervescent city. New York held its tongue and carried its pain with a dignified silence.

Jeff, Jessica, and Rico sat on a bench at the exit of one of the hospitals. Grief and destruction overwhelmed them, and they sat there, unable to talk or move, for a long time.

"She was right," Jeff broke the silence.

"Who?" Rico asked.

"My aunt."

"Your aunt?" Rico tried to understand.

"Yes! My aunt was right! We argued where it was safer to live, in Israel or in New York. Eve and I said Israel was a dangerous place to live in because of the wars and terror attacks there. She claimed that there was no safer place in the world, and certainly not New York. How right she was. She must be watching television now; she probably can't believe her eyes. She's probably trying to call us and going crazy with worry."

Jessica and Rico nodded in agreement. Silence fell again.

"Maybe she got home by herself?" This time, Rico was the first to break the silence.

"She would've called me," Jeff dismissed the idea.

"Not necessarily! It's been hard to get a signal since the attack this morning. Did you see how long it took you to contact Eve's parents? Let's go there, Jeff. Don't bar the possibility. We have to try everything," Jessica cajoled.

With no other option, the three of them drove to Jeff's apartment.

"No! I haven't seen her since you left this morning," the doorman replied when Jeff questioned him as to whether he'd seen Eve.

"Let's go upstairs anyway. We'll have a cup of coffee, regroup, and head out to continue searching," Jeff said.

When they entered the apartment, Rico's phone rang, and the three of them jumped.

"It's my wife," Rico said before he answered.

"That means communication is returning. We should try calling her again," Jessica suggested.

With a shaking hand, Jeff took the phone and tried his luck again, but to his disappointment, all he got was voicemail again.

"Damn! Who invented that crazy voicemail! I hear her voice, and I don't even know if she's alive!"

"Jeff, calm down!" Rico demanded after he finished soothing his panicked wife.

"Rico, it's been eight hours since the attack. It's already dark outside. If nothing bad did happen to her, where is she? And why the hell doesn't she call?" Jeff insisted angrily.

"Unfortunately, I don't have a clear-cut answer. There are a lot of possibilities. Let's just wait patiently. I'm sure we'll find out during the course of the night. Someone will call or come over," Rico said, confident that the mystery would soon be solved.

"Yeah. Someone will call and say, are you Jeff? We found your wife. Dead," Jeff said pessimistically.

"On the contrary! My logic says that every phone call that has anything to do with her will be positive. I don't think that if something, God forbid, happened to her, someone will be able to find her in the rubble, call here, and announce that she's no longer alive. Don't forget that she doesn't work in the World Trade Center, and apart from the fact that we passed her name on to the information center, no one knows about her presence there. If someone does call, it will only be her. Wait a bit, and you'll see that I'm right."

"Your analysis is logical, although there's no certainty that this is how things are. Let's assume she left the building, inhaled smoke, and died. According to what we saw, a lot of bodies were taken out of the building, and their families were notified. I wish someone would call. At least then, we'd know where things stand. The uncertainty is driving me crazy!' Jeff said in frustration.

"Try your mail! Maybe there's a message waiting for you there! Maybe she couldn't call and sent you an email," Jessica raised an assumption that sounded logical to Jeff. He ran to the computer in the home office, and to his surprise, discovered the inbox contained numerous mail. He scanned them all but was disappointed to see that they didn't shed any light on the mystery. He chose to ignore them, apart from a mail from Rivka in which she asked if everything was okay. "No, things are not okay," he wrote back. "Eve is missing since this morning. We're still looking for her."

After that, they returned to the living room.

"Maybe I'll make you something to eat? You haven't eaten since this morning," Jessica suggested in an attempt to ease the dark atmosphere.

"I'm not hungry. You can make something for yourself and for Rico. I'm good with a cup of coffee. I have a feeling we're in for a sleepless night," Jeff said, and Jessica rushed to the kitchen to do his bidding. Several minutes later, she returned with a tray with three cups of coffee.

"Let's think logically," Rico tried to put matters in order as he took a cup of coffee and sat in the armchair in the living room. "Eve was on the twenty-first floor of the north tower, right? From what we saw on television, the damage was to the top stories, maybe sixty floors above, and that's quite a distance, isn't it?"

"It is," Jessica agreed, as Jeff followed with interest what Rico was saying, as though the man held the power to change reality.

"So, that means that when the building collapsed, it's obvious that she wasn't hurt. Is that right?"

"Right!" Jessica confirmed again.

"This means that she had to walk down twenty-two floors, using the stairs, not a simple feat for a pregnant woman, but definitely possible. I think she needed something like ten to fifteen seconds for each floor. Which means that after four to five minutes, she should've been outside. The rescue forces outside probably—" The phone rang, cutting off his calculations.

"Now, we'll know if you're right," Jeff said as he leaped up and hurried to answer the phone.

"Jeff, what's going on? We've been trying to call for hours. Anything new?" Eve's father asked worriedly.

"I'm sorry! I've been out searching for her all day long. I'm losing it. I don't know what to do," Jeff replied, disappointed by the caller's identity.

"Stay at home. There's no point in you running around the streets. We're on our way."

"Okay." Jeff ended the call.

"Continue, Rico," Jessica prompted.

"Before you continue, I think you're wrong about the time required to go down the stairs and go out. Don't forget that the conditions weren't normal. Maybe it was dark? Maybe the stairwells were dark? We have to take into account that Eve is in an advanced stage of her pregnancy," Jeff corrected Rico's calculations.

"Okay, so not five minutes. Let's assume that she needed double that time. When she came out, she saw the rescue forces waiting outside and probably—" The phone rang again, cutting Rico off at the exact same sentence. Jeff ran to the phone, which had become so important that day.

"Am I speaking with Jeff Farmer?" a feminine voice was heard on the other end of the line.

"Yes, that's me," Jeff replied, his heart pounding hard. The voice was an unfamiliar one, a voice he hadn't heard in his life. His body turned cold, and his heart continued pounding. Deep inside, he felt the conversation would determine Eve's fate, for good or for bad. Was Rico right? Would this be the call notifying him whether Eve was alive, or was Rico wrong?

Life holds in store many surprises. In the unknown future, there are many mysteries, and no one knows what the day will bring. This is the secret of life. Every second may bring a knock on the door or a phone call, bringing news. Sometimes, that news will be good, bringing someone joy, and sometimes, it will be bad, bringing someone sadness. As was the news Rivka told him when she told him his beloved aunt had died.

Chapter 24

The band stopped playing, its musicians remained standing, helpless and embarrassed at the sight of the empty dance floor. The Hebrew songs they sang did create a pleasant atmosphere, but it wasn't enough to rouse the guests who remained sitting in place. A somewhat sleepy atmosphere had taken over the large venue, and Rivka was well aware of it. The profound feeling of disappointment was evident on her sad face. She felt as though she'd burst into tears in a minute. This wasn't how she wanted her wedding to look. It was only expected, she thought to herself sorrowfully. A celebration in which such an assortment of people participated, from such different worlds, was bound to fail. The profound fears experienced by her and Yoav—during the eve of the wedding and during the wedding itself—regarding the success of the party were realizing themselves before her eyes.

"I don't believe your brother's suggestion will succeed," Yoav expressed his fears one day before the wedding.

"So, what should we do?" she asked.

"There's nothing we can do. It's enough that we're getting married," he replied with a forced smile and kissed her forehead.

"From the day we announced we were getting married, nothing has gone to plan," she complained.

Indeed, they came across difficult obstacles until they found themselves beneath the wedding canopy. The wedding's troubles started months before when her family refused to come.

"I don't even understand why we're discussing this. No one's going to that heretic's wedding, no matter what," Yehuda, head of the opposition, presented a tough stance.

"You're right, brother," Margalit supported him as usual.

"If the wedding takes place according to our rules, I think we should participate," said Rueven, head of the doubters, which was the largest camp, and included Rivka's parents.

"We'll go, even if we're the only ones who will," declared Ahron and Miriam, who at that stage, were the only ones supporting unconditional participation in the wedding.

Ever since Rivka had left, the two had become much more tolerant. They started seeing the secular world in a different light. Newspapers, books, and computers were no longer considered bad words. As far as they were concerned, Rivka could celebrate her wedding any way she chose to, on the condition that the food served would be of kosher authorization that suited their faith. Ahron presented their stand before his father daily when they met at the mini-market.

"This is your daughter's wedding, your own flesh and bone. There's no sin in that she chose to live her life differently than ours. Millions of Jews live that way, and they're still Jews, like you and me. Would it have been better to marry her off to an insane or blind man? It's time to forgive her, and nothing would make her happier than seeing us at her wedding," he reprimanded his father.

"If we participate in the wedding, many family members will follow us. And if that's how things will happen, it's our duty to make sure the wedding happens according to our acceptable rules so, God forbid, we won't sin or cause sin."

"Papa, you're right! You're one hundred percent right! Call her yourself and tell her we're prepared to come en masse and ask her to consider our guests and us. Tell her that many will make the long journey in order to attend the wedding, and she has to consider that and have a wedding as customary in our community," agreed Ahron, who, at this stage, found it important that his father give his principal agreement.

"And if she won't agree?" his father insisted nevertheless.

"I think she will. I don't believe she'll pile on difficulties and prevent us from coming. During her conversations with me, she already agreed to serve food approved as *kosher lemehadrin*. First, you must tell her we want to come. Then we'll see how things go from there," Ahron urged his father.

And that was how the difficult argument between the two camps was decided. Ahron's persuasion worked, and his parents gave in and decided to be present at their daughter's wedding.

"I think that in this case, we have to go," Yehuda said bitterly when he heard of his parents' decision. However, he was forced, like the rest of the family, to accept the "verdict" and join their flight to the land of "heretics".

"Honoring your father and mother is the most important commandment. If your parents are going, you must put their desires before your own," was the opinion of the rabbi of the yeshiva, to whom Yehuda had gone for advice.

When one argument ended, another began. Rivka's parents conditioned their arrival on being allowed to celebrate according to their ways and faith. To do so, they even agreed to fund all of the wedding's expenses.

"We'll pay for everything, as long as the wedding will go according to our community's customs," Rivka's parents told her.

"I don't know," Rivka hesitated. "I'm not sure Yoav's family will agree."

"Try, daughter, try," her mother cajoled her.

And, indeed, Rivka did try. When she told Yoav's family that her parents wanted the wedding to be an ultra-orthodox one, they didn't understand.

"What exactly do your parents want?" they asked in bemusement.

"They want the food to be *kosher lemehadrin*, and they want the band to play and sing Hasidic music, and they want complete separation between men and women," Rivka specified her parents' demands.

"And you agreed?" Yoav's parents asked in shock. Rivka's parents' last demand made them very angry.

"I don't know anymore. I'm confused," Rivka replied.

A grave dispute broke out between the two sides, to a point that the wedding party was in jeopardy. Many arguments and discussions took place between the two families. Yoav's family insisted the wedding be a secular one and refused to hear of a wedding according to Rivka's parents' demands. As far as they were concerned, the main difficulty had to do with the music for the guests and how to distribute seating places in the hall. Regarding the food, they agreed the food be *kosher lemehadrin*, which wouldn't hurt the secular guests.

During those days of dispute, Rivka and Yoav found themselves between a rock and a hard place. On the one hand, they wanted to please Rivka's family so they'd come to the wedding, yet on the other hand, they couldn't ignore the desires of the other family members. They suffered many sleepless nights. Rivka daily called Ahron to tell him of their ordeals. Ahron rushed again to his parents.

"Because of all these unbridgeable disputes, you won't be present at your daughter's wedding. What does it matter what the band will play? If you don't like the music, we can always ask them to stop. Rivka promised that the band will sing only Hebrew songs. It's enough that we have kosher food and side tables, far away from wanton licentiousness, which I'm not even sure there will be. I have no doubt that with a little good will, we can reach an agreement," he urged them.

"We have a powerful desire to compromise. Convince them that at least men and women will be separated. This is crucial to us. This is, after all, the world into which Rivka was born. They shouldn't deny the bride's past," Yehudit claimed.

"You're right, Mother. I'm convinced that if matters depended only on Yoav, things would be easier. But don't forget he has a large family behind him, and a secular one. And if one agrees, there's always someone else who won't. There's nothing you can do about that! They have their wishes, too, and we have to consider them, as well," he said, reminding her that there was a second party participating in the wedding.

"They should also consider our feelings. What are we asking for? Small, inconsequential things. What's so terrible about splitting the venue in two, so men and women won't mix, huh?" Moishel insisted stubbornly.

"We have our logic, they have theirs. What we consider simple and logical, they consider complicated and complex, and vice versa. Believe me, they're not stupid. And anyway, I've heard people say that Yoav is a marvelous guy. A combat pilot in the Israeli Air Force. People in the know claim that these are the best men you can find. You understand that your son-in-law is one of the best?" Ahron tried another tactic.

"Yes, I have heard that they're good men," Moishel said, without bothering to hide the pride in his voice.

"And a combat pilot; isn't that dangerous?" Yehudit asked, worry for her future son-in-law creeping into her voice.

"Very dangerous. You know, Mother, that there are many wars in Israel. Combat pilots are the elite of the fighters. A combat soldier's life is always in danger. But don't you worry, Mother, God will save," Ahron continued praising Yoav.

"Then we'll go, son. You make sure that the wedding is balanced and modest," Yehudit consented. She hurriedly took a napkin and wiped tears of happiness from her eyes.

"Do whatever you can for the benefit of the matter, son, and God help you. And regarding expenses, tell Rivka we'll pay to the last cent," Moishel gave his blessing to the matter.

Thus, after a continuous process of persuasion of both sides, it was decided to accept the compromise, which Ahron and Miriam had toiled on together, which was that the band would play and sing at the beginning of the evening Hebrew songs, and end the evening with Hasidic songs. Regarding the guests, it was agreed that the hall be divided to three. The secular guests would sit in one half, men and women both, while in the other half, the Hasidic guests would sit. That half would also be divided in two, so that men and women, God forbid, wouldn't mix. In the beginning, when the conciliatory suggestion was accepted, Rivka's happiness knew no bounds. But the more she thought about it, the more she feared the emotionally loaded meeting between the two families would end in failure.

Thus, after a long, tedious ordeal, the family gathered and came en masse from New York, Jerusalem, and Bnei-Brak.

The wedding ceremony was actually successful. The rabbi who wed them did it wisely. When he saw his crowd, he asked the women first to sit on one side of the wedding canopy, and the men to sit on the other side. "Like they do in choirs when women sing on one side, and men pitch in from the other side," he joked. Then he spiced up his blessing with various quips to amuse the guests. When he finished blessing a Sephardi blessing, he immediately started an Ashkenazi blessing, and everyone was ecstatic. Finally, Yoav broke the glass to the sound of the guests' joyful cheering, and it seemed like things were working out in the best possible way. However, then the guests sat in their allotted seats, the band started playing Hebrew songs, and it seemed that they weren't lively enough to rouse the guests. Although some of the guests tried to sing along to the Hebrew songs, they were few, and their voices were swallowed in the noise and din of the other guests, who didn't stop chatting. With nothing in common among the guests, the dance floors remained empty. Minutes passed until they totaled up to an hour and not a soul ventured to the dance floor.

Things were so bad that it looked as though in another minute, the guests would disappear home, and the wedding, which so much work and thought had been invested in, would end prematurely. Sorrowfully, Rivka straightened in her seat and gathered her modest wedding dress, which had been made especially for her.

"I can't sit here any longer," she told Yoav and slowly walked to the women's section at the orthodox side.

There, a surprise waited for her. A bunch of women and girls gathered and welcomed her singing and dancing. The musicians pounced on the opportunity and started playing a series of Hasidic songs. The orthodox men swarmed to the dance floor and burst into a wild dance. The orthodox women and girls on the other half of the hall didn't sit around twiddling their thumbs and starting pumping up the beat. The young, secular friends cautiously approached the dance floor and watched the dancing orthodox men. After several minutes, they invaded the dance floor as well, joining the festivities as though they were born and bred Hasidim. The dancing became wilder and wilder as the evening drew on.

"Hay, hay, hay, hay, hay, hay," the band sang loudly.

It wasn't long before all the guests, women on one side, men on the other, secular and orthodox, jumped and danced in abandon. The previously occupied chairs were empty, and the dance floor became too crowded to contain everyone. The revelry swept away every single man and woman. Joy was so abundant that nobody cared any longer what sect others belonged to; everyone danced as one. When she saw the unexpected burst of joy, Rivka's happiness knew no bounds and tears of delight washed her face.

That's how they celebrated their wedding, Yoav on one side of the hall, Rivka on the other. Celebrations continued almost until dawn break. They would never forget the happiness of their wedding.

Among the dancers, were Jeff and Ahron. Like the others, they were swept away by the happiness, frolicking enthusiastically and tirelessly. When Jeff wanted to rest, he was immediately dragged again to the dance floor. His body dripped sweat, and he panted as though he'd just finished running a marathon. In the end, he broke away from the dancers and sat, exhausted, in one of the chairs next to the dance floor. After a long rest, he got up and approached the screen that separated the women from the men. He peeked at the women's side and then at the bride. She was sitting in a chair, women, from young to old, dancing around her. She was like a beauty queen. Her modern dress was tasteful, her hairdo and makeup intensified her beauty, and she stood out against all the rest of the women. Occasionally, one of the women would approach her and give her a juicy kiss on her cheek. Rivka looked happy.

Jeff took his eyes off Rivka and looked at Pam. Suddenly, his sister also looked like a handsome woman. She was still short and stout, but her skin had become tanned and smooth, making her look different, better. For the wedding, she bought a special dress that suited her body. Her special makeup and hairdo did wonders for her new look. And, perhaps, it wasn't the external things that did wonders for her. Since she'd arrived in Israel, she'd been happy, and lately, more than ever. Her self-confidence improved amazingly, especially ever she'd established her status at work and after meeting her boyfriend. Pam, like everyone else, jumped and danced. Judging by the expression on her face, there was no doubt she was on top of the world. This made Jeff sorry his mother wasn't here to see it. He offered to bring her to Israel with him, but she refused, and he didn't push too much.

Next to Pam, Eve whirled around dancing. Unlike the other women, her movements were somewhat reserved, as though she was a woman of nobility. Yes, Eve was also at Yoav's and Rivka's wedding. She'd survived the inferno. Miraculously. When he looked at her, he remembered the terror of that day. His heart raced. Even now, as she danced before him, hale and healthy, he felt agitated. Jeff removed himself from the noise and ruckus of the wedding and allowed his imagination to take him back to that day, September 11, 2001. He remembered the nurse's voice on the phone, notifying him that his wife was fine, and she was in the hospital. Jeff was so confused he couldn't understand why she was hospitalized if she was healthy. When he asked the nurse, she explained that Eve had been brought to the hospital unconscious.

"She suffered from smoke inhalation and lost consciousness. When she arrived here, we conducted a battery of tests—she's fine. So are the fetuses in her womb. She's awake now but in shock. Don't worry, Mr. Farmer, a few more hours of rest, and she'll be good as new," the nurse assured him.

When Jeff realized Eve was alive and that their babies were alive and kicking, he jumped for joy, and so did Jessica and Rico. They immediately drove to the hospital and stormed her bed. And then Jeff saw her white, frightened face, her bruised body that couldn't stop shivering. For hours, she stared at them without saying a word. The three of them and her parents, who'd arrived in the meantime, couldn't get her to talk. Then she fell asleep. Exhaustion and sleeping pills did the job, and she fell into a deep sleep. Jeff was so worried, he ran to ask a doctor what was happening.

"Your wife went through a very tough experience. She's reacting in a completely normal manner. Don't worry too much. Sit next to her. Support her and she'll be fine," the doctor assured him.

Jeff did as the doctor ordered. He remained sitting next to her the entire night, stroking her head, kissing her, and following her breathing alertly. In the morning, she opened her eyes, and when she saw him, she whispered as she did every morning, "Good morning, my love," and he jumped from his place, held her tightly, and couldn't stop kissing her.

"Good morning, love," he replied.

When the nurse came, he remembered to ask her why she hadn't called him before, why she'd left him so helpless, tortured with worry, for such a long time.

"When your wife arrived here, we obviously didn't know who she was. She had no documents. Her handbag must've remained there. First of all, we had to put her through a battery of tests to make sure she was okay. There was chaos here. Many nameless casualties were taken first to triage. It was crucial to treat them first, and only then, start clarifying and cross-checking with the information center. In your wife's case, we had no choice but wait for her to wake up. When she did, she was so frightened she couldn't talk. It was only after several hours that she took a piece of paper and wrote your name and number on it," the nurse solved his mystery.

Eve was released that same day. Although she was still in shock, she was in good enough condition to recuperate at home.

Family and friends heard about the miracle and came to visit. Even Miriam, Ahron, and his parents left the stronghold of Brooklyn in order to visit Eve in Manhattan. Still shaky, she told her many visitors the story in a quiet voice.

"We were in a meeting, and everyone was in high spirits. The subject of the meeting was a merger between two large companies. One of the company's shares were traded in the stock market. The atmosphere was pleasant and quiet. The conference room was located on the east side, so the rays of the sun shone inside, and it was very pleasant. One of the lawyer's told a joke, and we all laughed. We were joking quite a lot. Then the lawyers started laughing at their boss, who was supposed to arrive and start the meeting.

"When I saw that he was delayed, I went outside for a minute and called Jeff. When I returned to the room, the phone fell from my hand and the battery disconnected from the phone. I thought to myself that I had to turn off the phone anyway so it wouldn't disrupt the meeting, so I put it in my bag without putting the battery back in place and sat in my chair. One of the secretaries served drinks, and everything looked fine. In the meantime, the boss arrived, and everyone was silent.

"Suddenly, before we even started discussing the merger, we heard loud noises coming from above. The noises grew louder until we heard a horrible crash and the building started shaking. We didn't understand what was happening. Someone went out to the hallway to check, but then he came back and said he didn't see a thing. He said that everything looked fine.

"We wanted to continue, but the explosions continued. I started getting really scared. I suggested we cut the meeting short and disperse. I felt as though something bad had happened. Their boss refused. He said he didn't think it was anything serious. Suddenly, someone rushed into the room in a panic and said there had been an explosion in the building, and that there was a fire raging on the top floors. The minute he mentioned the word fire, no one cared about the boss anymore. We all ran.

"I grabbed my bag and ran out. When I got to the hallway, I saw people running and screaming hysterically. The offices had emptied, and everyone was running toward the steps because the elevators no longer worked. While we ran down the stairs, someone said a plane had crashed, and I didn't understand where. I thought the fire was outside, but like everyone else, I continued running down. In the beginning, there was light in the stairwell, and my progress was relatively quick. I almost managed to keep up with everyone. Later, it was so hard for me. I could still hear the explosions from above. It became really hot and dark in the stairwell. People ran and jumped like maniacs, hurting each other. Something hit my stomach, and I thought I was going to pass out. My stomach hurt and fear contracted it even more. I felt I had to get out of the building, or I'd die.

"I think when I was about halfway down, I started having trouble breathing. It was impossible to see anything, but I could feel that thick black smoke spreading in the air. I felt I was going to faint any second. My senses blurred. Then, the lower I got, the less dark it was. I realized I was approaching the exit. And then, I got terribly dizzy. Everything became blurry. Someone stood next to me and urged me forward. I remember he kept telling me, 'You can do it, you can, don't give up,' every time I stumbled because I felt I had no strength to continue. In the end, when I fell, I felt him hold me and help me get up.

"Somehow, I continued forward. At a certain point, he literally carried me. I don't think I would have managed to get out of there without his help. That man, I don't know who he is, but he saved my life. At a certain floor—I think it was the exit because I saw firemen—I lost consciousness. After that, I don't remember a thing until I woke up in the hospital."

Thus, in a voice choked with tears, Eve described these minutes of terror that she'd gone through, as everyone clung to every word she said in wonder. When she finished, no one said a word. Silence descended on the apartment.

"And do you remember what that man looked like?" Jeff was the first one to break the silence.

"No! No, I didn't see his face, but I think he was dressed like you," Eve replied, pointing at Ahron.

"Like me?" Ahron didn't try to hide his discomfort.

"Yes. Like you."

Days later, Jeff and Ahron made tremendous efforts to find that guardian angel who saved Eve.

They hung signs along the orthodox streets and neighborhoods, searched Brooklyn from top to bottom, and visited yeshivas and synagogues, but to no avail. The man wasn't found.

Jeff continued gazing at the woman he loved while she danced, noticing that her hips were slim again, as though she'd never given birth to their son and daughter. Her body showed no signs of childbirth. The twins stayed in New York, with Eve's parents. When he thought of his son and daughter, he was pleased that they were Christians. He decided that when they were old enough, he'd tell them his wonderful story, and proudly emphasize his and their connection with the Jewish people.

Epilogue

Eagles spread their enormous wings and glided in circles over the deep, narrow wadi. The shrieks of the birds, searching for prey, echoed between the mountain walls and could be heard in the distance. Once in a while, the exhausted birds rested in the crevices of the rock surrounding the camel-like mountain, uniting with the nesting birds. Their small, piercing eyes surveyed the yawning abyss, and they tensed their bodies, waiting for what would happen. In the background, one could easily hear the roar of the water, falling from a vast height, forcefully hitting everything in its way, splashing in every direction, leaving a path of pure slivers of water. As it fell, the water gathered in the stream that flowed down the mountain. On both sides of the stream, as though wishing to decorate the wondrous sight, grew dense, green flora. On the hard ground, up the winding mountain, a Montpellier snake quickly slithered, searching for food in the shape of rodents and lizards. A group of young hikers, walking along the dirt path toward the mountain viewpoint, started singing, and the songs erupting from their throats decorated the air in a variety of notes. Huge basalt boulders scattered every which way were a silent testimony to the existence of an ancient settlement, rife with stories of war and heroism that the residents conducted against the Romans. Among the ruins, rested silently the ancient synagogue, perhaps the most ancient, and wild weeds already grew from its walls. And in this gem of nature, stood with pride the houses of the settlement of Gamla, with its red-tiled roofs. A toddler emerged from one of the houses to the yard. "Daddy, look at the flower I picked!" she called joyfully, and her light-blue eyes shone with excitement.

She brought the flower to her father, who was sitting on a wooden chair, drinking from a can of beer and looking at the blue Sea of the Galilee. He turned his gaze to the little girl, smiled, reached out, gathered her to him, and kissed her pink cheeks. His eyes surveyed with unabashed pleasure the pretty child sitting on his knee, examining the purple flower in her hand.

"Beautiful flower, honey," he murmured, while wrapping the child lovingly in his arms. Then, he raised his head to look at the lake spread beneath him and paid attention to the rays of the setting sun, which reflected with much fanfare in the clear water, heralding the approaching Shabbat. His eyes became heavy. In a minute, his eyes would close, and only the magical sight of the golden autumn leaf, which had just fallen from the tree in the yard, landing lightly at its feet, would wake him up.

"Here's some sweet watermelon. Eat it now, while it's cold." The mother came out to the yard and, if not for her swollen belly, one would have thought she was a young girl.

"Mommy, look at the flower I picked!" The child broke away from her thoughtful father, running to boast to her mother.

"Sweetheart, that's a wildflower! We should let the flowers grow and not disturb them." The mother hugged the child tightly and kissed her.

"God, she looks so much like you," the father said, his eyes going between the mother and her child.

The woman approached her husband, kneeled on her knees, hugged him passionately, closed her eyes, and said in a soft, quiet voice, "I love you, Yoav."

He looked at the woman at his side, buried his head in her bosom, and said, "I love you, Rivka."

"And don't forget, love, we're invited to dinner tonight at Eve's and Jeff's," she reminded him before kissing his lips.

Made in the USA
Coppell, TX
25 September 2021